ORFEO

Orfeo

Hans-Jürgen Greif

TRANSLATED FROM THE FRENCH BY

Fred A. Reed

ESPLANADE
Books

THE FICTION SERIES AT VÉHICULE PRESS

Published with the generous assistance of the Canada Council for the
Arts, the Book Publishing Industry Development Program of the
Department of Canadian Heritage, and the Société de développement
des entreprises culturelles du Québec (SODEC).

Esplanade Books editor: Andrew Steinmetz

Cover design: David Drummond
Photo of author: Idra Labrie/Perspective
Set in Adobe Minion and Adobe Garamond by Simon Dardick
Printed by Marquis Printing Inc.

Originally published in French by L'instant même.

LIBRARY AND ARCHIVES CANADA CATALOGUING IN PUBLICATION
Greif, Hans-Jürgen, 1941-
[Orfeo. English]
Orfeo / Hans-Jürgen Greif ; translated by Fred A. Reed.
Translation of the French book of the same title.
ISBN 978-1-55065-231-4
I. Reed, Fred A., 1939- II. Title. III Title: Orfeo. English.
PS8563.R444507313 2008   C843'.54   C2007-904441-7

Published by Véhicule Press, Montréal, Québec, Canada
www.vehiculepress.com

Distribution in Canada: LitDistCo
orders@lpg.ca

Distribution US: Independent Publishers Group
www.ipgbook.com

Printed in Canada on 100% post-consumer recycled paper.

Contents

CHAPTER ONE

Tu che accendi questo core—Mi rivedrai, ti rivedrò
"You who set my heart ablaze—we shall meet again"

–Gioacchino Rossini, *Tancredi*, Act I

C ome quickly. I am dying. F.-O.
It could only be her. Those few words were enough. He had to obey, at least send a note. What excuse could he possibly claim: his wife, work, an upcoming business trip? And how old could she be? Seventy-five, eighty? Weber had not seen her for a dozen years, since her last student's début concert. He'd sent flowers afterwards. To her, not to the young pianist, who had shown little distinction. He'd been tempted to write what she had so often told him while he was still her student: "Not enough color, too little emotion! You don't let your feelings come to the surface! You strike the instrument like an enemy. Emotion, it comes from inside, inside!" But the following day, in the *Freiburger Rundschau*, he had written instead of his years under the tutelage of Anna Maria Ferrone-Oragagni, the celebrated piano teacher. He described her genius, her extensive musical culture, her brilliant career as a soloist, later, and unjustly forgotten, her pedagogical abilities (here he'd chosen his words with utmost care), her generosity toward students who were too poor to pay her normal charges. Out of consideration, he'd written almost nothing about her last, rather tepid protégé.

Weber still felt affection for la Signora. Everyone had called her la Signora, "the old lady," not out of lack of respect nor because of resentment against the inflexibility of her judgments, but because she had always seemed more like an implacable grandmother who could not bring herself to love her grandchildren. Despite her tyrannical ways, he almost venerated her. Many had fled from her to continue their studies under less exacting masters. Never did she attempt to retain a student whom she did not consider promising enough to make a career. Several had gone on to win reputations and some were ranked among the top concert performers. But as he listened to her last disciple, Weber found his mind wandering. Why had she kept him? The young man was no better than Weber had been when he was studying under her. Could it be that her judgment had faltered with age? The performer was a handsome, slender lad whose appearance made you want to spoon-feed him Viennese pastries. Who knows, perhaps la Signora had turned soft-hearted?

It was about fifteen years since she had told him, "My dear boy! Be reasonable, just listen to yourself. Your technique is acceptable, but the sound is not getting better. Find something besides the piano. You will never succeed. Stop going through the motions (*la commedia* was how she put it). You're not that bad; you like music (she called it *la musica*), but your hands won't do what you hear inside your head. They never will. It's time to think of something else."

He had turned pale; his hands froze on the keys. He heard her out. He had witnessed others before him rushing out of this same studio in tears. He had never seen them again.

"This is your last lesson with me. I am sorry, for you. You have talent, but not enough. You will make a competent amateur, and that's all. But you will never have a solo career. You can always try your luck with someone else, but I'm telling you, it's useless. Yes, find something besides the piano. I do not want to see you end your days as an accompanist in some ballet studio. Or in some wretched night club, making music you do not love."

On that day, as he dragged himself through the villa garden toward the station, Weber bid farewell to eleven years of hard work, including two with her. She was never wrong, and he knew it. She was right about his hands, about his inability to convey emotion. Technically, she had brought him along in spectacular fashion. But the more he had heard her play, the more he despaired. Her playing was so simple in appearance, yet it revealed the composer's intentions with a dazzling transparency, while he—he could barely rise above the notes, even though he would scrupulously obey the most infinitesimal indications of the score. He knew what had to be done; he could not execute it.

But she had instilled in him a sense of discipline, pride in a job well done. She had taught him not to give up in the face of adversity, to "keep his backbone straight"—one of her favorite expressions—whatever he did. His hardest moment came when he had to tell his parents that all the money they'd spent on lessons had come to naught. His father had gotten to his feet without a word and thrown a dark glance at his wife. His mother wept bitterly. Once he had recovered from the shock, he'd enrolled in the University of Freiburg and earned a degree in musicology. The music critic's position at the *Freiburger Rundschau* had fallen vacant. It was perfectly suited for him. The publisher, an old friend of la Signora and a regular at her receptions at the villa, made it a point of honor to support the arts in this corner of Germany so well known for its intense cultural activity and for its competition with Strasbourg, its French rival.

Etched in his memory: his weekly trips by the two-car train that carried him in twenty minutes to Bad Krozingen, the hot spring where thirty years earlier la Signora had purchased her great house after deciding to bring her concert career to an end. La Signora: those chubby hands of hers, with their astonishingly short, fleshy fingers, fingers more like those of a master chef, fingers that moved with phenomenal agility; her intelligence, which could encompass an entire interpretation in the blink of an eye; the way she understood a score; her enormous musical culture. Her raspy voice, the way she rolled her r's when she spoke the German that she'd picked up along the way, her unending grammatical errors, uncorrected even after all those years. Her personal dialect, a hodge-podge of Italian, German and French. The interminable exercises she would assign him, as demanding as they were exhausting. Her cutting tone when she corrected him, her rare encouragements. The sound of the piano beneath her fingers; that unforgettably round, full sound, with a sweetness that flooded the farthest extremities of the body. She could hardly be bothered to explain; instead she preferred to show what had to be done. As a pedagogue, she had been mediocre. But she could unerringly identify a student's weaknesses; more often than not she would recite them with an impatience that verged on anger.

* * *

On the night of the recital by her last, neither excessively bad nor good student, she had taken her usual seat in the small concert hall in downtown Freiburg, with its prickly acoustics, in a corner where the sound carried badly. Dressed in black, like a widow from the *Mezzogiorno*, she kept her hands hidden in the sleeves of her coat. She wore a hat of the kind affected by women in mourning during the 'fifties. La Signora had never lost touch with the city of her birth; throughout the concert she sucked on candies sent to her every three months, for decades, by a Neapolitan confectioner. During a lesson, when things weren't going well, she would crack one between her indestructible teeth. The sound of cracking candy was a danger signal: la Signora's temper would begin to flare, the pitch of her voice would rise, turn shrill, fill the studio. She would breathe her eucalyptus- or licorice-scented breath directly into the student's face. Her favorite victims were the ones who considered themselves advanced. Her tantrums came at regular intervals, like the recurring bouts of indigestion that made her look like a desiccated lemon.

"You know nothing yet! *Niente, niente*! Out with it, my little one! You dabble in music, not play it. You don't understand what's going on in this piece. Maybe one day you will. Now, I show you how it's done."

Weber used to emerge from her lessons crushed. It would take him an hour or two to recover. But he obeyed her blindly; by her alone he swore. La Signora even appeared in his dreams; at every hour of the day or night her gravelly voice echoed in his head. After a lesson, which could last twenty minutes or two hours, the finest reward was to breathe in the fresh air as he walked from the villa to the station. Even after a particularly long, exhausting session, la Signora never offered a snack, nor the slightest consolation after one of her descents into hell. She would simply show him the door, without ado. She preferred boys as students: "More obedient. With girls, too many tears. Not enough nerve. In this country, no guts. Think they're princesses, don't want to work. Can't stand criticism." But she obsessed the few girls that stayed on. It wasn't simply because she barked her orders, or kept silent at the end of a lesson, to show that her aims had not been achieved. La Signora was everyone's guilty conscience. She insulted them, told them they didn't work hard enough. Whatever they did, it was never enough.

And there was the omnipresent odor. Not only did the elderly lady consume an inordinate number of strongly flavored candies, but she also drenched herself with an eau de Cologne that smelled so strongly of musk that it made one gag. It was another of those products of her homeland that she seemed to possess in limitless quantities. Its powerful scent assailed the student even in the hall outside the studio, where he would wait his turn seated on an elaborately carved Louis XIII chair that dug into his back. To be precise, it wasn't exactly a hall, but a broad, short corridor where the only light filtered through the glass of the front entrance. Besides the carved seat, it was furnished with four armchairs whose time-worn leather upholstery had long lost its color. In winter, heavy wine-red felt portières hid the main entrance and the door to the studio.

The studio itself was a cavernous room that was also used for receptions. Damasked drapes in a floral motif covered the windows; la Signora lived in mortal fear of the slightest draft. Come fall, she would moisten a finger and draw it along the cracks between the sash and the window frame, checking for air leaks, "not to die of pneumonia in this country." Living in the south of the Black Forest region did not agree with her, it seemed. She complained of the damp heat in the summertime and of the cold winters, but did not want to return to Naples to live. "I've lived here too long. I'm uncomfortable everywhere. The immigrant's lot."

When he'd been her student, Weber heard of the lavish receptions held at the villa whenever a great musician would pass through Freiburg. He knew nothing but the dark side of that immense dwelling, and remembered waiting interminably in the "hall," where he could overhear the sounds of the great Steinway and la Signora's shrill voice. He remembered her odor; it hung in the air like an opaque cloud, and when la Signora leaned forward to speak to him or to correct a fingering error, he'd had to gasp for breath.

She would have been in her sixties when he began to work under her. His high school music teacher had spoken of her as a superb pianist. Her methods were outmoded, of course, but she was still capable of training her best pupils for concert careers. Even then, she hardly ever left the villa except to attend the few concerts given by leading artists, or for her students' first recitals. Her disciples were obliged to attend the first performance of a graduate; they were there "to learn". They would gather around her, forming a human shield. The scent of musk would permeate the hall, and the concert-goers, attempting to locate the source of this curious odor, would swivel their heads. At her last student's recital, she had not even left the hall during intermission. Her face had become hardened, her features were drawn, her eyes downcast.

This tiny, swarthy, ugly, wrinkled crone bore not the slightest resemblance to the pretty young woman in the numerous yellowed photographs displayed on a shelf in the studio. She had been fond of one in particular, a Polaroid snapshot of her with her last teacher, Lipatti, who was smiling at her sorrowfully. He had written on the photo, in large letters: *To my dear Anna Maria, and to true music.* The date revealed that it had been taken a few months before the death of the great pianist.

Weber would have liked to bring her up to date on what he was doing, to introduce her to Kirsten. He had planned to meet her after the concert and invite her to the house, the better to demonstrate his success—a daring gambit, for he feared her still—but she had already vanished, her former students had dispersed. A call to the villa had gone unanswered.

Her note could only be true; she never lied. Weber had received it at two o'clock in the afternoon. He taped a piece of paper to the refrigerator door: *F.-O. wants to see me. Don't know when back. Kisses.* Kirsten was planning to dine out with a new girlfriend, she would be back late. He called the paper. Nothing pressing, his story for tomorrow's edition was ready, he had no messages. He punched the elevator call button several times without success. Nothing new; someone was unloading their grocery shopping, or holding the door open to chat with another resident. Their compact apartment was in a large art-nouveau house overlooking the Dreisam, the small river that flows through the town. Kirsten had discovered the four-room attic apartment, with its pleasingly arranged and bright rooms, its view of the tiered grapevines that marched up the steep slopes of the Schlossberg, and the distant gentle hills of the Black Forest. The kitchen and bathroom were modern and there was a guestroom with its own bath. The spacious veranda, which had been cut from the roof, looked over the "garden," an attractive inner courtyard with a few aspens and lindens, closed in on three sides by the adjoining buildings. It was a pleasant apartment, but during the summer when the damp heat of Freiburg became overpowering, they moved out to their summer cottage near Bernau, not far from Sankt Blasien, an hour's drive from the city.

He decided not to wait and hurried down the five flights of stairs, jumped into his car, and took the road toward the highway leading to Bad Krozingen. The villa was situated close to the Neumagen, a peaceful little brook. He parked on a nearby side street, and strode rapidly past a row of prosperous houses almost hidden from the footpath by their bushy hedges and trees. When he reached the villa he pushed open the wrought-iron gate and walked past the two conifers that had been trimmed into spherical shapes. To the right and left of the path, on the edge of a sickly lawn, there were a few beds of ill-matched, loud-colored flowers. The lawn was suffering from lack of sunlight; la Signora had refused to allow the trees to be trimmed. Like the massive neighboring houses, hers dated from the 'twenties. Now it was overgrown with vigorous, invasive vegetation. Johann opened the door. He had hardly changed. La Signora had hired him as a handyman when she arrived in Bad Krozingen. He also believed himself to be a butler and liked to affect a green and yellow striped vest after his chores were done. His hands, with the dirt under the fingernails, his sunburned skinny neck, his bony face: everything was exactly as Weber had remembered it. The man said, as though he'd seen him the previous day, "Good day, sir. Madame will be happy to see you. She has asked for you several times already. But please wait for a moment; she is busy just now. Would you be so kind as to wait here?" He motioned to the four uncomfortable chairs, their leather upholstery even more worn than before, then disappeared through the door that led to the office.

Yes, everything was precisely as it had always been. From the cloying odor of musk to the gilt-trimmed occasional tables, from the woodwork to the portières and the portraits of artists she had known, in their shiny black frames. On the floor, the very same Anatolian carpet, now worn to the warp. As Weber remembered how he had been at age nineteen, his hands began to turn moist and he broke into a fine sweat despite the coolness of the room. He smiled. La Signora would forever cause him this kind of discomfort. She was still one of the few people in the world who could make him feel ill at ease. She, and Kirsten.

From behind the portière leading to the drawing room-studio, he could hear someone start to sing the Rossini aria "*O Patria! Dolce, ed ingrata patria!*" from *Tancredi*. Weber moved closer. He rummaged through his memory, but he could find not a trace of that alto voice. The interpretation sounded strange: the vocalises in the repeat of the cavatina "*Mi rivedrai ... ti rivedrò*" that he knew so well in the interpretations of Rossini mezzos were perfectly rendered. But instead of a display of cold agility, the voice seemed a perfect fusion of emotion and melody. Each vowel, drawn out longer than usual, seemed to shimmer; each attack was more vigorous. It was a strange voice, ranging from alto to soprano, effortlessly leaping twelve or thirteen notes, handling the glissandi with a dancer's elegance. Weber, who had heard many voices, was stunned. But there was more: the voice of this singer blended, with an extraordinary mastery, the vocal apparatus and the musical sensibility of a consummate artist.

The music came to a sudden stop. He heard the croaking voice of la Signora. "Repeat that last passage, will you? You do not give it enough *sentimento, capisci?* From inside, inside! Don't just plunk it down there! This Tancredi of yours, he wants to fight, so spare us the theatrical moaning and groaning!"

The singer immediately launched into the same passage. This time, the voice added to Tancredi's hope of freeing his country, a ringing call to arms, bristling with martial fervor, before turning to Amenaida, his beloved.

Weber could not restrain himself any longer. A few measures before the end of the cavatina he pushed aside the portière and cracked open one of the double doors . In the center of the room, next to the piano, stood a hospital bed. Around it were a chair and a low, book-laden table. Madame Ferrone-Oragagni was hardly more than a black-clad skeleton. From her voluminous skirts protruded two emaciated legs; on her feet she wore felt slippers. Her fleshless hands seemed longer now: in her right hand she held a white baton. She was wearing a slender mink stole around her neck. Her flat-faced head protruded from the fur collar like that of a bat. Her cheeks were sucked in against her teeth; her lips were thin and bluish; her gray hair was combed straight back. Had it not been for her black eyes that still sparkled just as Weber remembered them, she could have been dead. As he stepped into the room, the baton began to tremble violently, as though her body was convulsed with sudden fever, or chills.

At the other end of the room in front of the window, Weber could just make out the slender silhouette of the singer, dressed in baggy pants and a white blouse, with her head thrown back after the effort of the aria. Against the light, it was impossible to discern her features. Supported by her right hand, she leaned against a stack of scores. La Signora did not introduce her; it was as though the young woman had ceased to exist with her last note. Weber felt the mixture of fear and anxiety he'd experienced outside the door well up within him. The odor of musk swept over him so forcefully that his head reeled.

The Steinway, its cover down, still held sway in the middle of the studio. The absence of a feminine touch in the room was almost shocking. If his wife had seen the way the furniture was arranged, Weber mused, she would have left the room in a fit of depression. Against the wall at one end stood a random collection of bookcases piled high with musical scores, above them four ugly paintings depicting the Amalfi coast, and on the left, chairs pushed up against the wood-paneled walls like soldiers standing at attention. There was a buffet with a blood-red marble top that looked like the counter of a butcher shop. At the opposite extremity of the room was the old day bed whose color he'd never been able to determine. Next to the piano lay a Bukhara carpet worn through in several places. Everything spoke neglect, as if it had been thrown together pell-mell, without a care for harmony. With the passage of time, it seemed, la Signora no longer paid attention to the objects around her. And yet she was wealthy enough to afford a cook, a cleaning lady, and a handyman. Beside her bed stood a cheap floor lamp that shone toward the ceiling, casting a pallid tinge over the entire room. Weber did detect two additions: a large oval cheval mirror placed near the window, next to the singer, and a small upright piano at the far end of the room.

The baton pointed to the chair beside the bed. After removing two books, which he deposited on the low table, Weber sat down. He recognized Manuel Garcia's *Complete Treatise on the Art of Singing* in the new Minkoff edition, and the most significant modern work on the voice, *The Structure of Singing* by Richard Miller.

"Thank you for coming," she whispered with a labored smile. "I must speak to you. It is important. Do not touch the bed; it hurts me."

The baton rose, pointed to the singer, and then fell to indicate the door at the far end of the room that led to the first floor. The young woman stepped back from the window and made her way slowly to the door, muttering, "*Scusatemi.*" Weber thought he noticed a slight limp, but he could not be certain. Her ash-blond hair was combed back to form a bun, in the style of the Ancien Régime. The only word that she had spoken seemed to belong to a contralto, the tonic *a* echoed with a fine tone of brass, but he couldn't be sure of a thing. She threw him a sidelong glance, then lowered her eyelids as she passed. Strange eyes. Weber had never seen anything quite like them: they were large, dark green, and almond shaped, and they slanted upward toward her temples, against a long, narrow face.

He would never forget that first glance. In it lay a question, and a veiled, quickly given invitation.

Then the old woman said, in her southern Italian accent, occasionally struggling to find the German words, pausing to catch her breath, "I asked you to come because you are the only person who can handle what I consider is my greatest success. I have trained a few good pianists, it's true. But at the start of my career I often worked with singers. I could have become a professional voice coach. But I wanted a concert career.

"Then I discovered this voice, almost too late for me. I have done with it what I could. That is why I do not come into Freiburg any more. Piano recitals started to bore me. I can hear the best ones on the radio. Don't look at me like that. I do not have much time. I grow tired quickly. What I am telling you, you must know."

* * *

They met each day for several weeks. Weber pieced together the story of the voice. Only someone totally convinced of success could have done what she did. Weber avoided telling his wife; Kirsten would never have understood the old woman's passion for the gift of that voice, itself a result of pure happenstance, of violent circumstance, of years of dedicated effort, of a lengthy struggle between la Signora and her student, of an adoptive grandmother and a child the likes of which the world had not seen for two and a half centuries.

One fine Sunday in June, thirteen years before, a young man named Georg Teufel, his wife and their son Lennart had taken an excursion to Sankt Blasien. That afternoon, the little boy complained of thirst. An ice-cream wagon had pulled up in the shade of the cathedral; his parents hovered over him as he chose his favorite flavor. Suddenly there came the sound of impact and shrieks of horror. An automobile had crashed into the ice-cream wagon, leaving only a heap of twisted metal. Lennart had been thrown onto the hood of the car; his parents and the ice-cream man lay crushed beneath the wreckage. Three had died; little Lennart fought to survive. His pelvis had been so badly injured that his doctors held out little hope that he would ever walk again. His entire lower abdomen and his upper hips were in fragments, with bone protruding through the flesh. The father's sister, herself a mother of several children, told the neighbors, "The little one won't make it. Either he'll be dead in a couple of days, or he'll survive, but he'll be a cripple; he'll spend the rest of his life in a wheelchair. Better he should have joined his parents. I just don't know how I can look after that boy, what with everything that has to be done. He'd be better off in an institution. Our taxes are high enough already. A children's hospital should take care of him, isn't that so? But he won't live through it, I know he won't. He was always a weak, sensitive child."

And yet Lennart survived a number of major operations. He spent a year in the Freiburg University clinic, where he became the doctors' and nurses' pet. When he returned to Bad Krozingen, his aunt took him in, reluctantly. She had no idea of how to take care of this broken lad who could barely restrain his tears, and whose mouth contorted with pain whenever she put him to bed or bathed him.

19

"It's awful to see," she would say. "He's full of stitches running every which way. He's got scars as fat as sausages. His legs won't carry him, he'll never walk again, I can tell you that! And the rest of him isn't a pretty sight. Down there, he's nothing but a pulp; they could only save his penis. So to speak. What kind of a life can he hope for, poor kid?"

Unable to walk with crutches, he spent his days in a chair by the window watching his former classmates. They had stopped coming to visit him after he showed them his wounds (his aunt's stories had made the rounds of the neighborhood by then). One of them rushed off to the toilet and threw up his meal. The others turned pale and hurried out in silence. Left to his own devices, the little boy could do nothing. He could not play, could not read. He began to withdraw into himself. Sometimes he would sing to himself in a sorrowful voice. His physicians recommended something to distract him. His aunt had asked Gertrud, the housekeeper at the villa and a childhood friend, to ask la Signora if the boy could come to the villa and listen to the music. "He likes it. Plus, he knows the place."

In earlier days Lennart had often gone along with his father, who had tended la Signora's garden. Georg had been a professional, unlike the careless Johann. While Georg Teufel designed sumptuous flower-beds, and even contrived to cultivate roses in the few places where the trees would let through the sunlight, his son would sit in front of the drawing room window. Motionless, he would listen to the music that rippled through the air, mouth agape, eyes lost in the distance. His father would tell anyone who cared to listen that his son "imitated" whatever he heard in the afternoon, that he could sing exactly those melodies in his tiny high-pitched voice. "Pity," said Georg. "He's got such a lovely voice! But in three, four years he'll lose it."

After a brief hesitation, la Signora had agreed with the aunt's request that the orphaned boy return to the villa to listen to her play. Her last student had left her, she was accepting no one else. Her spare time was hers to use as she pleased. Why not do something charitable, and at the same time have a listener who asked only to sit there, still and mute?

Thus began Lennart's new life. Early in the morning his aunt wrapped him in blankets and plopped him down in his wheelchair at the entrance to the villa at nine o'clock. Gertrud wheeled him through the kitchen door to avoid the steps at the main entrance, and waited for la Signora to sit down at the Steinway to begin her day's work, for she continued to work, but for herself alone. And Lennart would listen, eyes closed, with a smile, an insatiable expression on his face. When la Signora asked him—she loved to hear his delicate voice—he sang back to her the melody on a single vowel. He never missed a note.

By midsummer he had begun to share the elderly lady's mid-morning snack, then her lunch. Together they would take an afternoon nap in the drawing room, she on the day bed, he in his wheelchair. When she returned to her work for another hour, she would treat him to a full-scale recital: a sonata by Beethoven or Schubert or Schumann. But Lennart liked most of all what he called "the bright things": Vivaldi, Mozart, Handel. He told her what he liked in this piece or that, using the only comparisons he could make: flowers, clouds, his own pain. And to make his point, he would sing a bit of it in his pretty voice.

More and more often la Signora would forget he was only a child. She spoke to him as she would to a musician. True enough, he was intelligent, and retained everything she told him, especially her stories about the composers of the 18th century. He was like a sponge, always looking for more, asking for details about music, about the theatre, about the singers. Soon enough he began to use the same terms she did, in Italian, French and German. When he was at la Signora's house, he forgot that he was little more than a rag doll. His eyes would glisten; often he'd be in tears by the time she'd finished the piece she was playing. He had wept so copiously on hearing a Chopin nocturne that she dared not repeat it. In his tenuous, highly charged emotional state, music was his only outlet.

There was only one drawback: he wasn't the least bit interested in playing the piano. He would invent any excuse to avoid it. His wheelchair was too low, his arms ached, or his hips; the notes blurred before his eyes. La Signora was almost hurt, but when she looked at his wide, dark eyes, she melted. "I'm getting soft," she said to herself. "This lad is turning me to jelly." And yet, often he would reach out to touch the sides of the instrument, eyes closed, as he hummed the melody he had just heard. He startled la Signora with his musical memory, his unerring ear; nothing escaped him.

Before the accident, he had been able to identify who was singing off-key in the school choir, to correct him, to sing the solos. At home, he had often sung to himself. His father had joked that he could "charm the birds in the trees." After the accident Lennart did not return to school. He would have had to repeat a year, but his former schoolmates had rejected him, and now he was afraid of them.

Not only did la Signora grow accustomed to the boy's presence; he was becoming indispensable to her. Lennart was as circumspect as a cat, and as quiet. He would never interrupt her as she played. Mornings, she waited for him to come. When they came to pick him up late in the afternoon, she felt sad. One evening, his aunt came later than usual. La Signora was reclining on the day bed; darkness had almost fallen, the villa was silent. Suddenly, in the silence of the end of that autumn day, when the sounds of the outside world had stilled, she heard a *cantus firmus* of utter purity, sung on a vowel fluctuating between *a* and *e*. It was the melody from a Mozart sonata la Signora had been practicing that morning. Then the voice fell silent.

La Signora told Weber, "His angelic voice seared my heart like a hot iron. It was the most beautiful child's voice I ever heard. It wasn't like that before the accident. Now there was something else, a feeling of serenity, of abandonment to music. The quality of sound? Magnificent. And a sense of harmony you'd swear he was born with."

Slowly she had raised herself upright. Lennart had leaned his crutches against the Steinway. He was singing Mozart on that single vowel that he had invented, head thrown back. Now and again he would stop, strike a few notes on the keyboard, and go back a few measures to make sure he had not slipped out of tune. When he had finished, the same smile suffused his face still. No longer was he an infirm and helpless child. In him lay a force that lifted him far above his tormented body. It was at that precise moment that la Signora understood the boy's true nature. He was the incarnation of song.

That night, a plan took shape in la Signora's mind, a plan as audacious as it was absurd. She decided to speak to his aunt. Impossible to tell whether or not she would succeed, she explained. The art of training such a voice had long vanished. The other woman did not understand what she meant by "such a voice." So la Signora launched into a lengthy medical explanation. Lennart's voice would always be that of a child. But with proper training she could make it more beautiful than anything that existed in the West. The aunt still seemed unable to understand. Then la Signora made an emotional appeal: she had become deeply attached to the lad, she, an old lady, a foreigner, childless, without family ties, nothing, alone in the world. Slowly the aunt began to grasp what she was hearing: the old lady was relieving her of a burden. No doubt about it, she'd been touched by Lennart as if he was an injured baby animal found by the roadside. The aunt, with her greedy peasant logic, wondered what the hitch was. Where she came from, there was no such thing as charity that didn't seek something in exchange.

As she spoke to the aunt, who she hoped would disappear from her life—and the boy's—in the shortest possible time, la Signora thought back to her best students. If she could train Lennart before she died, it would be her greatest achievement. It would not be ephemeral, not a circus act, but the *risorgimento* of an extraordinarily sophisticated art form, the fusion of the finest human attributes: talent, work, emotion, intelligence, culture.

One day she told Weber, enunciating each vowel, *"Beauty is born in suffering."*

Had she forgotten that beauty calls forth desire and love as well?

Nothing good could come of letting Lennart move to the villa, his aunt was convinced, though instinctively she hoped to obtain something "to make up for the loss." But the elderly Italian held her ground. She drew up a list of all the things she could offer the boy if her proposal were accepted: she would hire a special tutor, a retired teacher from Staufen, a small town not far from Bad Krozingen, for two hours a day. Lennart would have a room of his own; Maria would prepare his meals. He would have clothing, books, everything a child might need. Furthermore, she would see to Lennart's vocal education. "The woman had no idea of the treasure she was turning over to me," she whispered in Weber's ear. In exchange, she asked that the woman bother her nephew as little as possible by visiting him. The kind of education he would be getting could not tolerate distractions. But the aunt had already capitulated. On the one hand, la Signora had made it abundantly clear that hers was a take-it-or-leave-it offer; and on the other hand, the opportunity was simply too good to pass up. If it hadn't been for this Italian woman, she would have been stuck with the kid all the time. The woman was crazy, she was sure of it, just like most people in Bad Krozingen when they heard about the deal, for she showed la Signora's note around. "Dear Madame, I am doing this for the love of music, it is as simple as that. He has a pretty voice. It can become a voice of great beauty. One day he may earn his living by his vocal chords. We shall see." People read the note and laughed.

But the aunt had gone home with the nagging feeling that she'd been cheated. "You never know with these foreigners. They don't think like us."

La Signora's first step was to pull from her bookshelves the classics of voice teaching. The *Opinioni de' cantori antichi e moderni* by Pier Francesco Tosi, by way of Mancini's *Osservazioni pratiche sopra il canto figurato*, Grétry's *Essais sur la musique*. She had reread the writings of Charles de Brosses on the art of song in Italy, the essays of Herbst and Agricola. Voraciously, she sought out whatever she could about the four Neapolitan conservatories whose masters had, in the 17th and 18th centuries, trained the greatest singers of the day, the celebrated *primi uomini*. She ordered scores of the works with which these wizards of the vocal art had conquered their audiences: Monteverdi, Gluck, Zingarelli, Rameau, Hasse, Handel, Giacomelli, Cavalli and Mozart. On declamation, she studied the French texts of the baroque period. Slowly, surely, she rediscovered one of the bygone glories of her native land, which she merged with the art of declamation of the classical French theatre, considered superior to Italian practice at the time. From her own experience as a teacher of piano, she knew the risks that lay in wait for any serious musician. She knew, too, the inherent potential weaknesses of singers: the collapse of the trunk and dislocated vertebrae, bursitis from performing the same movement over and over again, faulty breathing, burnout, a lack of rigorous personal hygiene. In fact, she was feeling her way in a field that was not her own. The singers she had worked with in days long gone by had implored her to continue with them, but for thirty-five years she had not taken on a single singer. Ever since that evening when she had "heard and understood" Lennart's youthful voice, la Signora described herself as "possessed."

From now on la Signora told young pianists who wished to work with her that they could not; she was to be left in peace.

Based on the teaching methods of the Neapolitan conservatories, she could plan on a training period of from eight to twelve years, if not more.

The little boy balked at every turn. He refused to take his work seriously; he wanted to play. Not only that, he was a born manipulator. He pleaded his infirmity and his pain; he negotiated every minute of leisure. He didn't like his room at the villa. It was hardly more than an expanded broom closet next to the kitchen that la Signora had had prepared for him. But because of his crushed hips, climbing the stairs was out of the question. He wanted to go home, he said, to the aunt whom he suddenly took a liking to. When la Signora came too close, he held his nose, averted his eyes from her stern gaze, from those darting eyes of hers that picked up everything at a glance. It was simple: he had been forced to live with this old woman, therefore he was unhappy. He had come to adore Gertrud, until the day she told him that many parents would pay dearly for the opportunity for such a great lady to look after their child the way la Signora looked after him. She even ventured that Lennart should thank his lucky stars for his good fortune. She was quick to point to his near-paralyzed legs, his slight body, and his frail limbs. He had shut his tear-filled eyes, turned his wheelchair around, and for weeks said not a word to her.

La Signora told Weber how, for the first two years, and only during fine weather, she would take Lennart out into the garden. He submitted to the ordeal, first in his wheelchair, then later, dragging himself along on crutches.

"Now I have pains like his back then, so I know how much he must have suffered. And I even warned him not to grimace! But in the end, he succeeded, first with a cane, then finally, to walk on his own. At first, the physiotherapist would come every morning at ten-thirty. He would go about his work gently, but it was so painful that Lennart would scream. I had to cover my ears; I'd never heard anyone cry out like that. It was terrible. Finally, I would time his screams, to understand his lung capacity. That's inhuman, isn't it? But I was like a madwoman. All I cared about was how I could develop that little boy, and that voice. At night I could hear him crying in his bed, sometimes sobbing until the wee hours of the morning. I would often go downstairs to console him, to hold his hand. That was all I could do. And he would calm down. Maria's and Gertrud's rooms were in the attic. Like elderly countrywomen, they didn't like having this infirm boy underfoot. That's the way they are. The lad would be twisted for life, was how they put it. They thought, and maybe they still do, that I was stupid to pay for an instructor, a physiotherapist, and a physician. In their villages there were plenty of little boys with angelic voices, they said, much prettier than Lennart's."

Weber began to take the full measure of la Signora's efforts, and of her obsession to bring alive a voice from the past. He could not help but imagine the scenes that must have played out between the foster grandmother and the child as the two collided. How could Lennart have resisted her? How could he have relieved the tension that built up between them? In spite of everything that united them, in spite of their love of music, he must have at times been overwhelmed with anger at his jailer. But he must also have realized that the old lady had only his well-being at heart. After two years of torture it hurt him less to move his limbs. The therapist came calling less frequently. Lennart could climb the stairs, and he moved into a new room overlooking the garden. La Signora had prepared a surprise for him: twice she called in the paperhanger to replace the wallpaper because she had not been satisfied by the effect. She furnished the room with busts of musicians, two silk-upholstered Louis XV armchairs, a bed shaped like an ottoman, yellow brocade curtains, and candelabra. The room resembled an 18th-century boudoir, something between the baroque and the rococo. In a Freiburg antique shop she'd discovered a collection of engravings of scenes from 17th-century Italian opera. They represented gardens in vanishing-point perspective; trompe-l'œil landscapes; high seas raging around a tiny island atop which stood a figure in full armor, ostrich feathers flying from his helmet, unbending in the eye of the tempest that whipped the crest of the lone palm on the shore.

Lennart's new quarters were like a candy box lined with yellow and pink. Anyone else would have suffocated amidst the heavy drapes, the cream-tinted savonnerie carpet, and the arrangements of silk flowers. The bookshelves were crammed with history books and with scores still unknown to him. When la Signora carried out her final inspection before handing Lennart the key to his room, she was certain that everything was as charming as it was suitable. The lad threw himself with delight into his newfound kingdom.

Two years after the accident, he often got bored in that dark villa. La Signora had drawn up a strict work schedule. Up early, exercises to loosen his hips. Toilette. Breakfast. Dried fruits, and above all, nuts were forbidden. Their oils would make his voice hoarse, she claimed. He could eat only small amounts of food at a time; a heavy stomach would hinder his work. Nothing too spicy, nothing too hot or too cold. No ice cream, which he loved. He learned to beware of the sharp shifts in temperature that are so frequent in the south of the Black Forest. Whenever he complained of a sore throat, she would rub his neck with an ointment compounded by a local pharmacist according to her instructions and she made him wear a silk mask over his nose and mouth. She had the windows caulked and had felt weather-stripping applied to the bottoms of all the doors. To protect Lennart's voice she'd moved a small upright piano into the far end of the drawing room-cum-studio; it was tuned to a lower pitch than normally used by instrument makers and orchestras. Meanwhile, the Steinway, always in perfect tune, remained reserved for her own work, as well as for final rehearsals. She had the panes of the glass doors that opened onto the garden replaced with mirror panels. By standing next to the large cheval mirror Lennart learned to see himself from all angles, the better to observe his movements and keep his body trim and fit.

At first, she would have him work for no more than five consecutive minutes, and then, only a few times a day. After six months, she increased their work sessions to a half-hour, four times a day. She had delved deeply into the anatomy of the respiratory system. To bring about a harmonious interaction of the different components of this complex system would take years of intensive effort, with only one day of rest per week. On that day he was not to sing, but only to rehearse his movements, and to practice his declamation exercises at half volume in front of the mirrors.

Lennart no longer complained that he was being held captive; quite the contrary. He began to notice the changes in his voice. Occasionally he would reproach la Signora for not moving ahead rapidly enough. She had drummed into his head that anything that had no bearing on music in one way or another was of no consequence; that his entire life would henceforth be centered on his vocal apparatus; that he must sustain it in the best possible health; that he must develop mental balance, and the ability to concentrate rapidly. Between the ages of fourteen and seventeen, during the period of rapid growth that was so critical to the development of the lungs, she realized, with a pleasure comparable to that of a mother witnessing the maturing of her child's body, that his torso was expanding and now formed a powerful resonance chamber. She devised a technique of inhaling and exhaling that made it possible for him to sustain a note, to execute the celebrated *messa di voce* for longer than a minute, in the manner of Carlo Broschi, known as Farinelli, the singer of whose vocal pyro-technics at Naples, Venice, London and the Spanish court she often spoke. But Lennart's arms grew longer as well, almost preposterously, as did his lower abdomen. His face, though destined to remain beardless, became more angular; his nose took on a prominence that horrified him. Increasingly he avoided looking at himself in the mirror outside the hours set aside for his declamation exercises. La Signora did everything she could to reassure him that everyone went through this same awkward stage; how fortunate he was that his face hadn't broken out in pimples, like most boys and girls of his age. It took la Signora several months, and great difficulty, to convince him that there was nothing wrong with his face. In fact, everything seemed to have conspired to create "the singer's mask"—a particular configuration of the cranial cavities, the resonators. The shape of the nose, the power of the lungs, and the training of the vocal chords worked in harmony to produce sounds of far greater perfection than in an ordinary person.

La Signora had copied, down to the tiniest detail, the daily routine of the future Neapolitan *primi uomini*: voice warm-up exercises from eight-thirty to nine o'clock; with the old teacher from nine to ten o'clock doing the obligatory Latin, French, German and English and reading from the texts; from ten to eleven o'clock, solfege and counterpoint with la Signora. Like most singers, Lennart loathed his subjects, but he kept at it. From eleven to eleven-thirty there were singing exercises, with emphasis on vocalises, to build vocal agility. Until twelve-thirty, mathematics, physics and a bit of chemistry. Then, a light meal, with fresh fruit as a starter, a piece of grilled meat, vegetables cooked crisp-tender, a large glass of water tinged with a few drops of local red wine, a bit of cheese and a thin slice of bread. For dessert, a small sweet, perhaps a crème brûlée or a sliver of tarte, never tea or coffee. From two to three o'clock, geography and history, Lennart's favorite subjects. The teacher would leave the villa. Then, another voice exercise session until three-thirty followed by an hour of solfege and improvised counterpoint on a *cantus firmus*. Yet another half-hour given over to declamation exercises and movements in front of the mirror, followed by relaxation and concentration exercises. Then came lessons in piano, which Lennart proved able to master satis-factorily after several years. At six-thirty, games or a stroll in the garden. Seven-fifteen, dinner, begun invariably with a minestrone, followed by grilled fish or steak tartare, salad, and a light cheese. The rest of the evening, until ten-thirty, was given over to conversation in Italian, and to reading in history and mythology. Lennart was now perfectly at home in German and Italian; he claimed to dream with equal inten-sity in both languages. According to la Signora, his French was passable, his English acceptable, but, all things considered, the vocal repertoire that most interested her pupil in those two languages was slender. Lennart remained weak in Latin and in mathematics. His teacher had stated that he had "the temperament of an artist, of someone who couldn't be bothered with logic." Eleven o'clock: lights out.

And so it went, for twelve years.

La Signora was failing fast. When she had begun to tell Weber her story, she could speak for a half-hour; as the weeks went by her voice began to fade after ten minutes. With a wave of the hand she would motion to him to leave the room. Weber would stroll through the streets of the little town, sit on a bench on the banks of the Neumagen, and jot down what he had just learned. Then he would make his way back to the villa to see if she were able to go on. For an elderly woman, her energy was phenomenal: though she was dying she was still capable of enough concentration to tell Weber of all she had done with the singer whom she had made the centerpiece of her life, whom she had supported, fortified, cajoled for twelve years, but "without breaking him." What did she mean by that? That, for all she had done, Lennart had a will of his own? One day Weber asked her how she had managed to keep Lennart under her wing, especially after he had recovered the use of his legs. Any other adolescent would have done everything he could to escape such a strict regimen. She had answered, "What else could he do? He lived in music. From his earliest years, it was his life. Later on, he will work with other voice teachers. But I prefer not to think about it. The idea makes me sick to my stomach. I have written down the names of some colleagues of mine who could complete the work. I will pass them on to you. With me, he has mastered the tools he needs to make an exceptional career. You heard him only once. Just wait. You shall see what he can do. Take care of him after I die, he must not interrupt his routine."

As he reread his notes, Weber could not help thinking back to his own childhood, to his family, to the farm where he grew up. Could he have endured such a life? Alone, shut in all day long with a woman old enough to be his grandmother, but who understood nothing of the sickly little boy who was cut off from the world. La Signora loved Lennart, of that there was no doubt. But she loved him most of all for his voice, and for the faraway promise of a bright future. When, even as death hovered behind the closed door, she spoke of his immense musical talent, of his intelligence, his sensitivity, her eyes glistened with emotion.

Slowly, Weber grasped what she expected of him. Lennart's world had been restricted to a handful of people; he knew nothing of life beyond the villa. From his window he could see the rooftops of Bad Krozingen, of course; the trees, the foothills of the Black Forest. According to la Signora, he had accompanied her two or three times a year to Freiburg. At the time, he was growing so rapidly that he needed to replace all his clothing, which was made to measure by a Lebanese tailor who apparently worked miracles. For Lennart's twentieth birthday, she had ordered for him two stage costumes, cut from old silks. But aside from these excursions, and the occasional consultation with a prominent osteopath in Basel, all he knew about the world was what la Signora had told him. She had spoken to him about the competitions in which he would have to participate, but she took pains not to tell him how hard the world of music was, that only the strong survive. At that point, enter Weber. Using his position and his connections in the musical world, he could guide Lennart along the path that la Signora had laid down for him.

"No female has his register; no singer has his breathing capacity. He sings his arias with supreme finesse. Now, he needs only a few seconds to concentrate, a single breath to establish his inner equilibrium. Just wait, you shall see for yourself."

Over the years Lennart's register had broadened considerably. His tessitura now ranged from soprano to alto, from E below middle C to C in the second octave above middle C. More important, it was equally sweet and smooth at every level. La Signora was especially proud of his perfect fusion of the head and chest registers.

"Once you hear him, you will understand no one else will ever reach his level. In his low notes he can now make his head heard; in his highs, the whole of his chest. And he can move from one to another so easily! For years he has worked on it, the intermediate zone that is so hard to master. Together with his *messa di voce*, it will be his passport to success."

In the Rossini aria, Weber had heard the results for himself: he had sung effortlessly, flowingly, with no shift in timbre or intensity. The tone coloration had been constant; there had been not a hint of slippage in his voice.

But death was awaiting her "impatiently," as la Signora put it. From the day she'd received the verdict, she had but a single overriding concern. For her entire life, she reminded Weber, music had been the driving force. The handful of youthful suitors (Weber was startled to hear it from this crone), her adventures with this or that admirer, had never distracted her from her sole passion: music. And Lennart, in her eyes, had become her unique and true achievement.

"When I hear that voice, it is like I am in paradise. I know I will die in a few days. My only consolation is his voice. In the afternoon, after you've gone, he sings for me. I have nothing else to teach him, only a few minor adjustments to make."

La Signora spoke only once of her own illness. "A year ago, I had difficulty getting up from the bench where I'd been sitting. At first, I thought it was a twisted back. But it got worse. My lower back hurt so much that it was as if a torturer were slashing my pelvis with a knife. For the first time, I *truly* understood what Lennart must have suffered after the accident. And me, all I did was keep driving him. I was furious with myself, and I begged him to pardon me."

At the clinic her physicians told her the truth: she was suffering from cancer of the spinal chord. It had invaded her body; nothing could be done. It would spread slowly, until it reached the brain. From that moment, the end would come quickly. The pain would be so intense that the dose of morphine she would need would kill her.

The weaker she grew, the more insistent she became. "Take him under your wing," she said, in a breathy whisper that betrayed her anguish. "I have no children of my own; no family. Even if he loses his way, he will have enough to live comfortably. I am leaving him the villa, and everything I have. If he fails, it will be my fault, because I wagered everything on a single card, him, and on his talent. But if he succeeds, and I'm sure he will, he will be ten times wealthier than any other singer today. And that will be compensation for the life he never had. Now it's up to you to prove to him that the world awaits him. Me, I trained him. The rest is in your hands: Do not hire an impresario. I detest them; they are nothing but scum. They care nothing for talent, only for profit. You will have to do it yourself. You love music, true music, too much to deny me this last wish. You know the dangers that lie in wait for him, the flattery, the promises, the people who will go crazy when they hear him sing."

Again and again, she returned to the matter of greatest concern to her. "If you are not vigilant, he could turn into a circus act. Once people have heard his voice, the pressures on him will be terrible. All the concert halls, the great opera houses will fight over him. If he works too hard, he might break his voice, and be forgotten overnight. Up to now, his life has been as regular as the pendulum clock in the hall. No extremes, no strong emotions; never. He had all that in the first year after the accident. He has to be protected. Look after him.

"When his cat died, the one he couldn't bring with him from home, it threw him off for weeks. It was nothing, an insignificant upset, but his voice began to suffer immediately. He's so sensitive that the slightest error on your part could be dangerous. His stability is purely artificial, even technical. Deep down, he has two personalities: a little boy who is afraid of everything, and an adult fully aware of his powers."

She was radiant with joy when she received Weber for what would be their last encounter. Behind her stood a nurse, preparing an oxygen tank. On a small metal table lay a coil of tubing connected to a respirator and several hypodermic needles. She appeared to be little more than an assemblage of bones, but the skin stretched tight across her cheekbones was flushed with emotion. She wore a brightly colored headscarf, a kind of turban that lent volume to her bird-like head. The heavy gold ring she wore on her finger was now several sizes too large. A plaid throw covered her legs and her abdomen, but the outlines of her hip bones and knees were visible. She motioned him closer. Weber pulled up a chair, sat down and leaned toward her. Pausing frequently, she said, "Tomorrow will be the day, I think. I am leaving with great joy. Just before the end, Lennart came and told me his stage name. He will call himself *Orfeo*. Can you imagine a more suitable name? But it refers to more than mythology, that's for certain."

She closed her eyes, mustered her strength. Then, she took Weber's hand and squeezed it gently, "It's really a tribute to me! He took the first two letters of my surname, then the first two letters of my maiden name, and added an 'o', the fifth letter. He hasn't forgotten the traditions, you see? He knew that the greatest *primi uomini* always took stage names. Most of them studied with the support of patrons. It was a way to show their gratitude, taking a name that expressed their debt to their benefactors."

She stopped once again; her breathing was becoming more labored. The nurse got to her feet, oxygen mask at the ready. But la Signora waved her away.

"I don't want it. Leave me in peace. Why bother? This is no opera performance; the heroine must die. Ah, *Orfeo*! What a masterstroke! He'll have the world eating out of his hand, you shall see! That name! Now I know he loves me. He never told me so. As for me, I never could bring myself to say it either. You cannot imagine what it means

33

to me. With the rest of you, the pianists, I was only doing my job. With him, it was different. There is no one like him. And thanks to him, I shall live on."

When Anna Maria Ferrone-Oragagni died, a handful of specialized publications reviewed her career and her work as an educator in a tone that suggested that her methods, even though they harked back to "a bygone era" had nonetheless produced several decent pianists. The local press published only one eulogy—and it was written by Weber.

Just before the evening she died, he had returned to the villa to ask la Signora if she had any short-term plans for Lennart. Lennart refused to leave his room. He'd had a "nervous fit" that morning, Gertrud said; he wanted to be left alone. Weber jotted a note on the back of his business card to say that he would return to the villa after the funeral.

The memory of Lennart's slender silhouette remained, etched in Weber's mind. His curious, deliberate way of moving. The way he walked, as if he were floating. His penetrating gaze, focusing rapidly, as though he were about to ask a question. He could not decide how to approach this singer, who intimidated him with his ethereal voice, with his ability to slip into the skin of a character in a matter of seconds.

CHAPTER TWO

Deh, per questo istante solo
"Ah, for this single moment"

−W. A. Mozart, *La clemenza di Tito*, Act II

W eber returned to Freiburg, mechanically. He'd been thinking intently of how best to approach the young man. Then he would catch himself: Lennart only appeared to be a man, because he was tall. The first time he had seen him, he'd taken him for a woman, because of his voice. It was a curious kind of confusion. "Whatever happens," he thought, "the mystery can't last forever. I'll be seeing him as often as I wish; I must prepare him for what awaits him in the outside world. He must know of la Signora's arrangements, and the role I should play in his life." Weber was uneasy; la Signora had confided to him that the singer had a "difficult" temperament. But she hadn't added any further details. If he were to attempt to gain the upper hand, their relationship might quickly become problematic. Weber could be blunt, and he knew it.

Suddenly, he felt discouraged. The whole enterprise seemed meaningless; he was far too busy; Kirsten's and his lives were already full.

He had planned to take the main highway back to Freiburg, but he ended up following a twisting, curving route through immaculate villages where no one could be seen in the streets. This less traveled road would give him time to find the words to tell Kirsten that he would be looking after Lennart. Now and again, as he exited a small town, he could see the bluish line of the Vosges in the bright sunlight, or the massifs of the Black Forest, and in the distance the spires of Freiburg cathedral, bright red against the pink or slate rooftops. He had to lower the sun visor; it was late May, and the weather was already hot. Before long, they would be moving to their little house at Bernau.

He parked near the Dreisam. The municipality had built a narrow pathway along the bank where, by day, elderly people would throng the benches. By night, it was no place to go alone, what with the gangs of punks or "artists" daubing their incomprehensible graffiti over the retaining walls of the roadway that followed the edge of the ravine through which the river flowed. Weber and Kirsten liked to meet there at midday for a sandwich, as their own veranda was still in the shade. In the evening they preferred to stroll through the warren of pedestrian streets near one of the old city gates, the Schwabentor, and they liked to end the day in the Oenothek, with its exhaustive list of regional wines. In May and June, as the academic year was drawing to a climax, you could feel the pulse of Freiburg in the intimate eating-places where the serving staff was made up primarily of students. Weber had met Kirsten, a native of Holstein, in just such a little restaurant, eight years before. It was the way she took his order that had impressed him: courteous yet vaguely ironic, with her northern accent, her calm face, and her lustrous blond hair, like a princess forced to assume duties beneath her station.

He smiled as he thought of Kirsten's keen nose for business. He hadn't the faintest idea about money matters or investments. Once she completed her degree in art history she took over an antique shop in Oberlinden Street, next door to Bären, one of the town's best restaurants, and only a stone's throw from the Herrenstrasse, a street popular among Freiburg's better-off citizens as well as tourists. She sold paintings by minor regional 19th-century painters, hand-blown glass, French and German porcelain. The customers appreciated her. Weber had watched her at work; she was skillful enough never to force a sale.

Weber opened the gate, walked through the garden and took the elevator. When he reached their apartment, he noticed that she'd forgotten to lock the door, again. One day, he told himself, they'd return home to find their place empty. But according to the concierge, the punks had never robbed a house in the neighborhood; they were interested in other things. Weber didn't like these young people; he couldn't understand why they dyed their hair, or the weird clothing they wore. Whenever he took the train he was shocked to see that their incomprehensible signs had not spared a single structure belonging to the railway. It was as though they had a language all their own. What would become of them later, he wondered, when they would be thirty-five, his age? He couldn't fathom their music. At the newspaper, one of his colleagues wrote a regular column on the punk scene. But he was among the least popular journalists in the newsroom. Weber, who considered his reputation excellent, saw himself as a member of the middle class. For all that, he kept the other man at a safe distance.

Kirsten would be back later. Before he left for Bad Krozingen, she'd let him know she planned to join a new customer for dinner, someone who had made a substantial purchase at the shop.

Weber frowned as he rummaged through the refrigerator. At the sight of Kirsten's organic vegetables he thought back to the minestrone la Signora had so often told him about. At that instant, a blackbird broke into song in the aspen in the garden. Weber loved the bird, a venerable male who'd spent years perfecting his trills. As soon as the weather turned warm, he would take up a perch in the uppermost branches of the tree, where he would warble until after ten o'clock. The early summer evenings were already long; night seemed to be hesitating before it fell. It was common enough to hear the bird for three hours at a stretch. It was a prodigious, perhaps unique voice. At their country house, during the month of July, every evening two or three blackbirds would converse in melodious chirps and whistles. But the blackbird in the garden was in a class by himself; to listen to him was a physical pleasure. There was only a superficial resemblance between the arias that made up his repertoire.

Wishing to enjoy the concert, Weber pulled a part-bottle of white wine, a tasty Gutedel, from the fridge, placed a few slices of pumpernickel on a plate, added a pat of butter, several slices of cold meat, some pickles, a few leaves of lettuce, a tomato and a slice of cheese. The lettuce and tomato were a bow to Kirsten: she paid close attention to the variety of colors on a plate. As his natural proclivity to overweight had intensified after marriage, she had forbidden him to eat white bread. She did allow him dark bread, but he didn't like its molasses aftertaste. There were times when he would crave one of the rich, country-style dishes with plenty of fat and fried potatoes you could find in the Württemberg region. Sometimes he would duck into the greasy spoon where he'd eaten in his student days. Other times, with a colleague, he would nip over to Strasbourg. They would dine at a restaurant where they would surrender to the sauerkraut, the sausages and the fat-marbled meats. But these excesses would leave him full of remorse. When he met his wife for supper at Bären he would on occasion order one of its hearty peasant dishes. Kirsten no longer raised an objection, but she would sigh at his backsliding. Weber put everything on a tray, walked across the living room and sat down on the veranda. The sky was bright and cloudless. And the blackbird was still warbling.

So sublime was the bird's song that Weber had to stop chewing from time to time. Was it a freak of nature, nothing but pure chance? Perhaps there was a connection between the bird and Lennart? Were they both singing for lack of love? Weber listened closely to its flights of coloratura in wonderment at the creature's ingeniousness. Suddenly it seemed as if the bird were whistling the Rossini aria. The same purity was there, the same impulsiveness, the same impatience, the same desire to please. *Seduction by voice.* Kirsten, who was not a musician— she liked music, but of the modern variety, primarily from the 'twenties, the songs of Kurt Weill and Hanns Eisler—adored the bird as well. How would she respond to Lennart's voice? Weber, first hearing him in the aria from *Tancredi*, had been stunned, then moved to tears. Music, perfectly executed, had always had that effect on him. As a musician and a music critic—he vehemently rejected the notion that inside every critic lies a failed musician—he was familiar with the criteria used to classify voices. He rummaged through his memory in search of the precise term that could describe Lennart's singular voice. For starters he would describe it as round, magnificent in timbre, agile. But more than a few contemporary sopranos could sing the same aria in comparable style. So what was it exactly?

He wracked his mind. Then suddenly he believed he had found what set it apart: *nobility.* Precisely what the others were lacking. *Nobility*, and this too: *elegance.* His range was exceptional; even a singer whose voice fell between mezzo and soprano could not possibly have reproduced it. To go all the way down to a low E was prodigious in itself. La Signora had warned him: this was a voice to be taken seriously;

it was not a circus act. With a sense of irritation, he thought back to the stage name that Lennart had chosen. It seemed to him infantile, bold and yet pretentious. But if the lad truly intended to revive the baroque *opera seria* he was certainly not lacking in audacity.

As he thought about what la Signora had asked of him, Weber realized he would be able to hear Lennart on subsequent visits to the villa. At their only encounter he thought he'd detected a glimmer of curiosity or perhaps apprehension in Lennart's green eyes, although it was impossible to interpret his glance, as he had lowered his eyelids like a seminary student. Perhaps Weber had been mistaken. Lennart was a good head taller, after all. He'd never been able to rid himself of a slight sense of inferiority in the presence of people taller than he was, like Kirsten, who adapted to her husband's height by wearing low-heeled shoes.

Ever since their first meeting, and especially after hearing la Signora's account, Weber had read everything he could find on the subject of *primi uomini*. When she noticed the stack of books on his worktable, Kirsten assumed that he was preparing to write an article on commission, which would bring in a substantial sum of money. He borrowed treatises and medical texts from the university library, thick historical tomes he quickly set aside as they offered little or no information on the quality of the voice of a particular *primo uomo* or *musico*, in contrast to the *prima donna*, his great rival. In the way of literature, he turned up a French novel from the 1970s; he found it boring.

He learned that, in medical terms, the larynx of a *primo uomo* possessed particularities that place his voice in a distinct category: unlike a man after puberty, he never develops what is known as an "Adam's apple." The two membranes located in the center—the vocal chords, also known as the "glottal folds"—are part of an extremely complex apparatus. The voice itself resonates in the irregularly shaped and variable pharyngeal cavity that communicates with the nasal fossa that form a part of the singer's mask. But these were mechanical elements; alone they could not explain the quality of the voice he had heard that day. In Lennart's voice, the chest register was incisive and lustrous; his head voice remained brilliant as well. Lennart could reach high C, perhaps even higher. His voice was breathy, like the sound of a flute, but smoother. And how could anything explain the emotion that seemed to flow through his different interpretations of the same aria?

"Intensity and volume are not at all the same thing," he'd read in Garcia. It was possible for a sound to be faint, yet forceful. What gives a voice its specific character is the vibration of the vocal chords, the dimensions of the thorax, the larynx, lung control, the capacity of the pharyngeal, nasal and buccal cavities, and the disposition of the resonators. This complex apparatus, Weber concluded, could be reduced to three essential elements: the lungs, which function as a bellows, the larynx, which acts as a vibrator, and the pharynx and the nasal cavities, which reflect or modify the sound of the voice.

So much for the instrument itself. But the fundamental question remained unanswered: how had la Signora been able to shape the young man's soul so that it could express the sounds he had heard on his first visit? The malleability of his voice, the ease with which he produced it, would have meant little had it not been for the ring of truth Weber had heard in the aria from *Tancredi*. With each repeat, the singer had added a fresh dimension of character, each as credible as the one before. How was that possible for someone so young, entirely without life experience? His physical suffering aside, Lennart had known little unhappiness, protected as he had been by la Signora against any attack from outside forces, insulated by a cozy cocoon that ensured his stability. The thought occurred to Weber: could it be that Lennart was an empty vessel, without a personality of his own, able to slip into the skin of any character at a moment's notice, to change his role, like a blackboard on which words may be written, then erased, then immediately rewritten?

That must have been it. La Signora had helped him construct a suit of armor that would protect Lennart against the trials that would be soon to come. As soon as his voice became known, the great opera houses of Berlin, Munich, London, New York, Milan, Moscow and Tokyo would be fighting bitterly over it. Inevitably a bidding war would ensue, agents would thrust themselves upon him. Lennart was impatient to begin his career, Weber supposed. La Signora had intimated as much. But where could he obtain the assurance that he would not fall? How long would his voice last? His entire future would depend on the strength of those two tiny muscles in his throat, on a robust constitution, and on the technique acquired over twelve years of hard work. Lennart was no longer a sickly young man. Despite his barely visible limp, he moved with assurance; his tall, slender body seemed supple and resilient. But Weber knew what often happened to young voices, particularly to counter-tenors and tenors. Most of them burned out in a few seasons, to be forgotten, with hardly a regret.

Today, no male voice could equal his in brilliance. Competition, as it had in the past, would come from women. The title role in *Rinaldo* had been sung as often by *musici* like Nicolino or Bernacchi as by sopranos like la Barbier or la Vico. True, Lennart's larynx was almost identical to that of a *prima donna*, in its dimensions, the way it was formed and in the absence of angulations. Singing at the true feminine octave, he had the advantage that his larynx was as pliable as a child's. His was a hybrid instrument that could produce sounds of a brilliance, and, above all, of a range that no woman, no matter how well trained, could hope to achieve.

As he sipped a second glass of Gutedel, Weber began to speculate, with a mixture of excitement and apprehension. How would orchestra directors react to Lennart? What would the public make of him? How would people respond to his voice, so fully measured, so perfectly controlled that even in the *messa di voce* it could dispense entirely with vibrato, that relic of a 19th century obsessed with powerful voices.

It was getting late. The sky had turned a color halfway between dark blue and lavender; the blackbird had gone to sleep. Weber smiled at the thought that the bird's throat, after a concert of three hours, must be dry as paper. In the quiet of the evening, he could hear the distant sounds of the city, a hum that would only end when the nightclubs finally closed. A tram's wheels squeaked as it rounded the curve in front of the Ganter brewery across the Dreisam. To the left loomed the dark mass of Loretto hill; the Schlossberg seemed as though it was just across the courtyard.

Weber put the empty bottle and the plates on the tray. He was about to return everything to the kitchen when the apartment door closed softly. He hadn't heard the key in the lock. Kirsten slipped off her shoes. When she went out alone, she wore high heels. They clicked on the tiled floor of the vestibule. Weber didn't like disorder; Kirsten would drop her purse, her scarf and her coat wherever she liked—and not without pride. Weber interpreted her behavior as the vestiges of a little rich girl's childhood. Early on, he had learned to help his mother do the housecleaning. He knew how to cook. Methodical, orderly and ambitious, he had been at the top of his class in cooking school. He had always been the best. Except at the piano.

Kirsten was wearing a light-colored linen suit. Without turning his head, Weber recognized the garment from the way its lining rubbed against the fine-textured fabric as she walked across the living room to join him on the veranda. She seemed happy. Her silky hair was slightly tousled, her pale salmon-colored blouse wrinkled, as was her skirt. Linen is fine as long as you won't be sitting down, he thought. She kissed him on the cheek, and gulped down the wine left at the bottom of his glass. She told him about her new friend Vera, a rather resourceful businesswoman, a divorcée and owner of Freiburg's largest nightclub, the Unicorn, with a huge dance floor that was a favorite with the students. Vera had dropped by her shop because she wanted to open another bar, for a more mature, better-paying clientele. She was looking to decorate it with old objects "to create atmosphere." Kirsten had given her a good price on some paintings of doubtful quality that would do the job as long as no one examined them too closely, and a significant portion of her stock of hand-blown mercury glass, what they called Bauernsilber, "peasant's silver" in Württemberg. Vera was still looking for a suitable place to display her newfound treasures. In her new bar, only classical music would be played, mostly instrumental and generally neutral. Maybe, she'd told Kirsten, she would hire students from the Conservatory. She could get them for very little money. The kind of customers she had in mind would go for that, and the prices in her new bar would be set accordingly.

"And how was your day?" Kirsten asked Weber.

He decided this was the right moment to tell her about la Signora's last wish. After filling her in, he explained how uneasy he was about what he hoped to do with Lennart. Kirsten's words reassured him: he was not a legal guardian, he could withdraw whenever he wished. Weber added that the singer seemed to be keeping up with his work. According to Gertrud, Lennart was acting as if la Signora were not dead. Each day he followed the very same routine he had followed while his teacher was still alive. A few days earlier, for instance, Johann had been planting flowers not far from the glass doors to the studio when he heard la Signora's voice. The handyman had crept up to the door and peeked into the room. Lennart was bending over a small table beside an armchair, pushing the buttons of a tape-recorder. She must have recorded several lessons just before she died, in a final attempt to guide her student through the first days of his independence. Then Lennart had stopped the machine, stepped over to the piano to rehearse, returned once more to the table to listen to her voice, then repeated the passage. Weber told Kirsten that Gertrud said she was afraid that Lennart was simply denying that la Signora was dead, "He loved her so much, and he owes her everything." There had been a few minor changes at the villa, she reported. Lennart now took Saturdays off; he walked more frequently in the garden, and would even stroll along the banks of the Neumagen. One night, he had burned papers in the chimney. He refused to eat minestrone, and insisted on cooked meals. The villa had not yet been officially put up for sale, but it was only a matter of time; a real-estate agent had come calling. Gertrud overheard him telling Lennart that despite its age, and the repairs that had to be done, it would be quite easy to sell. Johann, Maria and Gertrud took turns guessing what price it would bring. Maria, the youngest, was concerned about her future. La Signora had bequeathed modest amounts to her servants. Lennart said not a word, which only deepened their distrust.

The next day, Saturday, Kirsten habitually closed her shop at two o'clock. On Saturdays they rarely ate at home. They had lunch at the Colombi, a horrifyingly expensive restaurant where Kirsten would encounter customers who looked forward to meeting her, something like a private club, and where, she reasoned, they could talk.

Weber noticed that she talked about Lennart as though he were a poor orphan in need of protection. Speaking in a detached manner, she allowed that she was curious to hear his voice. Perhaps when she saw him, she would be able to imagine "what to do with him." Weber loved his wife, but there were times when she was a bit too determined to take the initiative. He suspected that she would like to place Lennart in one of those rest houses deep in the Münstertal, which she called the "Monstertal"—the valley of the monsters—because of its high rate of congenital malformation that came from inbreeding. She grimaced when he described the accident that had produced Lennart's condition. Lingering on the penultimate word, she said, "He must certainly be a very ... particular person." Weber hadn't appreciated her tone. He thought he'd detected a touch of irony, and perhaps even disdain, as though the singer were a kind of pariah, and she were making fun of her husband's tender-heartedness. He brought her up to date on his visits to la Signora's without revealing his interest in Lennart, which had nothing to do with pity. When he mentioned his stage name, and how pleased la Signora had been, she paused for a moment, then, in a soft voice, said, "Not bad, not bad at all. If his voice is as remarkable as you say it is, he'll go far with a name like that."

Weber's schedule during the summer was different from the rest of the year. There were fewer concerts to be covered in town, but he was often on the road writing about the music festivals. He maintained his standards; festival organizers might well pay for his travel and accommodation and flatter him at post-concert receptions, but his critical articles remained fair and were often hard-hitting. Rarely did his judgment mislead him. Other newspapers frequently echoed his evaluations. Ever since joining the *Freiburger Rundschau*, he'd built up a solid network of connections in the German music world, an immense and flourishing industry. He knew the leading critics both in Germany and abroad. He was deluged with invitations. He didn't like attending out-of-town events alone because Kirsten could not stay away for more than two days. She did her best business at Christmas and between May and August, when Weber was out of town. But deep down he knew that "his" music didn't really interest her. More than once, she'd derided him as a "baroquist."

Weber realized that he'd drunk too much white wine; he decided he should have taken a red, a Spätburgunder, instead; at least you knew where you stood. Shouldn't have eaten the pickles either. He massaged his stomach. Although it was still early, Kirsten went right to sleep. Sleep came easily to her, as though to an innocent child, while he often suffered bouts of insomnia. When he thought of the blackbird's song, the Rossini aria took its place. Finally, all he could hear was Lennart's voice, practicing vocalises. The perfectly joined *a*'s, *e*'s and *o*'s had the effect of a lullaby, rocking him to sleep. He imagined Lennart in sailor's costume, singing the aria "*Vo solcando un mar crudele*" from Leonardo Vinci's *Artaserse*.

Weber dreamed a strange, disquieting dream that night. When he awakened he could still recall the details, but he pushed them into the back of his consciousness, and said nothing of it to Kirsten, although she loved hearing about his dreams. She believed they presaged events, and claimed to be jealous of them; she could never remember her own. But Weber envied her ability to forget. In his considered opinion, her liver was less atrophied than his, which gave her a deeper sleep, but although he had never told her this, he attributed her lack of dreams to her down-to-earth, even prosaic nature, to her businesswoman's life. Last night's dream was too fragmentary to speak about, he concluded. But for all his attempts to forget it, elements of it kept popping into his mind, exciting and yet unsettling all at once.

The dream would reappear, each time identical, persistent, as though intent on insinuating itself into Weber's nocturnal life.

Everything about the Colombi exuded luxury. The low voices of the diners blended with the tinkle of fine crystal and silver. The table service was choreographed like a ballet. Kirsten and Weber were concentrating on the food; they loved to eat well. Over dessert, he asked her if she would like to go with him the next day to Bad Krozingen to visit Lennart. It was a Sunday; they were free. She sensed his nervousness, and said, "I won't eat him up." He found her remark funny, especially after a fine dinner. She lighted a cigarette and looked around the room. A redheaded woman nodded at her. Kirsten waved; the woman got up and joined them. It was Vera. She was the only daughter of Scholler, who had made a fortune rebuilding Freiburg after the war. Something gave Weber the vague impression that this was not a chance encounter.

The two women greeted each other as if they'd been friends for an eternity. Weber took an instant dislike to this slender redhead who kissed Kirsten so effusively. There was something coarse about her, he thought. When she shook Weber's hand, she did so like a man, gripping it strongly. Her bracelets jangled discordantly against the gentle hum of the restaurant. Vera spoke loudly, rapidly, like a raspy-voiced fishwife. With her, there was no discussion; words dropped like guilty verdicts. Heavy makeup caked her broad face with its high cheekbones. Weber couldn't make out the color of her eyes, so thickly had she applied her eyeliner. And that lipstick of hers would scare off any man; it certainly turned him off. Her purple silk dress, held up by two fine shoulder straps, was a masterpiece of sensuality, suggesting curves whose real existence Weber strongly doubted.

Beside her, Kirsten looked like a schoolgirl. The redhead pulled a cigarette from a leather case and asked the waiter to bring her after-lunch drink to the table. It was clear that she was accustomed to giving orders, and to being obeyed. She spoke at length of her new bar and her plans for making a mint from it. When she learned that they were going to see a singer in Bad Krozingen, she immediately showed interest in joining them. Weber could feel exasperation getting the better of him. He intended to introduce Lennart to the outside world, but slowly, at least in the beginning. The singer was young and reclusive, he explained, and would resist too many new faces at the same time. He could feel Kirsten's knee under the table, but he ignored it. Now Vera's curiosity was aroused. She began to ask more pointed questions about the singer. But when she learned that Lennart sang only baroque opera, her interest quickly subsided. They chatted for a few more minutes. As Weber and Kirsten were leaving the restaurant, Vera strolled over to join a gentleman at another table.

Once outside, Kirsten gave him a piece of her mind. That was no way to treat such an excellent customer. But Weber stood his ground. Wait until tomorrow, he said to himself. You'll see.

As they stepped into the vestibule, Weber could see Kirsten putting on a mask of cold politeness, as if to conceal her dismay. The scent of la Signora's *eau de toilette* still hung heavy in the air. She had departed the house two weeks earlier, but her odor clung stubbornly to the walls. On their way through the garden at the villa, Kirsten criticized the invasiveness of the trees; they should have been properly trimmed years ago, she said. She pointed to the poorly kept lawn, the tasteless arrangement of the flowerbeds.

That morning, Weber had called the villa. When Gertrud handed

46

the telephone to Lennart, he told the singer how deeply la Signora's death had affected him. Lennart had cut him off, "I know, sir. I read your article. Thank you very much." All that was spoken in a remote, emotionless voice.

After a long silence, Weber ventured, "May I see you? We must discuss your future. You know that, according to la Signora—"

Lennart interrupted him again, this time with a tone of mild irritation, "Yes, yes, I know. I've already given it some thought. The main problem in the short term is the sale of the villa."

"I don't have a head for business myself, you know. My wife is much more the businesswoman. Would you mind if she were to come along? I've already told her about you. Gertrud tells me you work on Sundays. I would truly like to hear you again. Your Rossini of a month ago ..."

A long silence. Lennart waited, but Weber could say nothing more; he felt like a student facing his first audition with a new teacher.

"I'm not working on Rossini these days, but on a Mozart aria. La Signora told me you are a pianist in your spare time. If you wish, you could accompany me. I prefer not to play when I sing. In fact, I don't like to accompany myself at all. I'm not really gifted as a pianist. You would be of—" here the singer paused, then emphasized the word— "*appreciable* assistance if you were at the piano. I have the transcriptions, they're not too difficult. Would late afternoon suit you?"

Now Weber's main concern was that his wife's mood might upset Lennart. Kirsten rarely visited Bad Krozingen, which she considered a second-class spa full of elderly people suffering from atrocious illnesses; the clinics were reputable, of course, but second-class nonetheless. A complex of pools in abominable taste, a knock-off of Roman kitsch, knock-kneed old geezers dressed in rompers limping about, rest halls that looked more like morgues, and rundown grounds where they lay waiting for death, resigned to the certainty that the only way out was feet first.

"They die by the dozen every day," she said with a malicious twinkle in her eye as they made their way across a narrow bridge over the Neumagen. "Look, see how low-key the funeral parlors are? I've heard that undertakers disguised as attendants come to take the dead bodies away before dawn, while the old folks are still asleep. What a repulsive place! Look how clean it is, not a shred of paper on the sidewalks. Nothing but pharmacies, one after another. They must be making a pile, all the pharmacies in this hole. I haven't seen a single store with pretty things. They're not interested in such things any more, the oldies. What a miserable place, a real death house! It's so quiet it's scary. And dark too. So dark you can't even make out the houses."

They'd parked their car in the town center, close to a square covered with yellowish gravel and bordered with lindens. A handful of grandfathers were playing bowls, but there wasn't a trace of Mediterranean insouciance in the game; their faces were stern, they moved ponderously, deliberately. Kirsten was right: two banks, four pharmacies and a stationer's surrounded the square. Further along, in a smaller street, were a bakery and a tiny supermarket. Not a soul to be seen. It was as if the inhabitants had vanished. Thick greenish-black hedges concealed the houses. Yes, the whole place looked liked a ghost village.

Even their stroll along the Neumagen could not please Kirsten. In her opinion, the cascading little brook made the vegetation too luxuriant. "It's the Styx! I wouldn't even want to put my toe in that murky water." Certainly she would never buy a house in this place. The villas were more like mausoleums, shrouded in silence. It was a village of old people, of nursing attendants and dogs.

When Gertrud opened the door, Weber felt the same sense of irritation he'd experienced the previous day at the Colombi. Perhaps his whole sour mood was due to Vera; he thought he'd caught the same pouting look on Kirsten's face that he'd noticed on the other woman's the day before. This new friend of hers was someone to keep an eye on, he concluded.

The studio windows were open. Lennart, who was seated in front of the Steinway, rose to his feet, his hand resting on the cover. He was wearing a white shirt; his dark brown corduroy pants half-covered his sandals and bare feet. He looked at Weber, then turned to Kirsten. His eyes traveled the length of her light blue dress, paused for a moment on the opal brooch, a birthday gift from Weber, then came to rest on her flat-heeled shoes.

"Kirsten, may I present Lennart Teufel?"

Lennart, who had said nothing when they entered the room,

replied, "Orfeo. Since la Signora Ferrone-Oragagni's death, my name is Orfeo. You're aware of that, I think. I would be grateful if you would no longer use the name my parents gave me."

Weber noted the calmness of his voice: not a trace of irritation, no stress on one word more than another. He thought of the inner equilibrium of singers, the quality that la Signora had so often spoken of, an equilibrium that could only be reached by stilling the pendulum of the emotions. The result would be a sense of quiet assurance, with imperceptible warm vibrations in a register lower than what the listener could hear. A rested voice, ready for performance, a voice that suggested hidden powers.

The singer explained that he preferred to take Saturday off, with no declamation, no forcing his voice, and resume his vocal exercises on Sunday afternoon. Right now he was working on "*Deh, per questo istante solo*," Sextus's aria from the second act of *La Clemenza di Tito*. In a soft voice, he said, "Could you accompany me? That way, I can give my full attention to what I'm doing. I trust that Madame Weber will forgive us if we work a bit."

Kirsten's face had become impassive; Weber knew how profoundly bored and disturbed she felt. She eyed the room like a real-estate agent, overlooking nothing. Lennart had taken down la Signora's Neapolitan paintings. The four Piranesi engravings he'd hung in their place depicted immense, outlandish, hallucinatory constructions, with stairways leading to nowhere, corridors, strange torture apparatuses, and tiny characters watching executions. But the white patches on the wall where the scenes from the Amalfi Coast once hung were still visible. By daylight, the Turkish carpet looked even more threadbare, the curtains seemed to be covered in a film of dust, and the mirror beside the door reflected the bareness of the room.

Weber was delighted to provide the accompaniment. He had begun to speak rapidly, enthusiastically, his excitement growing by the minute; at last he would hear Lennart sing one of the great arias of the classic *primo uomo* repertoire. Vocally, it was less complicated than those of baroque opera, but it demanded of the interpreter great emotional maturity. With *La Clemenza di Tito*, Mozart bids farewell to the ancient *opera seria* form. In the opera, Weber explained, Sextus has been manipulated by the ambitious Vitellia, who convinces him to murder Titus, the emperor. Kirsten, who did not know the story, feigned attention as Lennart looked on in amusement. When the plot is discovered, the senate condemns Sextus to death. But Titus forgives his friend, for he cannot reign unless he feels that he is loved. Absolutism has come to an end; the emperor must sacrifice his own ambitions to the interests of the state. It was the same appeal that Mozart made to Leopold II when he was crowned King of Bohemia in 1791.

The aria "*Deh, per questo istante solo*" is undoubtedly one of the opera's most remarkable. Before he is hauled off to his death in the arena, Sextus harks back to his old, abiding friendship for Titus one last time: "*ti ricorda il primo amor.*" He complains of the emperor's scorn, his hard-heartedness; Titus would be less severe could he look into his heart, he sings: "*Pur saresti men severo se vedessi questo cor.*" This passage is the centerpiece of the aria: it is sung twice, almost unaccompanied, where the voice alone must transmit Sextus's remorse and sadness at having betrayed his friend. The words "*amor*" in the first stanza, echoed by "*questo cor*," suggest that Sextus is revealing his friendship for the first time. It is his last chance to open his heart, which he delivers unconditionally to Titus. The aria is Sextus's soul, plunged deep into despair and remorse.

Weber sat down at the piano. He leafed through the score, a transcription that he recognized as la Signora's handwriting. It would be easy enough to play the first part, but the second he studied for several minutes; it would be more demanding.

The moment Lennart began to sing, the resonance and the intensity of his voice all but paralyzed Weber's fingers, as he struggled to follow the score. Behind him, he heard Kirsten gasp for breath. Lennart attacked the aria with extreme deliberation, slowing down even more in the central passage, and allowing his voice to expire on "*cor.*" And when he reached the passage where Sextus confesses that Titus's anger and severity cause him to die of grief, so deep was the despair in his voice that Weber's eyes filled with tears. By the time he reached the "*disperato vado a morte*" Weber could not go on; his hands froze atop the keyboard; the voice had become transparent, with a constant, sustained breathing that made each note pure, effortless, unadulterated. When the aria shifted tempo and key in measures 25 and 26, from the "*disperato vado a morte*" until the admission of betrayal of a friend, and the chilling "*che fui teco un traditor*," Metastasio's text stood forth in all its glory, set off by the genius of Mozart, and by the smooth singing, the *canto spianato*, by the nuances, the precise intonation, the stability and the consistency of his voice. His *legato* was perfect, his *messa di voce* on "*cor*," in a troubling F-minor, was just long enough to reveal Sextus's inner torment. The aria then opened onto the *portamento*, where the singer joins one note to another without replenishing his breath. When Lennart used his *voce di petto*, with its bronze-like timbre, he perfectly conveyed the friendship between two men who were never able to speak their affection. Even as the fate of Sextus edges toward death, he makes only the briefest allusion: "If only you could gaze into my heart and feel what I feel toward you! You are my best friend; I love you. I was led astray by this woman, Vitellia; it was she who drove me to do what I did not wish to. I ask not for pardon. That would be futile, and above all, unworthy of the two of us."

Suddenly, at the beginning of the second part of the aria, Weber was struck by Lennart's transformation. He was no longer the young, raw-boned singer with the slightly unprepossessing face. Lennart had ceased to be himself; *he had become Sextus.*

At that moment Weber resolved never to call him by anything but his stage name again.

Picking up the score where he had paused for an instant, Weber noticed something else about the voice he was hearing; it was as though the singer was pacing himself. The first time he had heard him, in the aria from *Tancredi*, he had taken note of this restraint, a kind of half-voice that harked back to the melody that flowed with the music instead of pushing itself to the fore. Just as in the Rossini aria, the *flautati*, a series of notes strung together by inflexion, a continuity of small sounds of different proportions in a single breath, held together by a dizzying agility, astonished him. Now technique had taken over, with percussive notes produced by rapid compressions of the stomach and a dilation of the pharynx, and *staccati*, when the glottis separates one sound from another in rapid succession.

The aria came to an end. Eyes fixed on the score, Weber realized that all the contemporary voices he knew so well had taken the wrong path. In place of Orfeo's purity and lightness of emission, today's singing schools forced the sound, and drew attention to the vocal prowess and power of the interpreter. Manuel Garcia was right: "Intensity and volume are not the same thing." Here, in the Mozart aria, melody, voice and text formed a perfect whole, a harmony so flawless that the meaning of the aria asserted itself with a clarity that any listener could immediately grasp. What emerged was a blending of sensuality and distance from the subject: the purity of the sound joining the male affection of the character of Sextus, an emotion so difficult to express. Now it had become intelligible, precisely because the singer had not exceeded his function. Orfeo had actually conveyed what was happening at that very moment in Sextus's soul.

As if that were not enough, the singer shaped his gestures to the *cantabile* of the first part of the aria. His hand and arm movements were pared down to a strict minimum; he raised them only for the words "*duolo*" and "*cor*," in a weak supplication, and never above shoulder level. All was measured restraint, his body swaying forward and back in the second part, conveying the torment of Sextus, a prisoner of his patrician dignity, as he reaches the far limit of what his pride can permit. Orfeo had held his head at a noble pitch for the entire nine minutes of the aria, lowering it only once when he repeated that he had betrayed a friend. The muscles of his face spoke virtually nothing of what his voice expressed. His lips had briefly twisted on "*sdegno*" and "*traditor*," his eyes focusing on a point just above the main entrance to the studio. Weber had not even noticed his breathing: his loose-fitting shirt concealed the work of the abdominal muscles. The sound of deep breathing, the *respiro*, was all but inaudible. He held his head high, chest thrust upward, free.

When Weber let his hands fall from the keyboard, the notes echoed in the room for a few seconds. Overcome by the immediacy of that voice, it was impossible for him to speak. He could hear himself breathe, like a gentle hissing, and turned to look at Orfeo. The *musico* stood motionless for several minutes, fresh, with no visible sign of fatigue, then turned to Weber.

"I think I should have gone even slower in the '*Pur saresti men severo*,' where Sextus implores Titus. He's submitting to him at the same time, isn't that so? That instant has to be underlined; I skimmed over it too fast, but I was afraid I didn't have enough wind. It would be senseless to breathe there, it would break the emotional spell. I'll work on that passage some more."

After a pause that seemed to expect a response from Weber, he ended brusquely, "Enough for today."

It was the same tone la Signora had used to mark the end of a lesson. Weber resurfaced. He was so shaken he could find no argument to restrain the other man. And yet, he would have wanted to begin again, and again. Hear him. Observe his movements. Join with his artistry. Join forces with him. Get as close to him, physically, as he could. Explore his gaze, follow the tilt of his head. But Orfeo waved vaguely to an imaginary audience at the back of the room, where Kirsten was sitting, did not thank Weber, said not a word upon leaving, and walked slowly across the room, vanishing through the rear door. Weber could hear his footsteps as he climbed the stairs. He got to his feet, and turned toward Kirsten.

She remained seated, shoulders thrown back, head slightly tilted. For a moment Weber thought she might be ill. Her face was pale, her hair had fallen across her cheeks, her lips were half parted and pale, her hands rested motionless upon the hem of her skirt, her feet were close together. When Weber touched her shoulder, he felt her muscles contract as though making a supreme effort. He shook her gently; it was only then that she started to breathe deeply. Her blue eyes, usually so full of life, remained focused on the far end of the room, on the door through which the singer had vanished. Weber lifted his hand, startled; Kirsten's cheeks were wet with tears. He had never seen her weep. When he told her it was time to leave, she got docilely to her feet and followed him. There was not a sign of Maria, who was probably preparing the evening meal.

From start to finish, they had been there no longer than half an hour.

They turned onto the path that followed the Neumagen. It was cool in the shade of the tall trees beside the stream. As always, the pathway was deserted. Where it passed beside an open meadow, a wave of warmth swept over them. Kirsten pointed to a bench facing the field, in the sunlight. They had not exchanged a word since they left the villa. She took up the same position as she had on the chair earlier: neck stretched out, she seemed to be listening. Above their heads there was nothing but the chirping of birds. Across the Neumagen behind a hedge a dog barked. Kirsten was unable to regain her composure and could not stop crying. Her shoulders were shaking, her fists were clenched, her knuckles white. When he touched her shoulder she shook off his hand, stood up and told him, in a low voice, that she wanted to return to Freiburg.

Did she prefer the main highway or the road through the villages, he asked. She gave no answer, sank into her seat as though she wanted to sleep, and closed her eyes. Her eyelids were still wet with tears. Crouched there, she looked like a little girl who has suffered a great sorrow. On the trip back to town she did not say a word.

As he drove, Weber thought back to the moment when Orfeo had left the studio. In the silence that followed the aria, he had felt so deep a sense of abandonment that he could not shake it off. He thought again of last night's dream: in it, he had felt the same feeling of disorientation confounded with an acute excitation of his senses, not at all like what he experienced when he was with Kirsten. He tightened his grip on the wheel for fear that his moist palms would slip on the leather.

At the end of the aria, he had not been able to formulate the slightest response, even of the pro-forma variety. The singer would have seen through such a stratagem. Weber thought he knew Mozart well, but Orfeo had just shown him that he had never truly understood the meaning of the aria. He rationalized in his own defense that the composer had created a major obstacle by writing the role of Sextus for a soprano. How was it possible not to be troubled by the ambiguity of a woman's voice, playing a masculine role, telling a tenor that she has betrayed him, and that she accepts death? In Orfeo's interpretation, the confusion had been carried to such an extreme degree that his voice, in the feminine register, had merged with the masculine intention to form an inextricable knot: love and friendship had taken on a new, indeterminate meaning. Orfeo's Sextus was in love with Titus. The sensual inflections, his despair at losing the affection—no, the love and the respect—of the emperor, were clearly audible in his confession: "Unworthy of pity, it is true—*Di pietade indegno è vero.*"

His Sextus was truly Titus's lover, constantly at odds with women: Berenice, Sextus's sister Servilia, and the cold, ambitious Vitellia. Weber thought of Antinous, who had replaced the women in Emperor Hadrian's chorus. Pity that the subject had always made composers recoil.

To the clarity, the brilliance of his head voice, Orfeo had added the vibrations of his chest voice through a subterfuge that Weber was only now beginning to grasp. For the full length of the aria, Orfeo had maintained a drone, a kind of imperceptible, permanent reference, a touch rather than a sound, further down the scale than the register in which he'd sung it. It was this "under-sound" that embodied the singer's intention to be a man, while not forgetting his feminine side. Moreover, through the freshness of his voice and the immediacy of his emotions, he had brought to it the wide-eyed candor of the child. Weber was stunned: how was it possible for such interpretative perfection, such great spiritual maturity to exist in a person so young, someone who had not yet known a single passion?

Weber was tempted to turn around. Perhaps Orfeo was nothing more than a startling recomposition of the character of Sextus. His impulse was to return as fast as he could to the villa, pore through la Signora's library and find the titles that Orfeo had been required to read. Perhaps he could find an answer in Miller's book on the structure of singing. It might be that the mixture of purity and sensuality he had heard was nothing but the projection of repressed desire. Once again it struck him that Orfeo might be an empty vessel, someone who executed blindly what la Signora had taught him, without understanding its implications. But no. The accent of truth in the Mozart could not exist without a deep grasp of the music and the text. It was imperative for him to hear the aria once more, to ascertain if it was *la musica*, the one and true. For that, in the end, was all that mattered.

Behind Orfeo's willowy silhouette lay hidden a complexity that Weber had begun to apprehend, and that he felt drawing him on. Something that cast him into a combination of dread and delight he did not wish to explain. Already he had begun to fear the night, and his dream. And yet at the same time he summoned it, hoping that it would not end so brutally as before. To follow it to the end, to learn what was haunting him.

* * *

He stole a sidelong glance at Kirsten. She had drawn her feet up on the seat, knees almost touching her chin. When he parked the car near their building she got out and turned this way and that, as if she did not know where she was. She followed him into the apartment and fell into the sofa cushions that enfolded in her silence, while Weber threw open the doors to the veranda.

It was the hour of the blackbird.

CHAPTER THREE

Ah de si nobil alma quanto parlar vorrei
"Ah, how I would love to speak of such a noble soul"

–W. A. Mozart, *Ascanio in Alba*

Kirsten did not join him on the veranda. She was not feeling well, better to go and lie down. Her face had lost a bit of its pallor, but her pursed lips and hard gaze gave him to understand that she did not want to hear a single question. When the blackbird paused, he went inside to check on her. She was hugging a pillow, as she did when she was feeling sick. Shortly after nine o'clock he had wanted to suggest a snack, but she seemed to be asleep. While he was busying himself in the kitchen, he could hear her moving about in the bathroom. Then, silence. When he joined her in bed, she was sleeping soundly.

Weber snapped awake; his dream had turned into a nightmare. It was as if an iron band were tightening around his heart. This time he would tell Kirsten about it— not everything, of course. Perhaps she could interpret some of those strange things. He turned on the light; his wife was no longer there. The blue dress and the pumps had vanished. She was not in the living room, not on the veranda, where it was as warm and humid as high summer. It was almost five o'clock. When he realized that she had gone out, Weber let himself drop onto the sofa. He laid his head on the place where he thought he could detect her distant scent, closed his eyes and drew a deep breath. Kirsten rarely used perfume; he preferred her light, fresh natural odor, that of a little blond girl. He switched on the lamp on the end table, stretched out his legs and stroked the cushions. He found a few blond hairs, arranged them on his knee, then began to weave them together absentmindedly.

His handiwork produced a tiny, delicate braid. It shone like gold in the light of the lamp. Suddenly he felt tears well up in his eyes, then run down his cheeks. He did not attempt to wipe them. Unlike his wife, Weber was easily moved.

He loved Kirsten, for her beauty first of all. She was the only woman he had ever truly desired. When they would meet at noon on a bench overlooking the Dreisam for a brief picnic lunch, he was always overcome with a feeling of bedazzlement when he saw her approaching, with her energetic stride and her look of freedom. He had often wondered what had convinced her to marry him. He did not even know if she loved him; she had never spoken the words. Her glance was bright and open, her smile quick and broad, but she laughed rarely. Using simple, practical arguments, she would invariably come out on top in any discussion. She had become an expert in 19th-century German and French painting, but her expertise had not given her an artist's temperament and it in no way dampened her business acumen. Whenever Weber became outraged at a mediocre musical perform- ance, she would throw him an amused glance as if to say that he had no good reason for losing his temper. That would calm him down. She read his articles rarely; the longer analytical pieces he wrote for specialized journals, never. They only discussed the details of their professional lives with each other in a lighthearted way. She told him with a smile one day that both of them worked in the arts, but that their paths never crossed—"A good thing!" she'd added.

As he stroked the little braid, Weber realized that they lived separate existences which never really touched. Her work in the shop was a source of pleasure for Kirsten, that much was clear. She was calm and convincing and quickly established connections with her customers. She would even meet some of them, like that woman Vera. Occasionally she would accept the invitation of a faithful buyer and eat at the Traube, the Bären or one of the chic restaurants around the Münsterplatz. He had no reason to reproach her, nor did he check up on her, or wonder about what she might have been doing. That she might have been unfaithful to him never crossed his mind.

In this gray hour before dawn, he missed her, desired her. The fine texture of her skin, her silky hair that was almost cold to the touch, and her slender, muscular body excited him. She was an accomplished tennis player who often defeated her male opponents. Watching her play was a source of pride for him. Her movements were sure, fluid; she played well, and hard, and treated her tennis opponents with the kind of camaraderie that she restricted to the confines of the court. Kirsten exuded health, almost like an adolescent. She needed no makeup, only a touch of mascara on her pale eyelashes. She had the look of a young girl who'd been brought up in luxury, far above the hustle and bustle of everyday life. Plenty of class, which served her well in the boutique. She treated customers as though she were doing them a favor in letting go of an object. Her assistants she would hire or fire with the same distant amiability. Her instructions to the cleaning lady were really politely concealed orders. She had an inner hardness, Weber believed; an impenetrable quality that he had never been able to fathom. She would never give herself entirely. Perhaps he admired her for her resistance, even as he adored her. When he heard a piece of music played well, he could feel his throat constrict. But he'd learned to let his tears flow less freely when he was around her; he was concerned lest he displease her.

But she had wept when she heard Orfeo sing.

Doubts overcame Weber that morning, doubts about himself, his work, his life, about their decision to remain in Freiburg. He had received job offers from several major newspapers: *Süddeutsche*, *Tagesspiegel*, *Welt*, *Frankfurter Allgemeine*. They could have made their life somewhere else. If his musical criticism was appreciated and esteemed, it was because of la Signora's teaching. In the final analysis, he owed her everything. At university he'd learned nothing more than how to put his ideas in order. But *understanding* music: that he had gotten from her alone. Without la Signora, he would have continued to work away at the piano. He would have become a second-class clunker, never satisfied with himself, and— who knows?—he might never have met Kirsten.

His wife enjoyed success. Instinctively, she associated only with winners. Weber was convinced that his professional accomplishment was due in large measure to their relationship. When he told her that he would be working late to finish a piece commissioned by this or that magazine, a piece that would pay well, she was happy. His "mini-business," she called it. She would often speak of the offer she was patiently awaiting from the owner of the store. Her father had already assured her that if she wanted financial support to start up her own business, she needed only to ask.

Both of them loved Freiburg. It was a city small enough not to get lost in, but not so small as to be boring. With its thousands of students it was a lively place, and they particularly adored being so close to Alsace. Then there was the apartment, which for him was a real success, and the country house in the Münstertal. But Kirsten was convinced she loved Freiburg more than he did. He was the kind of person who could put down roots anywhere, it was true; he enjoyed travel, and felt at home wherever he happened to be. With his near-black hair, his receding hairline and his chunky build, he could blend in unnoticed in France and Italy, while men there would turn to look at her. Women, too. When she and Weber went out, she did not behave as though they'd been married for eight years. Only rarely would they exchange words of affection, and occasionally a diminutive that they both found ridiculous, and that made them laugh. In public, she would sometimes kiss him full on the mouth, as though he were a lover with whom she had finally mustered the pluck to show herself. That particular trait always caught Weber by surprise. He had thought that Holstein's traditional Protestant reserve forbade such behavior. But more than once it occurred to him that Kirsten's pluckiness had rescued her from her strict upbringing. She spoke rarely of her birthplace, a few kilometers from Husum, a gray town on the North Sea. After his mother's death a few years ago, he too no longer spoke of his village deep in the mountains beyond the Münstertal. But he was proud of his roots; he liked to return there and to practice the dialect he'd learned as a child. No sooner did he set foot in the place than he was speaking it fluently. But no, there was nowhere else he would rather live. Suddenly he found himself wondering, what if Orfeo left the region. It would be the normal thing to do. After all, Freiburg's little opera house did not enjoy much of a reputation. But Weber felt a pang, as intense as it was brief, at the thought.

He was exhausted, fearful. What could be the reason for his case of nerves? Was he afraid Kirsten had not simply gone out, but had decided on an impulse to leave him? Was it because of the previous day's visit? Now Weber cursed the idea of having invited her along. Orfeo had done this to her, that much was clear. Since Sextus's aria, she had not said a word to him. But Orfeo—in his state of disarray he found the stage name pretentious, preposterous even—would be a troubling experience for anyone who did not know the seductive powers of a voice, especially when it can be heard without artifice, without amplification, when it strikes the imagination, and stirs the soul. Then, too, there was the singer's body, and the deliberate movements that lent him a strange suppleness against the dark background of the room. Perhaps it was a combination of everything: his voice, Weber at the piano, the singer's physical presence, the sadness that emanated from him, the nightmarish Piranesi prints on the walls, the villa surrounded by its high, almost black hedges and its fence which brought to mind a refuge, or even a prison.

And yet she had heard exceptional voices before, counter-tenors, contraltos, mezzos, his collection of recordings was overflowing with them. But not one of them could compare with Orfeo. Weber attempted to drive the image of the singer from his mind, but it kept popping up like an irritating presence. His slender profile, the way he silently dragged his feet, his nonchalance when he took his position next to the Steinway. The glance, the quick agreement between them. Then the first note, the controlled emotion, that purity—*a purity he had never heard before*—in the production of the sound, his simple, often elegant gestures. The absence of vibrato. The detached manner in which he spoke of the aria, as though it were just another unexceptional piece of music. Weber had been as deeply moved as one might be by an ancient masterpiece of the goldsmith's trade. La Signora was right: Orfeo was unique, an anachronism. She had bequeathed to Weber a first-class *musico*, an 18th-century singer born of chance and of an accident with irreparable consequences for his existence as a man, a misfortune that had left him alone in the world, with nothing but music to turn to.

The little clock on his desk chimed seven. Weber got up, tossed the tiny plait into the toilet, showered, put on a pair of light trousers and a shirt, and brewed a cup of coffee that he drank on the veranda. The air was heavy with humidity; white mist was rising from the flank of the Schlossberg. The birds were already going about the day's business. The city was emerging from its slumber.

At seven-thirty he went downstairs. The street was deserted. He wasn't expected at the office until two o'clock that afternoon.

Kirsten could not be far away. The car was where he'd parked it the day before.

Vera had stayed at the Colombi until almost one o'clock in the morning. She left the restaurant in a foul mood. First there'd been the nondescript meal and that lout Weber had treated her like a rag-picker, then a vague acquaintance of hers, a customer at the Unicorn who liked to hang around looking for a pick-up, had attempted to seduce her, grossly at that, using the kind of talk you'd expect from a traveling salesman. She pleaded a prior commitment, a meeting with her current DJ, the latest of a long line of young men who occupied the console high above the dance floor. The place usually emptied by midnight on Sunday evenings because the clients' classes began at eight o'clock the next morning. She had gone over the books. Business was brisk. She could afford to sink a sizeable sum into the new bar. All that remained was to find a catchy name for it.

Vera usually went to bed late and got up around noon. Once she got home, she drank a glass of water and put on her pajamas. It was around three-thirty when the doorbell rang. She opened the door a crack; after one look at Kirsten's face, she grasped her by the wrist and drew her inside, sat her down in an armchair and poured her a glass of brandy. Kirsten drank nervously, in tiny sips. Gradually she relaxed, got up from the chair and moved over to sit beside Vera, a woman who knew how to listen and how to convince people to talk. Kirsten could take all the time she wanted.

"We went to that monstrous villa, in Bad Krozingen. I told you about Weber's old teacher, an Italian woman who got it into her head to teach a cripple to sing. Everything about the place is gloomy, the trees are so tall they hide all the light. When I stepped into the living room, or the studio—I couldn't tell what it was supposed to be, a huge room in any event—I wanted to stay as close to the door as I could. The whole place smelled so strong, it was enough to make you gag. Weber plumped me down in a chair at the back of the room. It was really sinister. There was this monstrous grand piano that looked more like a sarcophagus, and the walls are covered with dark paneling. The floors creaked like something out of a horror film. Right in front of the garden door was a large mirror. I don't think I've ever seen such a forbidding room. Oh yes, there was another piano at the far end, an upright, a black one. There were sheets of music everywhere, even on top of the sound system, and baroque engravings, Piranesi reprints, hung above the wainscoting. You don't find them on the market that often. It was his *Prisons*, if you see what I mean. Dreadful, really dreadful. Not a bit of color in the room, and it echoed like an empty concert hall."

The words tumbled out so rapidly that Vera had to lean forward to understand Kirsten's mumbling. Kirsten was looking not at her, but at a mirror that reflected a modern painting.

"I was expecting to see a disabled person, someone stuck in a wheelchair, with a squeaky voice, a kind of midget monster, a hopeless paraplegic or something like that. Weber told me about a terrible accident, the guy's pelvis was shattered. But get this! He can walk, he's tall, and he's handsome, I mean handsome! I would call him immense. When we went into the room, he was seated in front of the sarcophagus. But when he stood up, I could see that he did it in the most bizarre way. He moves in sections, you see? First the legs, then the hips, then the trunk, the neck, the head. It's like he has to concentrate on each movement before he can make it. His fingers were just touching the edges of the keys. And his hands! That was the second thing that struck me. Weber has nice hands; they're probably the best looking part of him. But those hands! Long, slender, fingers you'd swear had no joints, perfectly tapered. Much finer than yours or mine. And incredibly white, with a touch of pink. I know it sounds stupid, but all I could think of was the line 'rose-fingered dawn.' I was so struck by his hands that I didn't even notice his face. In any case, he was standing with his back to the garden door, against the light. He said almost nothing except during the introductions, when he corrected his name. He insists on being called by his stage name. Besides, Weber was talking nonstop, or so it seemed. It was cool in the room. The singer was wearing a white silk shirt, loose fitting, with buttoned sleeves, brown corduroy pants without a pleat, and polished leather sandals with little gold buckles, quite pretty really. His feet were as fine as his hands, his toenails were shiny, as if he polishes them every day. But what a body!"

She seemed on the verge of a nervous collapse. She was rubbing her hands up and down the sides of her skirt. Her mouth was dry, there were tiny splotches of foam at the corners of her lips.

Vera said, "Sounds to me like an Adonis. Pity about that unfortunate accident."

Kirsten did not pick up Vera's irony. "Let me try to remember. Yes, he made some remark about his work schedule. He looked at me when he said it. No, it wasn't me he was looking at; it was my dress. You won't believe it, but I was ashamed. His taste is exquisite, perfect simplicity. And there I was in that dress, with that big fat brooch of mine! I was wearing it because I wanted to please Weber; he really likes it. All of a sudden I felt like Cinderella at the wrong ball, looking totally out of place in my bright colors. But him, his shirt was so white that he stood out in the darkness of the room; around him everything looked softer. His eyes are green I think, almost black. But I'm not sure. Anyway, he looks me over, from head to toe, and stops at my feet. Until yesterday I liked them, these shoes; I thought they were elegant."

Kirsten fell silent, took another sip of brandy; Vera had refilled her glass.

"Before we got to the villa, I asked Weber what the cripple looked like. His body was no pleasure to look at, he told me. It's just not true. When I saw them standing there side by side it was Weber who lost out, in every way. When he sat down at the piano he looked small, and submissive. The singer took a few steps toward the garden door while Weber told me about the aria he was going to sing, and the opera it was taken from. All I felt was humiliation. I was the dumb blonde. I admit that baroque opera doesn't really interest me; him, he's always going on about it. At the store I would *never* allow myself to give him a lesson about something he doesn't know, in front of a stranger no less. I was so furious I felt like getting up and walking out then and there. When Weber talks about music, he's like the Pope in person. That know-it-all attitude of his makes me feel like an idiot. At home, he clamps on his headset and shuts me out. He has never tried to help me understand baroque music. How am I supposed to like something I don't even know about? He doesn't want me to go along when he meets other critics or musicians. It's like he's ashamed of me. But let me tell you, I hardly ever say a word. You ought to hear them: 'Magnificent!' 'What depth!' 'Great musicality!' 'Incomparable technique!' Or else they're utterly mean, with those 'superficial,' 'cheap rendition,' 'the mistakes are acceptable, but not the lack of professionalism' of his. Specifics? Forget it! If I'd ever tried to talk like that in my art history courses, my professors would have thrown me out!"

She put on a scornful face, which Vera found charming. For the first time, she saw Kirsten transformed; now she was a temperamental adolescent, misunderstood and sulking. Vera was enjoying her attack on Weber. She was used to getting what she wanted; instinctively she identified the breech through which she would enter Kirsten's life. Vera kept quite open company with the musicians and the DJs that she hired for the Unicorn, men a good deal younger than her, with vigorous sexual appetites. They never slept in her bed, never saw her apartment. She would take them to a small room she'd outfitted at the head of the stairs leading to the DJ's consoles. From a mirrored window she could look down onto the huge dance-floor. The men dropped like ripe fruit into her hands, but they never held her interest for more than a few nights. To conquer women like Kirsten was infinitely more exciting. She had to overcome their resistance, cajole them, reassure them. After a while she would cast them aside as well; even they ended up boring her. Still, men were easy prey, but a woman would usually yield only after a long, exhausting siege.

Her first impulse was to edge closer to Kirsten, to draw her hair back from her face with an elder-sisterly caress. She held herself back. Kirsten suspected nothing, better let her talk, get rid of her fascination for this guy with the woman's voice and the malformed man's body. He must have been really a strange one, but Kirsten's fascination with him would certainly dwindle with time. Vera was certain of that.

Her first task was to distance her gradually from Weber, whose mistrust was clear to Vera. Generally, the husbands of the women she seduced never imagined the role she played in their lives. With him it was different, given his sensitivity, his antennae. He'd looked at her with open hostility. Vera had resolved to avenge that look. The singer had made Kirsten see her husband in a new light. Weber's tics and manias would irritate her so much that she'd no longer wanted to share his bed. Soon she would *see* his pudgy body as an example of what Vera called "slobs who don't even know it." As luck would have it, the singer did not seem to have anything to offer her sexually. Once this realization had sunk in, Kirsten would be ready to be consoled. It was only a matter of time. Vera had learned to wait for the most opportune moment. She forced herself to hear Kirsten out.

"In fact, I never really understood what Weber was talking about. All I remember about the story is that the emperor's closest friend betrays him. He's the one who sings the aria. My Italian isn't very good, without the supertitles I never know what's happening on stage. But this time, I think I got it all. Everything, in fact! The aria's not long, but it was as if it lasted an hour. I would have gladly listened to it again and again. You just can't imagine it, that voice!

"Fine, so I'm no musician. I can barely read music. I played the triangle in the school orchestra because I was so hopeless on all the other instruments. You know, what I really like are songs from the 'twenties. Because of the lyrics, mostly, then for the rhythm. But I couldn't sing a single one of them. So, when it comes to sophisticated stuff like baroque opera, better forget about it. Weber figured it out when we went to the opera in Berlin. They were playing something by Monteverdi. *The Coronation of Poppea*, I think it was. I got so bored I couldn't stop yawning. But for him, it's one of the greatest masterpieces ever written. Me, I haven't got a clue, as you can see. So be it; I'm good at what I do, I've got to keep on telling myself. Otherwise, life with Weber would have become unbearable a long time ago."

Vera could not restrain a smile of triumph. Now there was no need to hold back. Kirsten was lost in her reverie. Her tone was more detached, with none of her earlier haste. But the fatigue showed clearly on her face; there were blue circles beneath her eyes.

"The other guy, the singer, when he speaks, it's like his voice is veiled, barely louder than Weber's. It really struck me. I was expecting him to clear his throat before the next sentence. And after that, how can I explain it? He's got the voice of someone who's absolutely sure of himself. Do you see what I'm getting at? The voice of someone who's been through a long psychoanalysis. Not a moment of hesitation. Serene. Calm. Right away I felt confidence in him. After the aria he looked at me, and all of a sudden, I felt safe and secure. How old can he be, I wonder. Hard to say. There's nothing young about him. Everything is mature, he's thought everything through.

"When he went over to stand beside the piano, he didn't walk, he *glided along*; I could barely see his legs move. Maybe it's because of his accident. Weber told me he spent years in physiotherapy."

Kirsten's hands had stopped their kneading.Her shoulders, which she had hunched forward as if to protect herself, gradually straightened, but her knees were still rigid.

Vera waited for her to let herself go. The end of the monologue was in sight. She had intuited a dramatic conclusion, a fight between Kirsten and Weber. That would be the ideal moment to intervene, to calm her, but only for the sake of appearances. Then, she would strike.

"I've thought back over every single minute of that half-hour at the villa. It's like a film playing over and over in my head. You know how sometimes you wake up with a melody in your mind, and you don't know where it came from? It just keeps coming back to you. That film, that music, I want to keep them in me until the end of my life.

"When he began to sing, Weber mixed up the music. Maybe he felt the same way, and if he did, he can't be blamed. That voice is like nothing I ever heard before; it's not a counter-tenor's voice, not a contralto, not a mezzo. It has something incredibly ... luminous, I'd call it. Something brilliant. Hard and soft at the same time. It's a voice that *glides*, just like the singer glides when he moves. *Elegant*, that's what it is. You probably think I'm out of my mind, but that voice of his is *celestial*. If that's what the angels sing like in Paradise, I want to be there.

"All of a sudden, I had the feeling the voice had created another body. First, he lifts his open hands in a gesture of supplication, palms up. Those hands of his, like something out of a Madonna by Leonardo or Raphael. The Emperor doesn't answer; his friend continues to humble himself. He bows his head, lets his arms drop. Then he curves his hands back toward his chest, and points to his heart, twice. That movement tore my heart out; I started to cry. Weber's never seen me cry. Now it's starting all over again. It's crazy, but it comforts me. Now, for the first time, I see what Weber means when he talks about 'depth' in an interpretation. I touched the inner depths of that music.

"Then the emperor's friend confesses. I could barely see the singer, only his silhouette. He was swaying back and forth, like he was feeling the deepest sadness. Excuse my big words, but that sadness of his, it was *palpable*. I could feel it, right in my body. I've never been so sad in my life, never. It was sublime; I'd give everything if I could feel it again, and again. I felt like I was *alive*, do you see what I mean?"

The tears flowed down her cheeks. Vera observed that Kirsten's knees were gradually relaxing. The younger woman breathed in noisily, looked around for a tissue. Vera handed her one. The crisis had just about run its course. Kirsten was more animated now, emphasizing her words; her breathing was almost back to normal. But Vera was feeling disappointed; the attack on Weber was slow in coming.

"When it was all over, there was a pause. Then he bent over and said something to Weber. I forget what it was. I'm upset I didn't pay closer attention. He bowed, and glided toward the other end of the room. Then all I could hear was the creaking of the stairs."

Kirsten took a long pause, crossed her legs, and sank back into the sofa.

"I thought I was going to faint. I couldn't move. Weber came over, spoke to me. I don't know what happened after that. When we got home I had a bath, and took a pill to help me sleep. It didn't work. The voice, that melody, they wouldn't leave my head. Now as I'm talking to you I can hear them."

In a soft voice Vera asked, "What does he look like? I don't have the slightest idea of his voice. I'd have to hear him, like you did."

Kirsten looked at her, for the first time. "I can't remember much about his head, just a few details. But I can still feel his eyes looking at me, those wonderful eyes. He's got a thin face, a long, straight nose. His hair is dark blond; he wears it long, in a ponytail. But I can't remember how all his features fit together. Everything is foggy in my mind.

"And then there's his name: Orfeo. Weber mentioned it the other day, and I didn't say anything. As if I had the right to! Sure, it catches your attention. But there's more. Firstly, he can hide his background. Can you imagine him taking the stage under his family name, Teufel? Can you imagine a singer called Teufel? Maybe it would work here in Germany, but outside? With that stage name, he becomes the son of music that causes wild beasts to weep, and trees to move about, just like in the myth."

She began to shiver again. This time, Vera reached out to smooth her hair, in a soothing gesture. Kirsten was not only one of the most beautiful women in Freiburg, but deliciously vulnerable as well. Vera moved closer, and breathed in her young girl's fresh fragrance. "Are you in love with him? Your first real love?"

Kirsten exhaled through her nostrils, and tossed her head impatiently. "All I know is that I can't live without him. It's hopeless, can't you see? He can never love another human being; all he loves is music. You should have seen him with Weber. For once, I wished I'd been in his place, accompanying him while he sang. I was jealous of Weber, of his piano playing, of everything he knows about the history of music. They made a pair, and I felt like I was shut out."

She lifted her hands, arranged her hair mechanically, encountered Vera's hand and pushed it aside as if it were a troublesome insect, then blurted out, "Good Lord! I must be a mess! I've got to be at the shop at nine, and I feel totally drained. When Weber realizes I'm not at home, he'll be beside himself."

"What if you told him the truth?"

"Sure, I should confess that I'm crazy about an illusion? He must be as shattered as I am. Look, up until yesterday I never even knew he *loved* music. When he listens to recordings he puts on his headset and shuts his eyes. His face shows nothing. Then he takes notes, and writes his article. For me, he was always classifying things, accepting or rejecting. Yesterday, it was love he was feeling, just like me. But now, I ache everywhere. I'm all tied up inside, right up into my throat. He's a cold fish. A clinical expert on music. Except for yesterday. You could see the happiness on his face."

Vera drew her fingernails through Kirsten's hair. "So, what are you going to do about it?"

"I don't know what I'll do. I need time. If I really listened to the voices inside me, I don't know how far I'd go." She turned toward the mirror. "Can you help me? I can't go to the shop looking like this. The customers will think I've spent the whole night on the town."

Vera looked after her. When Kirsten left, her sleepless night barely showed.

Vera brewed herself another cup of coffee. In the gray light of morning the outline of the Schwabentor, all brown and white, filled the window of her room. The clock showed almost nine. When she threw open the windows, the sounds of the city flooded in. Far below, people were going about their business. The restaurant busboys were sweeping the sidewalks, pushing the last traces of night into the gutters.

She lighted a cigarette, and smiled as she watched the smoke curl upward.

CHAPTER FOUR

Alma oppressa da sorte crudele
"A cruel fate burdens the soul"

–A. Vivaldi, *La fida ninfa*

Weber realized that he could confide in no one. Impossible to sit in a coffee house to pass the time. Show up at the office at eight o'clock and eyebrows would be raised. The combination of fatigue, grey sky and bitter coffee depressed him. He got into his car, but did not start it. Why had Kirsten left him? Where had she spent the night? With whom? Now he was sorry he'd thrown out the little braid. No point in waiting in front of the boutique. He strolled instead through the streets leading to the Schwabentor; the people he met there looked bizarre, lots of body-piercing. The day was warm, and some of them had already taken their shirts off, displaying brightly-colored tattoos. One man's decorations came right up to the neck; huge, convoluted flowers covered his entire torso. Weber turned around to look at the young man. "How can anyone make himself so ugly?" he wondered. "They are the people, they and their ilk, who leave the empty beer bottles, the greasy paper, the debris strewn around the public benches. So we can clean up after them." He felt like yelling at them: "Bunch of idiots!" but said nothing. All of a sudden, he felt old. The great square behind the cathedral was still empty; it was only eight-fifteen.

Suddenly, he was hit by remorse: it was all his fault. He should never have asked Kirsten to come along the day before. She was furious. They'd quarreled once before; she had criticized him bitterly for being embarrassed in front of his colleagues when the subject of music came up. True, once they stepped into the villa he'd almost forgotten her.

Weber had noticed the way Orfeo looked at her, without any particular sympathy; he was almost neutral, in fact. During the execution of the aria, he'd thought only of the singer. When you got right down to it, Kirsten was right: music was his private preserve, and the only people who could enter into it were the insiders. After all, if you want to talk about music you had to have an education, training, long years of work, an unconditional love for a subject that covers a multitude of fields, sometimes in direct opposition to one another. Kirsten wasn't an insider. She only knew a few composers, and most of them Weber looked down on. Once, she ventured she liked jazz. He'd started to explain how it had originated. He wanted her to appreciate what the songs meant, that was all. But Kirsten's face had gone hard.

"You know, I couldn't care less about the origins of jazz. What I like is the rhythm, the tunes, the voices. I like it, that's all. It stirs me up. You, you're always dissecting things. And at the end, after your explanations, all that's left is a handful of dry shells, and I've lost the pleasure."

It was true; he'd long lost that sense of naiveté. There were times, during a magnificently performed piece, when he could forget the interpreters and their technique, and listen only to the music, without reading the score in his head. At times like those, he felt like he'd been carried off into a world where calculations and computations no longer mattered. All would vanish; he no longer heard the coughing in the hall, a program being wrinkled by nervous hands. But that happened less and less. That was the reason why he had to seek out the voice again. For it had given him a shudder that was deeper, more tantalizing, more inexplicable even than what he experienced when making love to Kirsten.

He turned on his heel, hurried back to the car, and entered the flow of traffic in the direction of Bad Krozingen.

A "For Sale" sign was hanging from the gate to the villa. Weber paused for a moment and stared at it. Then the sound of scales being sung with increasing speed, reached his ears. When he heard Orfeo's voice, Weber's sadness vanished. Now the singer was taking a scale in G-minor over two octaves, gradually adding one note at a time, first lower, then higher. Weber walked around the house until he reached the garden door. The shutters were half open. In the darkness he could barely make out Orfeo's silhouette. He was dressed entirely in black, standing close to the small table beside la Signora's armchair. After completing his scales he bent over the tape recorder, pressed a button, and began again, this time with mouth closed. At the same time, Weber could clearly distinguish the voice of la Signora with her southern Italian accent and her rolled r's: "Open wide the resonators. Open wide, do not force your voice. Let the high notes and the low notes resonate. Attention, head *and* chest." Orfeo stopped the recording, sang the scale once more, then listened to la Signora again. "Always project the voice into the mask. Do not keep the voice in the throat, only in the resonators. Flatten out your tongue, not in a roll. Keep your tongue relaxed." Johann had been right; la Signora was still there, hard at it, from beyond the grave.

A surge of anger swept over Weber; he was jealous of la Signora and furious at Kirsten for not confiding in him. He cursed the idea of coming here, better to return to Freiburg straightaway. No, he would stay. He would call his wife from here. As he stepped through the garden door, the hardwood floor creaked beneath his feet. The singer turned and blushed when he saw Weber.

"Good morning, Mister Weber."

After a moment of hesitation, he added, "That's just la Signora's instructions. When I hear her voice, I don't feel so alone." He paused. "I was about to start work on two Vivaldi arias, from *La Fida Ninfa*. I wasn't expecting you so soon, but you couldn't have come at a better time. You know the verses of Scipione Maffei, '*Dite, oimè, ditelo al fine*' and '*Alma oppressa da sorte crudele*'? I really love these two pieces. The first one is an ideal warm-up."

Not a word about why Weber was there, not a word of polite conversation. Without a moment's hesitation he took a deep breath, raised and spread his arms, worked his jaws back and forth, stuck out his tongue. Even though he'd seen singers performing relaxation exercises, Weber found the sight rather graceless. His own tongue could hardly be as smooth and pink after the night he'd spent. He was in no mood to sit down at the piano. Ten minutes to nine. At nine o'clock he would call the boutique.

When he saw Orfeo pull the score from under a stack of sheet music, Weber saw the absurdity of his anger. He was looking for someone to listen to him, trying to get a grip of the situation by talking about it. Instead, here he was with this singer whom he barely knew, who didn't have the faintest idea what had happened. Orfeo smiled a distant, formal stage smile that didn't extend to his eyes. He must have looked upon him as his accompanist. As soon as Weber left, Orfeo would go back to listening to la Signora on the recording. But Weber, indeed, could not have come at a better time; he was the fumble-fingered pianist the singer needed at that precise moment.

Orfeo's face had taken on its normal color. He spread out the sheets of music, and placed them on the Steinway's music stand, then said, "Let's go!"

Weber sat down at the piano. The singer's tone of voice had been soft and imperious all at once. Weber rebuked himself for obeying the way he had. His wife had just left him, he reflected as he scanned the first sheet of the score, and here he was, about to play a baroque aria. "Baroque" matched the situation. There he was, sitting in front of the same Steinway where he had suffered years ago. Next to him stood a *primo uomo*, a living anachronism. Yet he desired only one thing: to hear that voice. He startled himself with the thought, "If I keep Kirsten waiting; too bad. What did I do? Nothing. She's the one who has some explaining to do. What got into her, getting up and walking out in the middle of the night?"

He turned his attention to the music. It would be easy to play, even though sight-reading had never been one of his strengths. The first aria was slow, melancholy, without ornamentation. No sooner had he begun to decode the music than a powerful sense of well-being rose in him as he sat there across from the singer. Kirsten had vanished; only the music remained, directly in front of him. And that voice, the voice he was waiting for.

Orfeo allowed him time to glance over the music, then nodded to him. They began. Weber's emotions were different from what he had experienced the previous day, subtler than those he'd felt with the Mozart aria. The melody curled around him, enveloping him. When they reached the plaintive words "*Dite, oimè, ditelo al fine,*" he had to concentrate on the score in order to hear the voice. In her transcription, la Signora had pared the *basso continuo* line down to its bare essentials;

the better to express the agitation of the character that reveals that he is prepared to die. Weber sneaked a glance at Orfeo. He had turned his trunk without changing the position of his legs, which were slightly spread. He projected his sound toward the far end of the room, into the shadows. Weber understood that it was a clever bit of staging. As he sang "*sta mia vita in sul confine*," as Morasto feels himself slipping away, all the light disappeared from his voice, as it led the listener down into the shadows of death. Weber caught himself. The figure across from him was only a singer presenting a number he'd honed to perfection. Suddenly the image of Kirsten at the boutique came into his mind. After the rehearsal he would have to call Freiburg.

Orfeo sang the aria four times in exactly the same way, with the same intonation, pivoting his trunk in the same way.

Weber said, "Excuse me, but I must call my wife. Where is the telephone?"

"Couldn't you wait a few more minutes?" Orfeo's voice betrayed a hint of impatience. "I would rather not interrupt my work session. You'll see, it won't take long."

From the piano he walked over to the garden door, executed another set of relaxation and breathing exercises. He was right, Weber had to admit. He would feel in less of a rush after they had rehearsed the second aria. He glanced over the new score; it was much more demanding, almost entirely eighth and sixteenth notes. He vaguely recalled the aria; it was rarely sung, and of extreme vocal difficulty, with wide, leaping changes of register. It was supposed to begin with a long entry, on a high E, pianissimo. Orfeo stretched the word "*alma*" over eight measures, increasing the volume without quite reaching forte, then returned to a sound so fragile that it was barely audible. Open-mouthed in admiration, Weber forgot all about Kirsten. The dizzying scales, on "*amore*" and "*catena*," struck him as perfect in their precision, but when Orfeo came to a stop he murmured in dissatisfaction, "No, no. Let's do it again. I'm making a hash of it. I'm not really into it. I've lost the rhythm, and when I do, it's a mess. I feel like I'm trapped in some kind of sticky pudding."

He looked tired. Weber noticed that the veins in his neck were bulging. He wanted to suggest they take a break, but Orfeo had already closed his eyes, begun to work his jaw back and forth, and let it fall limply. Then he threw back his head and took a deep breath. They began again, five times over. Orfeo resumed his vocalises on the *a* in "*mitigare*," experimented with several variations and finally adopted the one that Weber felt was the most difficult. He sang it without accompaniment, not altering a single note.

. This time, the aria seemed to be a success. But Orfeo still was not satisfied; he started over, with a determination that bordered on obsession. Then, all of a sudden, Weber interrupted him, "Let me remind you of one of la Signora's principles: never fight your instrument; turn it into your ally instead. What is your weakness? If you can't eliminate it, or conceal it, exploit it! I just don't see what's wrong; your scales sound perfect to me."

Orfeo threw him a dark, sidelong glance. He was about to speak, but resumed his relaxation exercises instead, while he walked through a semi-circle in the room. As he did, Weber noticed, he pointed his feet outward, like a dancer, drawing the sole from front to back. Instead of striding from the hip, he did so from the knee, which created the curious impression that he was hovering above the ground. As he moved about, he stopped at the same places, as though on stage, following the cue marks on the floor. Finally he came to a stop beside the piano, took a deep breath, and gave Weber a sign, "Ready!"

This time he did not break off. Weber was familiar enough with the difficulties of the score by now that he could turn his full attention on the workings of the voice. Finally, he grasped what had upset Orfeo: the vocalises, that had sounded as if they were detached from the aria, no longer broke the melodic line; now they formed an integral part of it, guiding the words instead of interrupting them. Here, the soul seeks to deceive its pain through love, but Licore has measured the risks. Better to suffer the chains of prison, reason tells him, than those of love when it seizes our hearts. That was why the vocalises on "*catena*" echoed those of "*mitigare*" and "*amore*." Together, they formed a framework, a matching of meanings that the singer must execute to perfection if he hopes to convey the intentions of poet and composer. Vivaldi is insistent: four times he returns to the vocalises on "*amore*" at the end of the first section. And each time, Orfeo introduced small variations, without altering its meaning. With the last rehearsal of the aria, he had brought text and melody into harmony, overcoming the temptation to shine through vocal technique alone.

Weber looked at his watch: ten-thirty. He wanted to get up, but sat staring at the music in front of him; the singer's voice was still ringing in his ears.

There was a knock on the door. It was Gertrud, carrying a tray containing a carafe of milk, a glass, some cookies and fruit. She set it down on the little table beside the tape recorder and left the room without a word. Orfeo filled the glass, took a drink, bit into a cookie and offered one to Weber. Then, unexpectedly, he grasped Weber's forearm, "You would make a good coach for me. You accompany me with a lot of finesse. I can even indulge in a bit of fantasy, like the ritardando in the last vocalise. To tell you the truth, these recordings—he pointed to a pile of cassettes on the table—are getting on my nerves. They don't give me any room to experiment. Yesterday, for example, I had more breath, and I don't know why. I could hold a note for more than a minute, with a crescendo halfway through. Here in the studio, it sounded good. I wanted to enjoy it. I stopped the recording; it was moving too fast. With you it would be perfect; you seem to know exactly what I'm going to do even before I do it; either that or you adjust very quickly. And I think you see music the same way I do. Nothing strange about that; we were both la Signora's students. But you're not as rigid. She hated my fantasies. I had to do what she was hearing in her head, not what I wanted to do. Do you really think I don't understand what a composer is looking for, in terms of effects? After all, I've been doing nothing else for twelve years."

It was the first time that Orfeo had spoken to him at such length, as one professional musician to another. But Weber had barely heard him: the touch of that hand, the child-like softness of his skin, had shaken him. It was nothing like Kirsten's caresses. He looked at Orfeo's fingers: they were long, slender, white and pink, with square-trimmed, shiny nails. His touch seemed to burn. Weber did not pull his arm away, but rubbed it discretely when the singer stood up and went over to the doorway where he finished eating his cookie.

In the silence of the large room, Weber struggled not to think about the hand. Suddenly, he remembered his dream. He focused all his attention on the score in front of him, but his forearm was burning.

"You could play the piano part from time to time, couldn't you?"

"Whenever you like. It would be a pleasure."

He felt he blurted it out clumsily. He should have found another way to put it, to make it clear that he felt honored to be able to work with a great musician, not merely a great talent who possessed a prodigious vocal instrument.

Orfeo seemed to appreciate his company. And for Weber, it was becoming clear that the invitation was not simply an indication of their nascent friendship, but also a way of establishing, in the short term at least, each of their roles. Orfeo perfectly understood his capacity as a musician. Weber had already accepted his genius, and his superiority. Henceforth, no misunderstanding could be possible. But in order to work together harmoniously they would have to see one another often. Weber's day began at two o'clock, at the office. Mornings, he worked at home. During the summer he traveled as the spirit moved him and worked on in-depth articles for the fall. All of which meant that he could see Orfeo regularly.

At the thought of long morning hours in the singer's company, his concern for Kirsten rushed back into his consciousness.

His eyes met Orfeo's. He sensed that the singer knew what he was thinking about, that he had read his thoughts. Orfeo smiled, much more warmly than at the beginning of the encounter. He was about to speak when Gertrud knocked. The real-estate agent was requesting permission to show a prospective buyer the villa. Three people entered the room. Orfeo led Weber out into the garden. They strolled back and forth across the lawn, following the white stones that Johann had laid down to mark out a path. They discussed the second aria. Weber was startled to hear Orfeo analyzing as coldly as the harshest critic the very same pieces in which he had found such intense emotion.

The would-be buyers stepped into the garden. The woman looked around perfunctorily and went back into the house, while the man examined the trees and the fence behind the hedge. He nodded solemnly in their direction, then joined the other two in the studio.

A few minutes later Gertrud informed them that the visitors had left. Maria would soon be serving lunch, she added. Reluctantly Weber declined Orfeo's invitation; he had business to attend to in town. When

Orfeo asked him about the following day, Weber replied: "I'll do what I can. Yes, like today."

He returned to Freiburg by the same route he'd taken the day before, without giving it a thought. He walked rapidly by the park bench overlooking the meadow where Kirsten had rested; he was rushing now, with a guilty feeling that seemed to be driving him to return to her. The sky was overcast; within an hour or two it would rain. Kirsten would explain everything, and they would act as though nothing had happened. And at the same time, the vocalises on "*mitigare*", "*amore*" and "*catena*" were rippling through his head. They were his property now, Weber reasoned: Orfeo never sang a vocalise the same way twice, and he had been the only one to hear them.

As he thought of the singer, excitement surged through him, a sense of unease that he had experienced only in the dream, with the new elements that had been added the night before.

As he stepped into the apartment, its smell, so at odds with that of the villa, struck him. Every space is impregnated with a subtle or not-so-subtle odor. At his house, the dominant smell was the murky whiff of the city, a disagreeable amalgam of wet stones and exhaust fumes, of flowering linden and damp earth. The door giving onto the veranda was still ajar. Weber closed it and looked around him. No one had entered the house; nothing had been moved. Then he noticed the blinking light of the answering machine. The first message was Kirsten's; the second, from Orfeo.

CHAPTER FIVE

Pallido il sole, torbido il cielo
"The sun has paled, the sky grown dark"

–J. A. Hasse, *Artaserse*, Act II

The rain hadn't begun to fall when he left the house. Weber wanted some time for himself before meeting Kirsten at the Bären. He walked along the Kaiser-Josephstrasse, the Gerberau, and the Augustinerplatz, giving the Schwabentor, with its flock of tourists, a wide berth. A guide had gathered them beneath the protective awning that sheltered the great fresco from the weather, the better to draw their attention to the high, half-timbered 16th-century houses. When Weber merged with the crowd of pedestrians on the Oberlinden, one of whose extremities gave onto the Herrenstrasse and the Salzstrasse, a fine rain was falling, the kind of rain the peasants call "sewing thread." With a grunt, he slipped on the wet pavement, barely avoiding a fall into the gutter. "No need to get my baptism as a Freiburger all over again," he thought. "I've taken too many falls in those damn gutters. They're obsessed with tradition here in Freiburg. These gulches are dangerous. Tourist traps." But deep down, he liked the narrow drainage canals that ran parallel to the sidewalks.

As he walked past the show window of Kirsten's boutique next door to the Bären, he noticed several eye-catching porcelain pieces, probably from Saxony. At the rear of the shop he could make out some paintings. Their old frames lent an air of distinction to the antique furniture around them, even if they were not of the finest quality. All things considered, he thought, the boutique could claim an honorable place among the numerous antique shops that lined the Oberlinden. As he stepped into the Bären, he sighed with relief. It is said to be the oldest inn in Germany. Everything was dark: the woodwork, the wall hangings and the floor. Weber adored the place, with its strong kitchen smells. It reminded him of his parents' house, not far from the Feldberg. Kirsten didn't mind it either, even though she found the decor kitschy and the cooking too heavy.

He scanned the handful of customers. For an instant, Weber thought he recognized a woman's silhouette, but forgot it the moment he saw Kirsten. She was seated at a table covered with a red-and-white checkered tablecloth, a glass of mineral water at her place, along with a bowl of salad that she had not yet touched. With her fingers she was rolling pieces of bread into little balls that she moved from one space to another as if they were chessmen. It was a nervous habit. Suddenly, when he saw how fatigued she was, with her drawn features and the dark circles under her eyes, Weber felt intense pangs of hunger. Other than a cookie at the villa, he had eaten nothing since the previous day. He gave the waiter his order, a *Bauernfrühstück*, a plate of fried potatoes, slices of ham, and plenty of onions. Suddenly he felt impelled to reach out and caress the hand lying inert on the tablecloth, but he brushed her forearm instead.

She said, "What perfume is that? You haven't been to la Signora's?"

That she had recognized la Signora's perfume irritated him. They never cross-examined one another. He felt as though he was under surveillance, with a vague sensation of guilt he could not account for. Weber realized that he wanted to keep everything related to Orfeo's music to himself. He had no wish to talk of his visit to Orfeo's. And yet if he didn't, he would be excluding Kirsten once again. The metallic sound of la Signora's voice came back to him, playing from the tape recorder. It was time for Orfeo to leave. Time to send his clothes to the dry cleaner's.

He related his visit to the villa, and summarized his work session with Orfeo. She interrupted him only to say, in a sad voice, "I wish I'd been there with you."

She looked up. Her eyes were red beneath her mascara-coated lashes. Weber noticed that her dress was wrinkled; it was the same dress she had been wearing yesterday. He didn't like the make-up and the lipstick; they reminded him of Vera. It was then that he understood where she had spent the night. He relaxed, offered no rebuke, asked no questions. As he spoke of his visit to the villa, she began to observe him attentively. In tacit agreement from that moment on, they used only the singer's stage name. As she began to eat her salad, she asked about the arias they had worked on. True to form, she pinched a few slices of potato from his plate, smoothed out the tablecloth and tossed the bread balls into the ashtray. He'd returned to the apartment to see if she had gone home, he told her—his only allusion to her disappearance, to which she did not respond—and found two messages: hers, inviting him to meet her at the Bären, and Orfeo's. She raised her head abruptly.

"He called our house? What did he say?" Suddenly Kirsten had come alive.

"It looks as though the real-estate agent has gotten an offer to purchase. The property will sell fast. It's just what rich people from the town are looking for. The same people I saw this morning; they're oozing money. Orfeo wanted to know if he should accept."

He realized that he no longer had any hesitation in pronouncing the name; in fact, it gave him pleasure. He was relieved that he felt no need to ask Kirsten about her escapade; he would have seemed spiteful. It was better to wait, to say as little as possible about Vera. Every time he thought of that woman he felt a sudden bitterness, an irritation rising within him. Kirsten wanted to know everything; Weber had to go over the details of their work on the second Vivaldi aria several times. She no longer looked tired; the make-up on her eyelashes stood out against her face, which now looked fresh again. As she ate, she wiped her lips, until the last traces of red were erased.

They agreed to suggest that Orfeo move temporarily to Bernau, should the sale be concluded rapidly. Weber would move the upright piano as soon as possible. Kirsten would call Frau Schäuble, who looked after the country house. When it came to the singer's diet, they would have to give her precise instructions. They would purchase the few items that Orfeo needed. As for the rest, they would wait and see. But they would go there as often as possible, each one whenever he or she could, to make sure that he wanted for nothing, before trying to find a definitive solution.

It was nearly two o'clock by the time they'd settled all the details. As they were leaving the Bären, Weber complimented her on the porcelain in the window of her store. It was a KPM service, from Berlin, she said, which made him laugh; he could never tell the difference between Meissen, Dresden and Berlin porcelain. He kissed her on the cheek and hurried to the newsroom in the Turmstrasse. The receptionist handed him a list of calls, several of them flagged "urgent." When he reached his desk, he put the list down beside a pile of papers, picked up the receiver of his private telephone, called Orfeo and gave him a brief report on what he and his wife had agreed upon. Speaking politely, the singer expressed his thanks, and placed himself entirely in the hands of Weber and Kirsten, whom he now considered to be his friends. The agent was pressuring him to accept the offer: the amount seemed astronomical. He had undertaken to do nothing until he had spoken to them. While he chatted with Orfeo, Weber felt light, happy. He dragged out the conversation, asked him about his midday meal, and what he intended to do for the rest of the day. A half-hour later he hung up with regret, stared absently at his desk, then set to work.

He opened the Monday mail, which was more voluminous than during the week, with its batch of press releases from the major recording companies, concert programs, new specialized publications, a handful of biographies, articles from big-circulation magazines. He picked out what caught his eye, threw most of it into the recycling box, and sent off for a few books on subjects that interested him. He was free to sell his critical commentaries to other dailies or weeklies; when he negotiated his contract, Kirsten had proposed an approach that made him almost a freelancer. His parallel publications ensured an appreciable supplementary income. Once again he thought of how marvelous she was, with her nose for business.

He noticed two invitations to music camps, far distant geographically from one another. One was at Husum, the other at the Weissenfels Castle in Bavaria. He examined the programs. The camp at Husum included a few 18th-century works. The organizers were emphasizing the classics of the 19th century, with incursions into contemporary music. His presence at the camp would provide an excellent pretext to encourage Kirsten to join him: they could visit her parents who lived not far from the pretty little seaside town.

But the second half of the Weissenfels camp, after a week of modern music, offered a program from the baroque. When he'd attended two years ago, shortly before the death of Count von S., a good friend and musical benefactor of the old school, he'd been delighted by the work of its guest conductors. The count's son had carried on the tradition of the musical camp, where some of the finest young musicians from the four corners of the world came to participate. Weber believed that the chateau might be the ideal place to spend a short week with Orfeo, alone. There would be no explaining to Kirsten. She didn't like "his" music in any event.

Weber examined the pamphlet from Bavaria. They could visit Würzburg, Bamberg, Nürnberg. The countryside would be magnificent at that time of year. Once they'd reached the chateau, a superb baroque construction, Orfeo would no longer be living amongst his etchings; he would actually be able to move about in the real stage settings of his operas.

He glanced down at his forearm. He'd scratched it absentmindedly as he was examining the brochure. Now the skin was visibly irritated. Some colleagues stopped by to exchange idle small talk. He rolled down his shirt sleeves and booted his computer as he continued to chat. He took his phone messages and listened while Litow complained about a punk concert he was assigned to cover. Litow had kept the nasal twang of his native Saxony; he would have liked to change his name to conceal his Polish roots. He didn't get much respect in the newsroom, perhaps because he wrote straight-up stories about avant-garde theatre and was the beat reporter for punk, funk, pop, hip-hop and straight-edge, a scene that no one else would touch. One look at him made you wonder how such a sickly-looking, sallow-skinned individual with wispy flaxen hair could possibly blend into a disorderly crowd shrieking at a group of musicians pretending to be possessed.

Weber and Kirsten would often run into Litow at lunchtime on the banks of the Dreisam. He would be hanging around with groups of punks, talking and gesticulating intensely, not even noticing his work-mate and his wife. He normally had little to say in her presence, but whenever they met he would devour her with his bug eyes. Weber knew nothing about Litow's professional training, but he did know that his colleague would often make penetrating remarks about a new classical release, which proved that he wasn't only interested in "what the young people are into," as Weber put it. But Litow's articles dealt almost exclusively with those often-ephemeral groups and their concerts. Sometimes the culture page editor would spike the stories, judging them poorly written. It was a humiliating experience for Litow, whose main objective was for his work to be acknowledged by his colleagues. Weber tuned out the lamentations of this pseudo-consumptive who looked like a hungry buzzard, then dialed the first number on the message list he'd picked up from the receptionist. An hour later, he'd begun writing his story for tomorrow's paper.

By eight-thirty he'd sent it off; it was a lengthy review of a recent publication dealing with the relationship between music and the plastic arts. He had researched the piece the week before and now, as he read it over, he noted with satisfaction that it was unmistakably his. In it he argued that the work's two volumes were well documented, but "as boring as granite." In other places, he used his favorite descriptive, "boring as two railway tracks," which he'd borrowed from a colleague. By the time they finished his article, his readers would get the message: that the two tomes were a grab bag of empty-headed erudition. Aside from a handful of university libraries, no one would buy such a book. In fact, Weber had been waiting for an opportunity to settle an old score. A few years ago, the author of the two-volume opus had written a less than flattering critique of a short book by Weber on gesture in baroque opera. It was a book Weber had been quite proud of. He'd never forgotten his outrage as he read the piece, the only unfavorable opinion in his clipping file.

The stack of papers, letters, announcements, and press releases had vanished. Weber tossed the CDs into his briefcase; he would listen to them later, at home.

He put on his jacket and slipped the Weissenfels brochure into his pocket.

At the restaurant, Vera had been observing Weber and Kirsten. Afterwards, Vera went to the boutique, where she waited for the younger woman to come back from lunch. Kirsten took her into the tiny room at the rear of the shop where she kept most of the paintings. Rents were high in Freiburg, and the landlord kept his warehouse outside of town. Kirsten had to make frequent trips. Vera had offered her the use of a large storeroom nearby in the Konviktstrasse close to the Unicorn. She had invited Kirsten to see the club. They had walked across the dance floor. It was empty of customers and silent; Kirsten found it a sinister, even threatening place. In the darkness, it was impossible to see where the room ended. Most of all, she loathed the trophy that hung above the bar: the "unicorn." In reality, it was the head of an Arabian white gazelle. The taxidermist had replaced its two horns with a single one, sharp and glinting like a long sword. Vera assured her that the customers loved what Kirsten called "that hideous thing." No matter which way she moved, it seemed to be staring at her with its glass eyes. According to Vera, the taxidermist had experienced great difficulty in disguising his work. But the horn was anchored solidly in the skull. It was strong enough "to hang a man from," she said. They let the matter drop there. Kirsten had not yet responded to her friend's proposal.

She was intent on stopping off at the apartment to listen to Orfeo's message. "Nothing in particular, I just have to hear his voice." Vera was ready to go along, she said. At this hour the boutique's only customers would be tourists; Kirsten's assistant could look after them.

It was Vera's first visit to Kirsten's house. After the usual compliments at the location and at the view of the Schlossberg, she waited. In truth, Vera was disappointed by the interior decoration. It was too cozy, too homey, with light chintz-covered armchairs, small mahogany side tables, antique paintings that stood out against the white-washed walls, and the exposed beams in the ceiling that betrayed its original function as a hayloft. She didn't like the courtyard either, surrounded by the window-studded walls of the other apartments. Even the view to the Schlossberg repelled her; it was only a hillside covered with grapevines. She threw a quick glance at the brown stuffed chair in the corner, the sound system next to it, and the numerous shelves of recordings above a writing desk. That would be Weber's corner. She turned away and walked over to the answering machine where Kirsten stood.

It was Orfeo's voice. He was speaking to Weber, first of all with thanks for helping him that morning, then with the exact price the real estate agent had presented him. He had no experience in such

86

matters, he said. Could Weber meet him later that day, or the next? He left his number.

Despite the distortion caused by the machine, his voice was pleasing to the ear, Vera had to agree. Kirsten listened to the message several times, until she had memorized it word for word. Though she found it childish, Vera went along with the game. Then Kirsten removed the incoming message cassette, inserted a fresh one, dialed the number of the villa, and asked Gertrud to let her talk to Orfeo. As soon as he came onto the phone, she pressed the "record" button. Blushing, she told him she had just come from lunch with Weber, who had spoken to her about the sale. As the matter seemed urgent, she could come right away. She would like to bring a friend, a business-woman who knew about such things. During the conversation, she tugged on a lock of hair behind her ear.

Vera forced herself to turn away for a moment to regain her composure. Kirsten was extremely beautiful, so desirable at that very moment. She couldn't have cared less about her Bauernsilber or the minor 19th-century century masters of hers; she wanted her, in her own apartment, far from Weber; he didn't even deserve her.

Kirsten hung up, removed the cassette, replaced the original one and went into her bedroom where she slipped it into a dresser drawer among her underwear. Then she stepped into the bathroom where she washed her face, and applied her usual eyeliner. She was pretty without makeup, Vera assured her. She did not say that her features looked drawn, that she should have applied a good foundation. When they got into the car for the drive to the villa, it was after four o'clock.

Vera intrigued Orfeo, or so it seemed. He looked her over from head to toe. In a neutral tone, he observed that his workday had already been interrupted several times. Gertrud and Maria were out for the afternoon, and he had lent Johann to his neighbor. The real-estate agent had just called to find out if he was going to accept the offer. Vera asked him to show them the property. She didn't say a word as they moved from one room to another, from one floor to another. But nothing escaped her scrutiny: windows, doors, hardwood floors, ceilings, bathrooms, kitchen. They went down into the basement, where they shivered at the dampness from the nearby Neumagen.

Orfeo opened the doors for them without a word. Each time they stepped into another room, Kirsten snuck a look at Vera's expression, then Orfeo's. When they entered the singer's room, she was taken aback. How she would have loved to have had a nook exactly like this when she was a little girl, with a four-poster bed, yellow silk curtains with white lace trim, small pieces of furniture with delicate, curving legs, a carpet in sky-blue and cream tones. A perfect cocoon for day-dreaming, far from the empty room where she had slept, and where the only decoration had been sailing scenes. Every time she visited her parents, she felt sad when she entered "the tomb of my youth," as she called it. As her eyes avidly took in the feminine decor, she regretted never having created an interior to suit her tastes. Even their house in Bernau was entirely Weber's inspiration. Their Freiburg apartment wasn't her doing either. At first, they'd camped out, like students. Later, after an interior decorator had finished with it, they found themselves overnight in a place in which she recognized only the furnishings, which had come from the boutique or from other antique shops. Over time, she'd added what Vera would call bric-a-brac: colored glass lamps, bronze statuettes, and, of course, a few old oil paintings by local painters, which she would part with as soon as she could sell them in the shop. Creating a space for herself and Weber had never interested her. But here, in Orfeo's room, she felt as though she were in a doll's house, built for her alone. She wanted to stay there, to stretch out on the bed, to dream that beyond the curtains stretched woodlands out of a Watteau.

They walked to the far end of the garden. From there, they could see the whole house. Then they returned to the living room, where Vera told Orfeo that, in her opinion, the offer was far too low, and suggested a much higher counter-offer. She advised him not to back down if the agent raised objections. While he called, Vera stood close by so as not to miss a word. Surprised by Orfeo's firm attitude, the agent promised to call tomorrow. If the buyers agreed, Orfeo would be rich. With all that money in the bank, in addition to the various investments that Weber had discussed with him, Kirsten calculated he would be able to live comfortably.

Kirsten tried to contrive a way to induce Orfeo to sing for them. Blushing, she told him how powerfully the Mozart aria had struck her. Orfeo listened politely, impassively, but said nothing. She felt Vera's glance and suddenly began to stutter, her voice echoing in the room. Embarrassed, she repeated a few words, then fell silent. Orfeo refused outright; his day had ended, he was in no mood to sing. His tone remained polite, as if he were speaking to a spoiled child.

Kirsten felt humiliated in Vera's eyes; she could only think of leaving. In the car she burst into tears, certain that she'd spoiled everything.

"Can't you see what he does to me? I just can't control myself."

Vera drove back, turning onto the highway because, as she explained to Kirsten, she had to get back to town before the club opened to meet one of the members of the rock group that was itching to perform at the Unicorn in the fall. For more than a year she'd been looking for a hard-rock group, one that would be a match for the fantasies of a celebrity DJ she'd hired in England. He would organize a rave the likes of which had never been seen in this part of Germany. It would last all night long. Young people would come from everywhere, and the Unicorn would be the magnet that drew them. "They'll be unforgettable nights," the DJ had assured her. "Your customers will remember them even on their death bed! You'll see. But find me the best group you can. You'll see what I can do. I promise you a night to end all nights."

Kirsten wasn't listening. She'd drawn her legs up under her chin and was staring ahead at the road.

The night before, Vera had felt flattered to be the confidante of the young woman who'd won her over with her natural reserve and quiet self-confidence. Now, Kirsten came close to infuriating her. She simply couldn't understand what she was getting so worked up about; her response was as outlandish as an adolescent's to some pop idol. She found Orfeo—the name reminded her of Cocteau's film in black and white, but she could see no connection between the singer, the character played by Jean Marais, and the bizarre story—repulsive. "He's like a string bean," she was thinking. "Everything about him—his body, his head, his nose, his arms, hands and legs—is too long." He slithered along like an adolescent who didn't know where to put his oversize feet. She was used to exceptional voices, from falsetto to deep bass, from hoarse to tender; voices with the kind of vibration that would excite her in her bed in the little room high above the Unicorn's dance floor. Orfeo's speech was full of mannerisms, with the saccharine inflections of a youthful snob.

She disliked everything about Orfeo. Her preference was for men who advertised their virility: a few days growth of beard, rough in a nice way, hard hands calloused from frequent workouts in the gym. But him! Nothing but an empty, beardless face, skin smooth as a baby's, with too fine a texture. His hips were too broad, like a woman's. When he shook her hand, she'd felt a sense of repulsion; it was the hand of a schoolboy, tender, a bit damp, limp. One detail had struck her, though. The singer's eyes had unhurriedly dissected her, with distant amusement, like those of another woman for whom she could never be a rival. No man had ever looked her over quite that way, without desire, without a hint of sensuality; it was nothing but a quick evaluation, an examination she could not hope to pass. For all that, his dark eyes were striking, with their long lashes and their almond shape, like those of an oriental dancer. Vera could not tell whether he was timid, or arrogant. "He must be as cold as a dead fish," she reflected. "A closed book. Without feelings. Very much taken with his own affairs." He looked upon the sale of the house as though it were totally unimportant. But his brief discussion with the agent had revealed a natural talent for business; he'd spoken in a calm, firm voice.

She'd hated everything about his bedroom, with all its frills and flounces, overloaded like a bridal gown, straight out of an old tart's imagination. And yet there was nothing effeminate about him. Elusive; even shifty perhaps. He reminded her of a monk or a priest, who would only dare to look sidelong a woman. The odor that permeated all the rooms made her nauseous; to her it was the odor of death. The whole villa was a huge tomb.

But above all, she must keep her mouth shut, not say a word to Kirsten, not lose her temper. She was anxious to be alone.

When she parked in front of the building, Kirsten invited her in for a drink. But Vera declined with the smile that she controlled so well, with an appearance almost of warmth. She would get a bite to eat at the Unicorn; then would come the interview. As they parted, she asked Kirsten, "Why don't you write him a letter?"

Then, slyly, she added, "You'll feel better."

Kirsten flung open the veranda door. The apartment was suffocating. She felt like smashing things; strode from one room to another, threw open the windows. Orfeo would find the place over-decorated, stuffed with crap. At his house everything was bare, except for his bedroom. Even the scent of musk she'd found so disagreeable on her first visit seemed pleasant to her now. She wanted to wipe the slate clean, to throw every single one of these meaningless objects, most of them purchased with Weber, into the trash can.

"Poor little rich girl!" she muttered. "You're nothing but a poor spoiled little rich girl. With your rich little husband. You can't tell him a thing, because you don't even know what's happening to you. Not that he'd understand. You'd like to dump him, just like you'd like to clear out all this junk. And you're going to spend the rest of your life selling idiotic things to rich idiots."

At the villa Vera had been the star attraction, no doubt about it, with her red hair, her flashy jewelry, her femme fatale look that reeked of money and success, all thanks to that hideous nightclub of hers. Sure Vera had spunk, and a nice body, "but she's not as well built as I am," thought Kirsten. But Orfeo hadn't taken his eyes off Vera, "I might as well not have existed." Kirsten didn't like Vera's frown as they left his bedroom. But the room was ravishing, a pure fantasy! Ah, what a miserable idea, to try to convince him to sing! She wanted to show off his voice to Vera, like you'd do with a dog you've taught a new trick. Perhaps if Vera hadn't been there he would have sung an aria. A simple warm-up scale would have been enough for her. But he wasn't one of those vulgar singers who'll croon at the drop of a hat for a handful of compliments.

Kirsten recalled that in the car Vera had said not a word about Orfeo, although she wanted to hear nothing else. After everything she had told her, all except how she'd felt when her husband had touched her shoulder. She could have hit him. She'd never felt anything but scorn for his submissive, admiring gaze when they would meet on the banks of the Dreisam for their boring little luncheon ritual; the fearful look on his face when the youngsters with their shaved heads got too close to their bench. Did he really believe their fake leather jackets with the fascist slogans didn't bother her? Weber loved what he thought was her dry humor, the way she sized up other people, her fearlessness. Truth was, the punks and the skinheads terrified her like a pack of hungry rats. She could feel their eyes on her when they hung around in groups of five or six, their eyes touching her hair, then sliding down over her body, with particular attention to her legs.

If Weber had tried to reach out to touch her the night before, she would have screamed. Orfeo's voice had lodged in her like a knife; on the way back in the car, she had only been able to bear the pain in her sex by crouching in the seat. From that moment on, nothing else existed for her, nothing but the voice, the gaze that pierced her through.

At the beginning, she simply ignored Weber and that faithful dog's devotion of his. She resisted his clumsy advances. Like the evening he left a small bouquet with a stupid note on his seat at the restaurant where she worked part-time as student. Other times it was chocolates. It was all too middle-class, too humdrum. When she'd come home from work in the wee hours of the morning, she would pretend not to see him, half hidden under the porch of a neighboring house. But he'd worn her down with his timid ways, his bourgeois courtship, his dogged determination.

She was cautions by nature. She never experienced real love, and had walled herself up in splendid isolation. In the end she concluded that, all things considered, Weber would do, better than anyone else. He could be funny in company; he was at ease with strangers. He was from the area and knew all kinds of people, and he introduced her to some who helped her. He was only timid with her, and when they went to Husum. When she'd presented Weber, her parents had been polite. But she knew they didn't like him; he was too short, too heavy, he gesticulated too much. He was ill at ease around these taciturn people. She and Weber had received them only once in Freiburg. They hadn't liked the city, "a pot where you stew slowly." They missed Husum, and the wind that swept the seashore and the flatlands.

Yes, she had married Weber for personal gain, at least to an extent. Up until today, she had not regretted her choice. She could not find fault with him. He was not sporty, but he had had an athletic body, at least at one time. She liked kissing his thick neck, touching his broad shoulders, his muscular thighs. Over the last two or three years he'd developed a pot belly she didn't care much for. He had begun to lose his hair, too; although his chest, his stomach, and his arms were covered with thick black hair. One night she mentioned it.

"What am I supposed to do about it? That's how we are in my family." And he showed her photos of his father and his uncles: all short, stocky, bald men.

No, she'd never really known love, not with him, not with anyone else. He must have suspected it. Otherwise, he wouldn't get that anxious look on his face when he looked at her from across a room, at a reception. Until yesterday, their life together had unfolded pleasantly, uneventfully. But when she thought of the years to come, consumed by a job she now saw as meaningless, accumulating like ants for a comfortable retirement, she felt like screaming with rage. In a few minutes Orfeo had swept it all away, had reduced her efforts to a farce, with nothing more than his presence and the beauty of his voice. She could never have believed her life could be turned inside out so quickly.

She had been raised never to lie, as a matter of duty; she had to tell Weber the truth. Yet to do such a thing seemed inconceivable. What was happening to her was not his fault. If she told him she was wildly in love with a singer who could never love anyone, he wouldn't believe her.

Talking any further with Vera was impossible. Vera had been patient last night, but she didn't seem to appreciate Orfeo; at best he had left her indifferent. Otherwise, she would have said something in the car.

Kirsten made up her mind to proceed cautiously, cleverly. Concealing the truth was not the same thing as lying. It wouldn't be easy, especially with Vera; she already knew too much. Weber? He could wait.

In Weber's bookcase she found a recording of arias sung by a counter-tenor. It was exactly what she was looking for. She knew neither the singer nor the pieces. To her relief she discovered a German translation of the texts, most of which were in Italian. First, she listened to Bertarido's aria in Handel's *Rodelinda*, "*Vivi Tiranno!*" in which the hero lashes out at a villainous rival. But when she came to the title of Artabano's aria *"Pallido il sole, torbido il cielo"* in Hasse's *Artaserse*, she saw an almost perfect mirror of her own frantic emotional state. According to the libretto, Artabano is a traitor and a criminal; his aria expresses his remorse and despair when he is confronted with his misdeeds. "The sun has turned pale, and dark clouds cover the sky. Anguish hangs over me, death draws near. All inspires in me remorse and terror. Fear grips me with its glacial cold, pain has turned life bitter, and I loathe my heart."

In the aria, taken at a brisk tempo, the counter-tenor showed considerable skill, avoiding excessive coloratura. It was a succession of ascending notes, in several variations, each one expressing his growing anguish. But she took an immediate dislike to the voice, which the author of the text compared to one of the greatest *musici* of that bygone day, Senesino. To her ear it sounded forced, a fabrication, an imitation of a woman's voice sung by a masculine character. For her, it was a colorless, lifeless caricature of Orfeo's. Weber had once told her how the voice of any of those celebrated *primi uomini* would overwhelm a contemporary voice. Even in those days, bearing in mind the stratospheric purses that some *musici* could command, several composers had begun to use counter-tenors. But the outcome was never satisfactory.

How would Orfeo sing that aria? Kirsten wondered. She stopped the machine. After a lengthy silence, she played the piece again. This time, the voice seemed even less acceptable, but she closely followed the text, which struck her as being particularly noble. She admired the repetition of the notes that seemed to express her own feelings, then listened once more, intently, stopping the recording on *"rimorso"* and *"orror,"* then on *"contro il mio cor."* When she came to *"pena minaccia, morte prepara"* she shuddered; she too was a criminal, she too deserved punishment for her outburst of mindless passion. Kirsten could feel dark clouds gathering over her head. Sadness flooded over her, the tears began to flow.

Impatiently, she put the recording back in its box, stopped the machine, picked up a note-pad and began to write.

* * *

When Weber opened the front door, she glanced at the pendulum clock. In a little over two hours she'd filled a dozen sheets of paper. She tore them from the note-pad, hurried into the bedroom and hid them in the drawer next to the cassette. Softly she closed the drawer and returned to the living room. Weber appeared to be in an excellent mood; he was starving, he told her.

When he kissed her on the cheek, she repressed the urge to recoil. She didn't like his scratchy beard. He had a disagreeable odor of paper and dust about him. While he was mixing the salad dressing and opening a bottle of wine, she ripped apart the lettuce leaves and slashed the bread into slices. As her husband wolfed down his meal, her stomach knotted. A bit of bread and a glass of wine were all she could manage.

Normally they related their day to each other before going to bed; not tonight. Nor did either of them mention Orfeo.

Weber awakened early. He had slept fitfully. Kirsten was still there. When he left the apartment, she still seemed to be asleep. He stuck a note to the refrigerator door: "Gone to B.K. for work with O. See you tonite. XX." A fine rain was falling; they wouldn't have been able to meet for lunch on the park bench in any case. He was whistling the aria from *La fida ninfa* but stopped abruptly when he got into the car and caught the scent of a perfume he recognized immediately. His irritation bubbled up so quickly that he began to sweat. Under the guise of a good customer, then of a friend, that redhead was beginning to stick her nose into their lives. It occurred to him that Kirsten might have taken Vera to the villa. But why didn't she tell him anything? He recalled that he'd also omitted to tell her about his conversation with Orfeo. Yesterday evening Kirsten had looked sad. And yet, at the restaurant, she'd been excited about looking after the singer. But why had she taken Vera to the villa?

His anger subsided, but so did his upbeat mood. The two of them were up to something behind his back. He opened the window to dissipate the smell.

On the other hand, when you got right down to it, turnabout was fair play; yesterday he'd had the pleasure of spending the entire morning at the villa.

He parked on the other side of the Neumagen, whose volume had doubled overnight after heavy rains in the mountains. The water was murky and brown, and thick with broken branches. The "For Sale" sign had been removed. Inside the villa, all was quiet. Orfeo was not yet at work. Instead of ringing at the front door, Weber entered the studio by the garden door. No one. The room was dark. He stepped into the kitchen. On the table were a plate of croissants and a cup of coffee. The *musico* hadn't eaten breakfast yet. Suddenly Gertrud came in, looking like a nurse in her white smock. As if it were the most natural thing in the world, she said, "Go upstairs and see him. He's having a breakdown."

The yellow curtains were still drawn, creating the impression that the weather outside was perpetually fine and sunny.

Orfeo lay on his back. His "Come in" sounded weak. He turned his head toward Weber, forcing a smile. He pointed to the edge of the bed, and pulled the quilted coverlet up to his chin, as if chilled. Then he placed his right hand atop Weber's. His face was pale, his hair clinging to his forehead; he looked feverish.

"It's nothing. Happens to me from time to time, when I get an anxiety attack. I have to rest. Work is impossible. I should have called you to cancel, but it was too early. Forgive me. It's not my fault."

It was the voice of a disappointed child, a tiny voice about to break into sobs. Weber wanted to leave.

"Stay with me. I need you this morning. I waited all night for you."

The distress in his voice touched Weber. He took Orfeo's hand and attempted gently to warm it, without speaking. In a few minutes Orfeo's face began to relax, his breathing was calmer now.

"My insides are tied up in a knot. If I force myself to work, I might damage my voice. I've learned to let these fits run their course. La Signora did exactly as you're doing; she sat on the edge of the bed and held my hand until I began to feel better. You'll see; in an hour everything will be fine."

Now his voice was just a high-pitched thread.

"Yesterday, quite late in the evening, the agent came and I signed the offer. At the last moment, I lowered the price a bit. The agent told me major renovations would be needed to put the house in shape. It was a convincing argument. I hope your wife and her friend won't be too upset with me. They told you they came yesterday, didn't they? They insisted I should stick to my price; they warned me the agent would do everything he could to get me to sell for less. It seems the buyers, the ones you saw yesterday, think the ground floor is too dark. It's true, the trees are tall. La Signora never wanted Johann to trim them. Whenever we worked in the studio, we always had to turn on the lights, especially in the summertime. Who knows what they'll do with the trees, and with the house. I think I was wrong to sign."

He paused, took several deep breaths, but cut off his breathing high in his throat, which made it sound to Weber as if he was choking back tears.

"Last night, I realized how much I love this house. La Signora always told me she would leave it to me, just in case I had an accident that would make it impossible for me to earn my livelihood. You know what can happen in my profession; you're never sure of anything. I cried when I thought maybe I'd betrayed her by selling the villa so fast. We always lived here together. Now it's too late; I signed. Maybe they'll say I didn't love la Signora. But she was the only person in the world who loved me. She always believed in me. Sometimes we didn't get along. I'd had enough of the work, enough of the routine. Her discipline was tough. But she wouldn't force me; we would simply take a break for a few days. If she hadn't loved me, she wouldn't have kept me with her all those years. Sometimes I really think I'm having a fit because I want her to be near me."

The tears welled from between his eyelashes, flowed across his temples and vanished in his hair. No longer was he the singer, so self-assured, so confident in his artistry.

"I don't know what's going to happen. I've lived my whole life here. The agent told me the new buyers want me to leave as soon as possible."

Slowly he turned his head aside, and for several minutes said nothing. Then he slowly opened his eyes. In the light of the lamp, Weber could see for the first time his huge irises, dark green like laurel leaves, flecked with brown.

"You told me you might be able to lend me your country house.

But I maybe should move into a hotel in Freiburg. That way, I could ... I could ... get to know—" he hesitated, "the world, the people in your circle. Plus I would be close to you. Your wife seems very kind. I would like to see you more often. Leaving the house is like falling down a hole. Everything here reminds me of my work, can you understand? When I wake up in the morning I know exactly how my day is going to unfold. When I leave, the only thing that will be left of la Signora will be her memory, a few audiotapes, and that perfume of hers that nobody likes, except me. Maria and Gertrud tried to get rid of it, but I use it every day. I discovered flasks of it in her wardrobe.

"Since last night, I don't want my life to change. When the agent left, I panicked. And yet, I did exactly what I had to do. When I sell the house, I can let the staff go; I'll give each of them a cheque, and that will be the end of it."

His hand was still cold; there was no response to Weber's comforting movements. Seeing Orfeo's hurt brought back memories of a late fall day on the farm. He would have been eight or nine years old, bedridden with a nasty flu. His mother was seated on the bed. She was a strong woman, who worked hard on the family's scattered fields at Menzen-schwand, between the Feldberg and Sankt Blasien. As a little boy he often went with her to the fields. In summer, she left him alone beneath a tree where he could play with whatever he found, branches, insects, pine cones. Later, he would bring along his first books. He would wait there quietly, while she worked alongside a field hand. She knew he was more gifted than the other children. One day, the schoolmaster had stopped her in the street: "Mrs. Weber, your little one will go far. When it's time, he should be sent to Sankt Blasien, to the monks." She never forced him to do farm work. He was only happy with his books, and with a violin he'd found in the attic. He would saw away at it until he found the melody he was looking for. Later on he'd learned piano, at boarding school, under a teacher who was amazed at how quickly Weber mastered the difficulties of the instrument. When his mother heard him perform a solo during a school concert three years after entering the academy at Sankt Blasien, she beamed with pride. He'd never let his parents down; always at the top of the class. Sometimes his father, whom you would have sworn was mute, so little did he speak, would look at him out of the corner of his eye, as if he couldn't believe that this child was really his son. But he'd left him alone. During summer vacation, Weber liked coming back to his room, on the second floor, with a tiny window. From there he could see the Feldberg. The noise of the barnyard animals from the other side of the old house, the acid odor when they smoked the hams in the fall, the sound of the wind in the oak trees across the yard, all of it came back to him in the yellowish light that reminded him of the light that filtered through the calico curtains of his childhood home. Except for his books, there hadn't been a hint of fantasy in his room. When he ran out of space on his dresser, his father had built him two bookcases.

The reason why he and Kirsten had bought the little house in Bernau could be found there, in the little room that had never really been his. No sooner had he left for Sankt Blasien than a younger brother took it over, to vacate reluctantly when vacation time arrived. Weber had furnished it with meager memories; the most precious was of his mother cradling him in her arms when he'd been sick. He'd remained deeply attached to the land. He'd told Kirsten one day that he couldn't survive without the odor of the forest and the fields, and the view toward the Feldberg.

After a coughing fit his mother had taken him in her arms and held him tight for a long time. Weber could never forget the blend of odors his mother exuded; he could distinguish the smoke of the burning fields after the harvest, the smell of oats and of the stable, the fragrance of supper being prepared, the brittle air of the first frosts; the warm room, the pot-bellied cast-iron stove cracking from the heat, the acrid smell of the silver paint on the chimney pipe that would chip off at winter's end and would have to be repainted come summer. He could still remember, from that particular afternoon, the blouse his mother was wearing, with blue and yellow stripes. The softness of the fabric, the distant, pleasing discomfort caused by one of the buttons as it pressed against his plump cheek. He had lain there motionless. In his mother's silent embrace, as she clutched him tight against her stomach, he felt safe. He had absolute confidence in her. He hoped she would never get up. When she finally left the bedroom he had begun to drift off to sleep. He had seen her back: straight brown hair gathered into a bun, rounded, slouched shoulders, a wide skirt made from a heavy brown fabric that swung back and forth like a bell, muscular calves burnt by the summer sun, grey wool socks, worn-down shoes. When she disappeared, his only physical memory was the imprint of the button of her blouse. Impossible to tell how long he had run his finger back and forth over the tiny depression it had left in his skin.

Weber never experienced that sensation again.

In his first or second year at boarding school he was forced to share a seat with a classmate who was particularly stunted, the result of a spinal malformation. The other children called him "the hunch-back." Because he could not run and play like the rest of them, they wanted nothing to do with him. He was gentle and soft-spoken and would confide only in Weber. At night, Weber could often hear him sobbing. He would get up, go over and sit on the boy's bed, and take his hand. The result would always be the same: his friend would sob in silence. But after a few minutes his tears would cease and he would fall asleep. They never said a word about the night-time visits during class, but Weber remembered with startling clarity, there in Orfeo's room, the boy's damp, warm hand, and the emotions he'd felt when he heard him cry. And when the boy's hand fell from his, when he began to breathe regularly again, he was happy. On those nights, Weber slept deeply. And the next evening, he listened alertly for any sound from the hunchback's bed.

His seat-mate did not return to school after the summer holidays; no one heard a word about him. How Weber would have liked to know what happened to that boy, even today. After that, he had found no one to console. For him, his remaining terms at boarding school were the empty years.

As he stroked Orfeo's hand he thought of his wife. He had seen Kirsten only cry once. He could do nothing to help her; she was inconsolable. But faced with Orfeo's distress, he did what his mother used to do, and transformed the room, bathed in yellow light, into an island beyond the world. Weber took Orfeo in his arms. His slender body seemed almost weightless. Through the fabric of his pajamas he touched his neck, his startlingly broad, deep chest. Orfeo's head slipped onto his shoulder. The touch made Weber shiver. Happiness welled up in him, alone with the *musico* in his room. Orfeo stopped shaking.

For a long time they stayed there, motionless. Orfeo appeared to be sleeping. Weber did not dare move, for fear of awakening him.

CHAPTER SIX

Questo è il soggiorno de' fortunati eroi
"This is the abode of happy heroes"

–C. W. Gluck, *Orfeo ed Euridice*, Act II

Once they set up house for Orfeo at Bernau, Kirsten and Weber traveled there regularly. It was an easy hour's journey. To Weber's enormous satisfaction, Vera begged off helping them with the move. She was too busy at the Unicorn. When word got around that she was organizing an all-night rave, a lot of groups came knocking at her door. She thanked Weber for putting her in touch with Litow. She was surprised at how well informed he was about what was happening in the field: "He's not much to look at, but he gave me solid advice. He knows exactly what's hot right now."

Weber was hardly listening. He hadn't a clue what a rave was.

Vera's mind wasn't quite made up. Three groups were in the running. In the meantime, she started rumors that one well-known group or another would be appearing, to whet her customers' appetites. But life had taught her not to rush things. After their visit to the villa, she had only seen Kirsten on the odd occasion. With her, there was no need to make haste.

The movers began work shortly after the contract of sale had been signed. One week later, the villa was empty. With no visible emotion, Orfeo related to Weber how, on the stairs, he'd found the shards of the little plaster cherub that had hung at his bedside for nearly ten years, a plump little boy whose open mouth was either singing or calling out for food, like the beak of a baby bird. This *putto* had been hung in such a way that its rosy head with the curly golden hair gleamed in the light of his bedside lamp. Hands full of pieces of plaster, he'd hurried from room to room, collecting the remains. When he left the house, he threw them into the bucket Johann used for his yard work. The head, which was still intact, he kept. Before his first night in the bedroom, la Signora had given him the little angel, with the promise that it would always bring him happiness.

Orfeo gave most of the furniture to charities. Everything else, including the Steinway and la Signora's huge closet—"my two sarcophagi," the singer called them—was stored in the barn of a farmer whom Weber had known since childhood, in Altglashütten, quite close to the house where Weber had grown up. As Kirsten saw it, it took a local to know how to save money. Ever since the villa had been sold, she'd begun to perk up. On their first trip together to Bernau, in the face of the singer's silence, she insisted that, all things considered, the big house was too sinister for him to live in any longer. The fresh air of the Black Forest highlands would do him good. And Frau Schäuble's cooking would be far more nutritious than what he'd been accustomed to from Maria and la Signora.

What she did not tell him was that Frau Schäuble, a tender-hearted grandmother, loved to take care of anything frail and sickly, man or beast, and that she could brew magic potions that were sure to have an effect on him. After her husband died, she no longer worked in the fields around the Schafberg; her son-in-law and her daughter looked after them now. People from the neighboring villages, from Oberlehen, Riggenbach, Weierle and Hohfelsen, came knocking at her door for remedies. At their first meeting, Frau Schäuble brought a smile to Orfeo's face when she cried out, "Ach, how skinny you are! Just you wait; I'll put some meat on your ribs!"

Weber had already moved the upright piano, the four-poster bed and the few items that Orfeo still wanted to keep. Frau Schäuble would tell anyone who cared to listen that the guestroom looked completely different now, that it was prettier even than the church. When, on the *musico*'s first Saturday morning in Bernau, she brought him a cup of hot chocolate, she was almost speechless: "He looks like the Christ child in that bed. You'd swear it was a Christmas nativity scene with lace all around!" Her remarks quickly spread from one end of the valley to the other. In their curiosity and thirst for news, people begged her to tell them everything she knew about this singer with—as she claimed—an angel's voice. Weber had told her about Orfeo's fragile health, about his moods and his work. From that instant, her mind was made up. He was "a young man, gorgeous as a rare bird. When he sings it makes my head spin; if you only knew! And how sweet he is in the bargain!"

Thanks to a generous separation settlement, Maria found work in Freiburg. She was "happy to live in town, where there was always something going on." Gertrud's cheque was even more substantial. Too old to find work anywhere but in a cafeteria or a down-market restaurant, she moved into a small apartment in Staufen, not far from Bad Krozingen, where she re-established contact with her friends. She became a regular at the Café Decker, where she liked to over-indulge in the café's celebrated pastries. At around four o'clock she could be found there with a group of widows who would get together at this venerable regional institution to celebrate the demise of their husbands. As for Johann, he read and reread the numbers on his cheque several times over before folding it and depositing it in the bank. Maria claimed he'd proposed that Gertrud move in with him, but she liked her freedom, she said.

They thanked Orfeo politely. The person that they had always seen as an intruder, whom they had been made to serve for twelve long years, had done nothing to deserve his fortune; by rights it was theirs, in fact. Gertrud and Johann came around to Maria's opinion: that he had used his accident, the loss of his parents, his constant illnesses, his fits and his crises, to bewitch la Signora; her mind wasn't really functioning at the end. He should have divided up the proceeds of the sale into three parts. He deserved nothing; considering the way la Signora had looked after him, just like a mother, he'd already eaten up his inheritance.

Orfeo never saw them again.

The Webers' country house was a former stable that had belonged to the Michelis-Hof, the Schäuble family farm. There were hundreds like it throughout the region. Strictly speaking, Bernau wasn't even a village, just farms strung out along a road. There was no school, no church.

But Sankt Blasien, whose great baroque cathedral and academy were still in the hands of the Benedictines, was not far away. Weber knew the Schäubles well; it had not been difficult to persuade them to sign the stable over to him. In their eyes, the Webers were model neighbors; they made no demands and paid handsomely. As year-round caretaker of the country house, Frau Schäuble could count on a modest additional income. When they'd come for the first time to inspect the property four years earlier, Kirsten had immediately appreciated its location: at an altitude of more than one thousand meters, the air was always fresh, even in summertime. There were no fields under crops, only pastures. And the view was breathtaking: from the Scheibenfelsen heights, which were only a few minutes' walk from the house, you could see the summits of the Rabenstock and the Silberfelsen. To the north loomed the Feldberg, and to the south, beyond Todtmoos, you could make out the Dachsberg massif.

In the course of restoring the abandoned building, they'd come close to giving up. Stones had fallen from the walls; only a few rotten boards remained of the door; weeds had taken root in the cracks of the walls. The interior consisted of a single large room that stunk of mold. In one corner lay a heap of rusted metal and rotted oats were scattered across the floor beneath the smoke-blackened beams. But the thatch roof was still solidly in place. The contractor, a friend of the farmer, assured them they could get off easy: "The walls are thick and solid like a fortress. We'll connect the sewer to the farmhouse's, add inside walls to make rooms; there's nothing to it, you'll see." Needless to say, the restoration had cost three times more than planned, but all things considered it had been less expensive than renovating their apartment in Freiburg. And, thanks to the slope of the land, one only saw the roof of the Schäuble's farm.

Kirsten fell in love with the place. The stable had been transformed into a comfortable apartment, with a spacious living room that overlooked the Dachsberg. Two rooms in the back were connected to the living room by a narrow hallway, with the bathroom to the right and the kitchen to the left that opened onto the main living space. Now that they'd completed their summer residence, Weber and Kirsten wondered what else they could wish for in life. Some of their friends had bought properties in Tuscany, others in Provence, but those places were too far away. Not to mention that the southern Black Forest, especially in summer, was much more pleasant than the sun-baked earth of Italy or the south of France. Weber added a few modern armchairs and two antique cupboards discovered in abandoned barns. Kirsten hadn't interfered. The living room, with its yellowed photos of members of the Weber family and views of the Feldberg, had a pleasant country feel. They fitted the upright piano in beside the new sound system.

Orfeo had moved in with a bulky case of musical scores and books, two trunks of clothing, and a satchel containing medicines and toiletries. His bed replaced that of the guestroom. He really liked the yellow calico curtains, he said. They were a reminder of his childhood that Weber did not want to part with even though Kirsten complained that she did not like waking up early in a room full of golden light. Frau Schäuble's simplicity and personality pleased the singer immediately. Orfeo behaved charmingly toward everyone. That first evening, he surprised his hosts by singing a few 17th-century German melodies by Hagen and Albert, and the magnificent *An die Einsamkeit* by Johann Philipp Krieger. They explored the countryside around the farm. Looking out over the peaceful landscape, he said quietly, "I would like to spend the rest of my life here."

On his bedside table, beside the miniature Ancien Régime pendulum clock, he placed the head of the cherub.

For Frau Schäuble it was clear that the *musico*, despite his height, was a fragile creature, someone who needed care and protection. She came early every morning to prepare breakfast, which she lay at the foot of his bed, and lingered to chat with him, and encourage him to finish his plate; then she went about the housework, sometimes tarrying at the far end of the room while he worked. She could not stop saying, "He sings like an angel! When you hear him, you'd swear you'd gone to heaven." Later, she would say he had a "celestial" voice, borrowing the term she heard Kirsten use. In mid-morning she prepared him a snack. At lunchtime she would stand at the entrance to the kitchen; from there she could see whether her ward was doing justice to her cooking. Following Kirsten's advice, she had gradually introduced venison, more substantial sauces, a glass of red wine, nourishing desserts. To fortify his long, slender body she gave him, immediately on waking, a raw egg mixed with Port wine. In the afternoon, after his work session, he would often join her on one of her expeditions to the farmhouses scattered throughout the valley. These outings were particularly beneficial, and brought color to his cheeks. It wasn't long before the farmers became acquainted with him, their wives especially, who adored him. They found him pretty, with his fine-textured skin, his large almond eyes and his bashful smile. On rainy days he stayed inside, listening to the recordings of music from outside his repertoire that Weber had passed on to. He discovered French, German and Italian 19th-century opera; before long, he could not do without it. A bit after five o'clock Frau Schäuble would leave, after preparing him a cold supper. He spent his evenings reading, everything from history and travel books to biography. Or he would watch the news on television. On rare occasions he would pay a visit to the Schäubles. The farmer, who was a stocky, taciturn type, spoke in grunts that Orfeo could not understand, and Frau Schäuble's daughter was continually busy. But her two granddaughters wouldn't leave him alone; whenever he went out for a walk they tagged along at a respectful distance. As he barely noticed them, they didn't dare speak to him.

Weber and Kirsten observed that the change in climate and diet, along with Frau Schäuble's care, had a rapid effect. In only three weeks, Orfeo's cheeks filled out, his neck grew thicker, his skin ruddier. Now he had a healthy, country-boyish look about him. Frau Schäuble, who was quite proud of herself, would exclaim, "He looks good enough to eat, don't you think?" Then, for the umpteenth time, she would re-tell the tale of the cat.

Not long after the singer's arrival, Frau Schäuble noticed that the farm's tiger-striped tomcat, a powerful, standoffish animal that wouldn't let anyone come near him, would take up a position in a window box planted with geraniums a few minutes after Orfeo began his vocalises. He would groom his fur scrupulously, and, when the "concert"—as Frau Schäuble called it—began, he would sit motionless until the session was over. When fine weather finally arrived, in early June, she left the front door ajar. The cat then deserted the window box, to take up a position on the threshold, peering into the room where the singer sat at the piano. Frau Schäuble was touched at the sight, and stooped down to scratch his head. The cat hissed and spat at her furiously, and fled. A few days later, Orfeo had gone to stretch his legs in the nearby field. The cat had followed along behind him, his tail sticking straight up; the next day, he had mewed at the door. No sooner had it been opened than he took up his position to hear Orfeo sing.

"I've never seen anything like it," Frau Schäuble told Weber. "You'd swear he is in love. He follows him everywhere. I wonder when he'll move into the living room."

But the cat never stepped over the threshold. He waited just outside the door, tail curled about his paws. After a month, when the vocalises and grooming were over, he began to flop over on his back, stretch out, extend and retract his claws, and roll around on the rough, sun-warmed stone. When Orfeo stopped, you could hear him purring, as loud as an idling motor. Orfeo gave him a name that everyone found curious, Singer, pronounced English-style, as if he were a sewing machine and a singer all wrapped up in one. The cat would only raise his head when Orfeo called. If anyone else called him by name, he would not react.

Two weeks after he had begun his daily visits, the tomcat deposited a dead bird on the threshold. When Frau Schäuble rushed over to "throw that thing in the trashcan," Singer arched his back, hissing, then darted off in anger. From that day on, he would bring gifts almost every day: mice, blackbirds, and the occasional squirrel. Orfeo asked Frau Schäuble to leave the little corpses exactly where the cat had dropped them. She could only remove them when Singer trotted off to accompany his idol on their stroll in the fields.

Orfeo was thriving. Since arriving in Bernau he had become far less tense. But Weber had begun to worry: their *musico* had precious little to say about his future, and even less about whether he even wanted to make a stage début. Frustrated by his charge's indifference, he said to Kirsten, "Well, he can't just stay here forever! He absolutely has to make a name for himself, in competition for instance. What are we going to do with him, after all?" But she didn't see things quite that way. "Time will tell, you'll see. Let him breathe a little. His life has been turned upside down, and now you want to go leaping into some competition?" Since Orfeo had come to live in the country, Kirsten was her old self again, full of verve and common sense. In Orfeo's presence she remained circumspect, speaking only a little. She rarely heard him sing, usually on Sunday mornings. On the third Sunday in June she was seated in the living room, near the kitchen. They hadn't seen the cat on their previous visits and had trouble believing Frau Schäuble's cat story. Orfeo, who was working on an aria by Hasse, pointed it out to them. This time, he'd dropped a bird's head at the doorstep. Weber interrupted the session with a laugh. You had to admit it was funny: a cat biting off the heads of songsters to lay them at the feet of the most beautiful voice in the world!

Not once did Orfeo ask what had become of the villa, of Maria, Gertrud or Johann. But there were times when the Webers caught the distant scent of musk in the house. One day, Kirsten caught the odor quite distinctly. It came from Frau Schäuble, who told her that Orfeo had given her some perfume as a gift. It was too strong for her at first, and she only put on a drop. "But I got used to it," she said. "At first, I wanted to please him. At the farm, they like the smell, and when I put it on, the cat lets me come near."

The notary deposited the money from the sale of the villa in Orfeo's bank account in Freiburg. Weber knew they'd begun work at the villa. The new owner took advantage of his connections: the Bad Krozingen mayor's office gave them permission to chop down several trees. A group of workers set about the task, to the consternation of the neighbors who had to put up with the whine of the chainsaws and later, with the shouting of the bricklayers. The buyer, a Freiburg businessman, wanted to do things in a big way.

Orfeo had never asked after Vera.

At the beginning of the second week in July, a few days before the start of the music camp, Weber and Orfeo set out for Weissenfels castle. Weber had a surprise for him: a visit to Würzburg, with its architectural jewels from the medieval period, the Renaissance and the Baroque. They took two rooms at the Mainz, an inn famous for its restaurant, then climbed up to the top of the fortress, where Orfeo admired the

Riemenschneider sculptures. After crossing back to the other bank of the Main, they mingled with the tourists in front of the great manor house of the Prince Elector. Orfeo spent several minutes studying the huge Tiepolo fresco in the main hall, whose tones of blue recalled the sky of the painter's native Venice. Looking for some refreshment they stopped off at the Heiliggeistspital, whose function as a hospital was now reduced to quenching the thirst of modern-day wayfarers with a few draughts of Bocksbeutel, the fruity, easy-drinking white wine of Franconia.

They made their way through the lively crowd and down the stairs into the cellar. It was impossible to talk. They were surrounded with the hum of conversation, the wails of crying children, and the din of live music from the gallery. The air was thick with the odors of fried food, smoke and wine. Weber could see drops of sweat beading Orfeo's forehead. Did he want to leave? he asked, almost shouting. The singer shook his head, but sought out and clutched Weber's hand, then tossed back a glass of wine. "It's just a little panic attack. Don't let it bother you." As he rubbed the sweat-covered hand, Weber noticed the startled glances of customers at the neighboring tables.

He got up and led Orfeo over to the staircase. Once in the street, he guided him back to the Mainz, accompanied him to his room, and told him to rest until suppertime; he'd reserved a table in the dining room of the inn. At eight o'clock, as Orfeo was still indisposed, Weber had the food brought to the room: turtle soup, grilled lobster, pear sherbet, stuffed quails, vegetables au gratin, a selection of cheeses and dessert, all to be washed down with Bocksbeutel. The sounds of the street could be heard through the open windows.

Weber visited the bathroom. As he was soaping his hands, he was irritated to note that his hairline seemed to be receding more rapidly than he had noticed before. He was discouraged, he was growing old; he examined the bags under his eyes, the fine wrinkles around his mouth. All at once, he wondered why he would bring the singer to Weissenfels in the first place. When you got right down to it, he really wanted to keep him—he avoided thinking "imprison" him—at Bernau. He would put on a display of concern in Kirsten's presence when he talked about the *musico*'s future. But his stomach began to churn at the idea that an opera house director could steal him away, or that some wily impresario might organize a concert tour for him. That would be the end of their encounters at Bernau. For the time being at least, the singer was his: at Weissenfels, only instrumentalists could participate. Again and again Weber assured himself that his only purpose in taking the trip was to please Orfeo, by immersing him in such delightful surroundings.

But his worries would not relent. He could not hide Orfeo much longer, and he knew it. The singer would go on to enjoy a brilliant career; he would forget about him just as he had forgotten Maria, Gertrud and Johann, all of whom had served him for so long. He would move from success to success, the world's greatest opera houses would compete for him. There could be no doubt. What would come of the *musico* when his career ended? How long would his voice last? Some *primi uomini* had sung well into their sixties. But then what?

He mulled over what he knew about the lives and deaths of the *musici*. Farinelli, he knew, had died friendless and alone in Bologna. For years he lived in a luxurious villa, long since demolished, amidst his collection of objets d'art and harpsichords. He never sang in public again after returning from the Spanish court. Almost all the others had come to the same sad end, with the exception of Gaetano Guadagni, who was ruined by his own generosity. Separated from their families, who had almost all rejected them, the *primi uomini* were unable to maintain ties of friendship with their admirers from their days of glory. Almost all of them had been wealthy. What they would earn for a single performance far exceeded the annual wages of several laborers. But in retirement, they could only await the end. They were seen by the world as monsters; their entire existence had been concentrated in their voice. From the end of their career until their death, they trod the path of solitude. Many of them reached a near-biblical age, which led many physicians of the day to speculate that loss of virility might possibly prolong a man's life.

Once they left the stage, the public forgot them. Some even attempted marriage. The most beautiful women of the day offered themselves. In Dresden a *musico* had died of grief when his marriage with a young woman, who was wildly in love with him, was annulled for incompatibility. Another became the laughingstock of London when he claimed paternity for a child his mistress had just given birth to. Yet another submitted a petition to the Pope, claiming that he was *treorchi*, meaning that the surgeon had not noticed a third testicle, and that he was able to engender his own descendants. The Pope rejected the petition, brushing aside the supplicant with a disdainful wave of the hand, "Let him find a better surgeon next time!"

Orfeo was becoming more enigmatic. There were times when the singer would act like a lost child and would cling to Weber. But on other occasions he displayed a striking intellectual and emotional maturity, and sound professional judgment. He knew exactly how far he could carry his repertoire, and precisely how to approach his music. But he would not let his emotions show. He never spoke of his physical condition; the loss of his virility didn't seem to bother him. It was as if he had put all dreams to rest, eliminated all desire to be young. He had a sure nose for other people. Weber remembered, not without satisfaction, his remark about Vera: "She's a Christmas tree that could catch fire any minute. Better keep your distance."

Even during his periods of anxiety, Orfeo revealed nothing about himself. All that came to the surface at such times was fear of his first stage appearance, of presenting his voice to the public. Weber's arguments reassured him, but only for a while. Weber wondered whether his feelings for the people around him were anything other than social convention.

Weber returned to the room. As soon as the waiter had set the table and drawn up the serving cart, he dismissed him and sat down on the divan. Orfeo pulled up an armchair. The singer's weakness had vanished. He served up generous portions, adroitly sliced the quails. It was as though he had never experienced any other life, though until recently he had been following the strictest of diets. Now, he seemed to be ostentatiously turning his back on the fare he'd been forced to eat at the villa, or even on Frau Schäuble's cooking. At meal's end, all that remained were crumbs, quail carcasses and dirty dishes. Due to the wine, Weber felt heavy-headed, drowsy. As he pushed himself back from the table, he felt more confident: he would help Orfeo emerge from his cocoon without betraying la Signora's confidence. Kirsten was right; time would tell.

In the comfort of his room, after the sudden relaxation of the tensions of a full day, he slipped into his dream.

* * *

He is waiting his turn in the vestibule of the villa. All is silent. Slowly the door swings open; someone exits the studio walking backwards, soundlessly, in his direction. It is not la Signora. This strange person quietly closes the door. Weber watches as he takes several steps backward, lifts his arms and gently draws the heavy red curtains that muffle the sounds from the studio, where la Signora is waiting for him. In the dim light of the vestibule, he can see that the man is wearing a white jabot, a lace tie, a light blue silk frock-coat narrowed at the waist, decorated with embroidery and precious stones. His pants, of a dark red shade, fit tightly about his thighs, reaching just below his knees. His patent leather pumps have high heels; white stockings accentuate the bulge of his calves. In his left hand he holds a flute, a handsome instrument that glints silver in the dim light. Without turning, the man waves his right hand slowly, in a rotating motion. Then he swivels his trunk to the right, toward a door Weber has not noticed. He opens it, waits. Weber gets up from his chair with great difficulty; he feels as though he were drugged and could only move forward deliberately. The other man is already waiting at the foot of the staircase, but Weber had heard no footsteps on the wooden stairs. Slowly, against his better judgment, he makes his way down the flight of steps. Together they walk down a long corridor, doors to the left and to the right. Above each door is a burning torch; the smoke makes him cough. The other man comes to a stop and, without turning, points to the fanlight. Weber looks in: it is his childhood bedroom. There is someone in his bed, a child, his hunchbacked little friend from boarding school. Crying, he stretches out his hands, then throws aside the covers and displays his scrawny naked body. All the tenderness he had felt then comes back to him, the urge to protect the child, and the desire to do whatever the sickly little boy might wish.

Through the next fanlight he glimpses la Signora seated at the piano, surrounded by a group of students. She is playing Scarlatti, striking each note cleanly, separating it from the notes that precede and follow. She is at the peak of her form: her shoulders are barely moving, her arms relaxed, her hands moving over the keys as her fingers strike with extraordinary acuity. He sees her in profile, imagines her furrowed brow. Her eyes are all but closed. When she has finished, everyone around her applauds. But Weber can already hear another melody, from far away, an Italian aria sung by a female voice. La Signora stands up, walks toward the fanlight, presses her stern, wrinkled face against the glass and stares at Weber. He steps back in fear of what she might say. The old lady hisses, "You don't even come up to their ankles, any of them! All you're good for is to smear ink on paper criticizing them." She pauses, then shouts, "You're useless!"

The figure ahead of him seems to be floating several centimeters above the floor. Weber can still not make out his face. He reaches out, takes Weber's hand and leads him to the next door. Weber sees himself seated at his desk in the newsroom amid stacks of reference books, a sheaf of paper in front of him. He fills one of the sheets with sentences, then crumples it and throws it to the floor where it joins many others like it, scattered about. Weber wants to cry out, to put an end to this futile task, when some men burst in and gather up the discarded paper. Then they walk out, holding the sheets against their chests as though they were protecting a treasure of inestimable value.

But already his guide is urging him on. They pass by several doors, then come to a stop. Weber sees the bedroom of the apartment in Freiburg: Kirsten and he are in bed together. He is on top of Kirsten— he pumps away as she stares off into the distance. He appears ugly to himself. His prominent pot belly, hairy back and shoulders—black hair down to his ribs. Hair that is too long at the neck but thinning on the top of his head. Her attractive face is motionless. She does not love him. As he watches the couple, a wave of distress floods over him, an overwhelming need for affection, for love, for tenderness wells up inside him. He wants to turn back, to open the first door, but behind him the corridor is as black as the abyss. Fear begins to overtake him; behind him the torches have gone out one by one as they passed.

There is no one to console him but his mute guide, but he refuses to turn, and his silhouette seems occluded, as the remaining torches begin to flicker out. It is at that moment that his guide lifts the flute to his lips. Weber hears a slow, sorrowful melody; it is telling a story he feels he knows, though he has no idea where he has heard it before. Suddenly, he recognizes it: is his own life; a life that seemed full, but in reality was empty, and infinitely sad. He hears in it the sadness of his sickly young schoolmate, of his mother after his failure with la Signora, of the hard work he had devoted to his studies, of his dread of losing the woman who is the proof of his success yet who has never loved him, whom he had desired and conquered for reasons that now escape him. He can hear an occasional happy note, but it is quickly swallowed up by the melody of the flute now mingled with the other voices, voices as sharp-edged as knives: those of la Signora, of his co-workers at the newspaper, a cacophony of strident cries. Gone, gone are the blissful days of his childhood, his early success at the piano, his school report cards that proclaimed him best student of the year, his pleasure at his growing reputation, his joy when Kirsten had accepted his marriage proposal. Nothing can resist that melody. It invades him, wraps itself around his chest, suffocates him. He can hardly swallow; tears are flowing down his cheeks. Behind him all is darkness; in front of him, the bottomless pit of sorrow into which he wants to throw himself as he follows the call of the flute that sounds like the cry of a child in despair.

Singing on an uncertain vowel, between "*a*" and "*e*," the music of the flute gives voice to his feelings, overlooking not a single one.

The armor that he has painstakingly constructed over time from a life without conflict, of respectability, of concern for appearances, begins to shatter piece by piece. With an immense effort, he throws himself upon the flute player. But his feet seem caught in a viscous slime that holds him to the floor. When he places his hands on his guide's shoulders, the man turns to face him. Weber breathes a sigh of relief: it is Orfeo, but his gaze looks right through him, focusing on a point in the darkness behind him. The presence of his familiar face is enough to make Weber, throwing caution aside, embrace him, sobbing. Orfeo strokes his shoulder with a comforting hand. Slowly Weber grows calm. When he breaks free from the embrace, he sees that the *musico* has raised his hands and cast aside the flute, which vanishes in the darkness. Then the last of the torches flickers out. Orfeo leads him to the foot of the stairs. Together they climb back to the surface. The door swings open.

* * *

When Weber awakened he thought he could hear sighs, moans and cries for help from somewhere far below. Orfeo was cradling him in his arms, his face pale, in his eyes a look of panic that Weber had never seen before. He was swabbing Weber's forehead clumsily with a dampened washcloth.

"Are you feeling better now? Good Lord, you really gave me a fright! I thought you were having a seizure. I was about to run down to the desk to have them call a doctor. You've been unconscious for a while now."

Weber smiled weakly, sat up, and took a drink of water. When he saw the remains of the meal nausea almost overcame him. He looked up and saw two Canaletto reproductions on the wall, scenes of the Piazza San Marco and the Grand Canal in Venice. He thought of La Fenice, of the impact that Orfeo's voice would create there. He reached out and took the *musico*'s hand. The touch of his fine-textured skin was so intensely pleasurable that it disturbed him. He shook himself. "It's nothing. Just had too much wine, ate too much. I had a nightmare that I managed," he exhaled as he pronounced the word, "to get through. You were in it; it was you who led me out of there."

Orfeo's eyes gleamed with delight. "I was in it? I just love dreams, especially nightmares. How nice it is when I wake up and realize it was only a dream. You know, I've had lots of them since my accident. Sometimes I would cry out so loudly that la Signora would wake up, to calm me. She was a sight, with a hairnet on her head, dressed in her dark red bathrobe. She loved velvet, except in the studio, because of the acoustics. She would stay beside me, sitting there on the edge of the bed, and I had to tell her what I'd seen in my dream. At first, I had lots because they were giving me sleeping pills at night. I'll never forget the pain in my pelvis and my right hip. When I moved in with my aunt, it all started up again. Every night I would cry out in my sleep. No wonder she was happy to get rid of me."

"When did you stop having nightmares?"

"But I still have them! Except that they're not the same ones. I had the last one, a really terrible one, when you came to the villa. If only you knew how alone I felt that morning! Then, you did exactly what la Signora used to do. You took my hand, and I felt safe."

"What was going through your head?"

Orfeo averted his eyes. Then, with effort, he said, "Oh, nothing in particular. I was alone, that's all. La Signora was at the cemetery; at the gate was a group of people, shouting at me to leave. I could make out the voices of Johann, Maria and Gertrud. They were shouting louder than the others. They really hated me, those three."

It was the first time Orfeo had spoken about himself. But even then, as he looked at the reproductions, he changed the subject. "I'd love to visit Venice one of these days. Would you come with me? I'd be afraid of getting lost, all alone."

Weber picked up the shift in tone. Orfeo had spoken to him in the intimate form.

"If you like, we can drop the formalities, especially since we're working together. Anyway, I haven't yet reached the age of respectability!"

Orfeo clasped his hand. At that precise instant Weber understood how true his dream had been: he needed Orfeo's physical presence in the same way that he could not do without the sound of his voice.

He avoided the singer's eyes for fear he would betray himself. Softly he caressed his hand, his throat still knotted from the dream, feeling an impulse to let himself go. All was collapsing around him; only Orfeo's presence meant something. For the first time he admitted to himself: he loved Orfeo. He had fallen in love with him the first time they met. A flow of memories surged over him, memories he'd suppressed ever since his first days in boarding school.

Weber took a deep breath, with a halting sigh, like a child unable to bear his heartache. He desired that mutilated body, wanted to caress it, more than he had ever wanted his wife. He attempted to sit up, but could only manage a shoulder movement that caused Orfeo to remove his hands.

In the silence of the room, the singer said, in a playful, barely forced voice, "You know, I used to think Weber was your first name. It struck me as curious. I'd never seen anyone with the first name 'Weber' in the telephone directory, until I realized that Freiburg was full of Webers! Even Kirsten calls you by your last name. Why? When it comes to names, there's no reason to hide anything from me. I know my family name is common enough in Württemberg, but all the same, to be called Teufel! Nobody would be happy with a 'devil' on stage, don't you think? So, tell me, what's your first name?"

It was true. Nobody except for his parents and his brother called him by his first name. He said, "I don't know when I began calling myself just plain Weber. At school, perhaps, or at university. Like a pseudonym. My name is Horst. But Kirsten doesn't like it."

"Horst? Why, that's a fine name! 'Eagle's nest!' You'll be my refuge, and I'll be protected by an eagle."

During the night he did not return to his room. He listened to Orfeo breathing, calmly, deeply. The *musico* hardly moved in his bed. Weber felt shattered. With a simple movement of his shoulders, he had sent the wrong message. For an instant, he'd believed that Orfeo had understood. He had wanted to sit up, to take him in his arms. But the singer had retreated rapidly into himself; he had outmaneuvered him with that business of the name. The opportunity was lost. He had no idea of how to turn back, to re-experience that luckless instant.

Orfeo had avoided asking him about his dream.

Weissenfels castle is one of the last great private estates in that part of Germany. In the late 'fifties, the owner, a dedicated music-lover, founded the summer music academy, which had been popular ever since. Each year, dozens of young musicians from the four corners of the world converged there to perform, primarily chamber music, but also in several full-fledged gala concert events. The mere invitation to participate could be an excellent springboard for the instrumentalists, all of them on the competition level. After Weissenfels, other summer academies were founded across Germany. The public loved them. It was not long before they began to attract agents, impresarios and journalists on the lookout for fresh talent.

The huge principal building, in the form of a U, faced the former stables, the Marstall, which had been made over into a hotel several years earlier. Behind them were located the farm's outbuildings. Since the inception of the Academy, its concerts were held in the great ceremonial reception room known as the Marble Hall, with a capacity of more than four hundred. Weber and Orfeo shared a room at the far left of the Marstall. From their window they could see the façade of the chateau, with its central block in ochre and white that contained the main staircase. The entrance hall had thick columns and its ceiling was decorated with playful frescos. It led to the great hall. Throughout the festival, from mid-July to the end of the first week in August, the chateau resonated like an immense stringed instrument; the breeze would waft the music across the green, rolling countryside as far as the village. The earth was rich, the farmers too; foremost among them was the Count von S., an affable, cultivated man.

Orfeo and Weber sat in on the rehearsals for the first great baroque concert. The orchestra was working on several pieces by Bach and Handel, and an overture by Gluck, under the direction of a Hungarian conductor. Agents moved discretely from one group to another, taking notes, like handicappers before a horserace. Here, all that mattered was music. Weber suggested they take a side trip to Bamberg, but Orfeo preferred to stay close to the chateau. He mingled with the instrumentalists, disappearing for hours on end. The next day, Weber began to worry; the *musico* appeared to be feverish, nervous. On the morning of the third day, Weber surprised him in a small room behind the marble hall in the company of two girls, one of whom quickly hid a garment cut from sumptuous cloth. Orfeo seemed irritated by Weber's intrusion. He told him curtly, "You'll have to learn to give me a little more freedom. I'm not a child, you know. I'll call for help before I collapse."

Weber was hurt, and returned to his colleagues. He had lunch with the count who, with a broad smile, questioned him about his protégé. He was startled to note that he felt irritated. To raise his spirits he called Kirsten. She told him there was nothing new in Freiburg, that she hardly ever saw Vera, who was completely caught up with finding groups for the rave and for the opening of her new club. When would they be back? How was Orfeo doing? Weber had difficulty keeping his voice under control. Nothing had been worked out between him and the singer, who seemed to be in a bad mood, and appeared to be avoiding him.

From the window of the room he mechanically counted the windows of the façade. Eight on either side, five on the main building. Three stories. The yellow gravel of the open area between the chateau and the stables was dazzling. It was stifling in the room. They'd had difficulty sleeping the previous night. He would have to take a shower before this afternoon's concert, at four o'clock. Doors slammed shut in the hallway. From outside, he could hear the sound of automobile tires on the gravel. Weber breathed deeply, dressed and went out, alone.

In the great hall, the marble floor seemed to radiate coolness. The count had reserved seats for them in the front row, close to one of the two doors that flanked the portrait of one of his ancestors. Weber's eyes swept from the crystal chandeliers to the painted tableaux depicting scenes from Greek mythology, the heavily-ornamented ceiling and frescos, the plaster painted to imitate marble. He shook himself back to awareness: he was here to report on concerts for his newspaper. The hall itself was of extraordinary quality, composed of a judicious mixture of marble and stucco that lent it perfect acoustic properties for this kind of music.

He waited for Orfeo, but the *musico*'s seat remained empty.

Weber began to be concerned. The previous evening, after the chamber music concert, Orfeo had vanished once more, showing up much later that evening without a word of explanation. After a barely audible "good night" he'd gone to bed, pulled the covers over his shoulders and switched off the bedside light. The *musico* was doing everything he could to avoid the kind of situation that had arisen at Würzburg, Weber was sure of it. His behavior suggested that he did not want Weber to do anything that might put his inner harmony at risk.

For an ensemble whose members had only been acquainted for a few days, the orchestra sounded remarkably good. But Weber couldn't concentrate. Nevertheless, during the intermission his colleagues would be expecting him to produce intelligent commentary. He shuddered. The audience was already applauding the last work on the program. The musicians were bowing before exiting stage left. Suddenly Weber's stomach was in turmoil, his head was spinning; he thought he was about to faint. The marble tiles began to rotate slowly beneath his feet. Around him, people were getting to their feet and moving toward the main exit. One of the musicians stepped back onto the stage, and called out several times: "Ladies and gentlemen, may I have your attention for a moment, please!" Then, when the crowd had fallen silent: "We have a surprise for you. Our baroque music ensemble will be performing several virtuoso pieces that do not appear on the program." With a wave of his hand, he indicated a door through which several of the performers now entered, dressed in period costume, carrying their instruments. They were delightful to see, the young men in blue and cream; the two girls, dressed as men, wearing white wigs. The surprise drew a murmur of approval from the hall. This was going to be something extra; people were on vacation; it was time for some amusement.

Then Orfeo took the stage, in formal dress. His tall, slender frame loomed over the others. He'd applied a beauty spot to his cheek, quite the insignia of the era.

Weber shuddered: Orfeo was wearing the same garments that he had worn in his dream, right down to the finest detail. He remembered having actually seen them—la Signora had had two such costumes made from a bolt of antique silk that she claimed she'd found in Venice—in the great armoire in the villa. But Orfeo had never worn them. He must have planned the whole thing, and concealed the costume in his suitcase. Hadn't Weber repeatedly told him singers were not accepted at Weissenfels?

Instead of being irritated, Weber could not suppress an intense feeling of satisfaction. This singer of his was displaying a striking sense of self-promotion. He had totally underestimated his determination to appear in public at last. Weber was sweating profusely. He wiped his palms on his trousers. This would be Orfeo's first performance in front of an audience of knowledgeable concertgoers, connoisseurs, agents and journalists. But Orfeo could well crack; you could read the jitters on his heavily made-up face. Drops of sweat had begun to run down his cheeks even before he began to sing; his eyes glistened. If he sang well, it would be the climax of the concert; if he failed, he would be a laughingstock, or an ephemeral diversion, just as quickly forgotten.

Weber felt his heart contract in sharp spasms. Now the pattern on the floor turned into a glutinous mass into which he was sinking. He looked around for the best escape route. But the crowd was too thick; it was too late to slip down the central aisle without disturbing people. From the other end of the row, the count threw him an amused glance that irritated him far more than his knowing smile of the previous evening.

The musicians took their seats. The harpsichordist raised the cover of his instrument, on which Weber could distinguish a bucolic scene. Orfeo motioned to the first violinist, then turned his head toward Weber and flashed a brief, frigid, barely perceptible smile.

The first notes rang out. Weber immediately recognized the aria from *Orfeo*, in the second act: "*Che puro ciel, che chiaro sol, che nuova serena luce è questa mai!*" It was one of Gluck's loveliest pastorals, a masterpiece of expressiveness that would break the hardest of hearts.

Desperate to regain his calm, Weber attempted to recall the words, but kept losing passages in his state of nervous excitement. Having crossed the borders into the World Beyond, Orfeo addresses the spirits, seeking the whereabouts of his wife. "How bright the heavens! How clear the sun! But what can mean this new extreme serenity of light? How sweet is this composure! What alluring concert doth the bird's soft song, the riv'let's bubble, the zephyr's murmur, altogether form? Surely this is the abode of happy heroes." Suddenly, the mood shifts. Orfeo sings his sadness at having lost Euridice. In desperation he cries out, "If I can't my idol find, ah! I can't flatter myself with such hope. Her sweet accents, her bewitching looks, her pleasing smiles alone can be a delightful Elysium to me!"

It was not the kind of aria that would display a *musico*'s vocal capabilities: there is nothing truly spectacular in the voice range. When Gluck staged the first version of his opera in Vienna, he deliberately chose the voice of a *primo uomo*, the alto Gaetano Guadagni. By selecting such a voice, one of the era's most beautiful, Gluck made a deliberate decision: instead of an Orfeo who would represent man and husband in the flesh, as he would do in the Parisian version of 1774, the composer had settled on the poet, the magician of sound. The French had never accepted the presence of *primi uomini* on their opera stages. They found them "against nature"—except at Versailles, where the King maintained a small troupe of *musici* for his chapel. The Viennese version was Weber's favorite. Up until today, he had heard only recordings with female altos in the role of Orfeo, and hadn't really liked any of them.

From the aria's first measures, he could barely contain his emotions. First the oboe prefigures Orfeo's lament in a hauntingly simple melody. Then the flute joins in, in a series of rising and falling scales, sustained by the strings, while the harpsichord lends texture, and the double bass underlines the musical structure. Ultimately, it devolves into a series of resolving chords and immediately accessible harmonies that the listener can easily fasten upon.

Orfeo's voice emerged, rising higher than that of the oboe, to float above the ensemble without ever abandoning it. At the first repeat of the introduction, on "*dell'aure il sussurrar*," the oboe launched its own *messa di voce*, drawn almost unbearably taut in its clarity—free of all vibrato—a piercing cry in the solitude. Twice the dialogue between instrument and voice was repeated. When Orfeo sang his despair at being alone in Elysium, his beloved lost to him forever, he slowly spread, then raised his arms, then let them fall gently to his sides.

He let the oboe guide him, responding in turn, resting for an instant on "*diletto Eliso*" and "*in qual parte ei sarà*." But instead of stopping abruptly, as the aria is traditionally performed, Orfeo let his voice fade slowly, with a long *mise de voix*. His final lament, "*Euridice dov'è?*" was followed by three sustained chords that lingered before vanishing into silence.

From "*I suoi accenti, gli amorosi sguardi, il suo bel riso*," Weber had closed his eyes. With the first measures, he let his tears flow freely. Orfeo was singing for him, he was certain; the voice tore him asunder and pieced him together anew, seized his heart in a grip so powerful that he thought he would faint. Suddenly he realized that he was hearing only the music and the text—he had forgotten to observe Orfeo's technique. "Her sweet accents, her bewitching looks, her pleasing smiles alone," Orfeo sang to him. His voice was remarkably sustained; it moved from register to register with consummate ease, without the slightest trace of transition between head voice and chest voice. The lightness of his sound, the seductive roundness and purity of his low and high notes, sweet yet penetrating, the absence of vibrato, of the slightest mannerism blended with the playing of the musicians in this perfect hall as the sound radiated outward and upward, weightless and fresh.

When the last chord had stilled, the public did not respond. Not a sound, not a movement, not a cough. The hall waited with baited breath. Weber opened his eyes. Before him stood Orfeo, motionless, his eyes focused on a point above the main entrance to the hall. The violinists had lowered their bows, the oboist and the flautist had laid their instruments on their knees. They stared at Orfeo. Suddenly, from the rear of the hall, a hoarse voice—it could only have been an Italian—cried out: "*Bravo! Bravo! Bravi tutti!*" then another voice picked up the refrain, "*Viva Orfeo!*" touching off a fury of applause. Never had Weber witnessed such an explosion of enthusiasm at Weissenfels castle nor anywhere else. It was the first time that he had beheld an emotional outburst to match this one, and from an audience that could be demanding, often frigid; that could be condescending too, to the point of arrogance. Here and there, people were standing, gesticulating. When Weber finally stood up and looked from side to side, he saw the count and his retinue erect, leaning forward, applauding like men and women possessed, as if stretching toward Orfeo, who stood impassive. The singer barely nodded, did not smile like the other musicians who had already gotten to their feet several times to applaud him. Cries of "Encore!" echoed through the hall, growing in volume. Soon the entire audience was chanting: "Encore! Encore!" People were stamping their feet, banging their chairs. A respectable-looking gentleman in the first row tore his program to shreds, which he flung at the musicians. Others followed suit.

Someone else was shouting over and over: "More *music*! More *music*!"

Orfeo motioned to the musicians, who flipped through their scores. Quickly they launched into the aria from the first act of Handel's *Partenope,* in which Arsace sings the exquisite "*Sento amore.*" "I feel the newest darts of love, but the sweetest is the first. And of one hundred flaming glances, the most vital is the first." If the text of Gluck's opera mirrored his feelings for Orfeo, what else could this aria be but a translation of what the singer wished to, but could not, say to him? "The sweetest dart is the first," went the text. And with what sweetness he had sung those words, with what inflection! Weber felt a sense of joy welling up within and suffusing him, a sense of fulfillment he had never known before.

In the hall, the trance-like atmosphere reigned once more. The same long silence, followed by an outburst of pandemonium. This time, the audience had remained standing. Several people had left their seats and pushed their way to the front, where they gathered around the musicians. For his second encore Orfeo sang Telemaco's aria "*Se per entro nella foresta nera*" from Gluck's opera of the same name, then, finally, he relaxed and, for the first time, smiled. The group had nothing left to give. How could they have known beforehand how the audience would respond? Once more they repeated the first Gluck aria, once again in absolute silence.

But the audience would not release them. Hundreds of hands were clapping in the same cadence; the shouts of "Encore!" sounded more like threats.

The crowd had understood: the voice they were hearing had no connection with the laws of nature. These music-lovers knew that they had witnessed one of the overwhelming moments of their lives, a *Sternstunde*, a "star-filled instant." It had been planned as an afterthought, a little surprise to end the concert. But the surprise had been transformed into a musical triumph. One woman had collapsed; another lay down on a row of seats where several gentlemen fanned her with their programs. The Italians clustered around Orfeo, grabbed his hands, shook them, laughing with delight. The turmoil in the hall finally got the better of Weber who slipped in beside the harpsichordist. "Stop, quickly! We've got to get out of here, fast!"

The audience would not relent. Weber finally convinced the musicians to lead Orfeo through the backstage door that led to the castle's Chinese room. In the hall, the count attempted to calm the crowd. The audience had lost all semblance of control.

"What you did just then was dangerous, really dangerous! Why didn't you tell me anything? There at the end, I was afraid they'd tear you to pieces. It was madness! Collective madness. And such respectable people! But it was good, it was superb, you were extraordinary. *Do you have any idea what's just happened?*"

Weber was striding back and forth across the room. Orfeo was lying on his bed, staring at the ceiling. The count had ordered a meal delivered to their room, but the *musico* hardly touched it.

"La Signora told me that's how people would react. Bizarre, isn't it? The women, especially. For a moment, after the first Gluck encore, I was frightened a bit. Everywhere I could see open mouths and teeth. For a moment, when they came so close to me that they were almost touching me, I was afraid they were going to bite. But it was exciting. Do you think they *really* liked it? The music, I mean."

"You've got to be joking! You never worked on the Gluck with me. I was as astonished as everybody else. I had to shut my eyes. Why? Because that aria is truly sublime. And the way you performed it made me forget how you sang it! Maybe what I'm going to say isn't very polite, but I stopped thinking about you. I could only think about the music."

Orfeo blushed with pleasure, and propped himself up on his elbow, "Didn't you catch how I cheated in the Handel? I ran out of breath at the end of '*prevale*,' so I made do with what I still had in my lungs, by lowering the volume. It didn't sound bad at all. But as I was doing it, I told myself that la Signora would have bawled me out. And yet, I worked on '*Sento amor*' for months! That bit of Gluck is my sturdy steed. I could even sing it with a nasty case of laryngitis."

While Orfeo expostulated, Weber's excitement evaporated. The singer was talking only about himself. For the instrumentalists, whose names he probably could not even remember, he had not a word. When Weber raised the matter, he answered, "Sure, they did a fine job. They made room for me with their *diminuendi*. Imagine, we couldn't even rehearse in the hall, only in a smaller room in the back, in the count's private apartment. When he heard me sing he shook my hand. He told me how sorry he was that he couldn't allow singers into his academy."

Orfeo kept on talking. Weber no longer bothered to interrupt him. The singer was not listening to him; he was launching into an analysis of the arias, piece by piece. Weber was right: the *musico* was interested only in his own artistry, in the effect it had on others. He had mentioned la Signora only once. Not a single nod to his work with Weber. It was as though all the hours they'd spent together at the villa had never existed. Weber no longer cared. He interrupted Orfeo a bit more sharply than he should have, "We're returning tomorrow. Better get some rest."

The singer answered, suddenly brought back to earth, "You're right, let's be on our way. There's nothing left here for me."

Not once did Orfeo call him by his first name. Weber knew that he was not sleeping; he could hear the singer toss and turn in his bed. But he said nothing more.

CHAPTER SEVEN

Cara speme, questo core tu cominci a lusingar
"Dear Hope, you begin to flatter my heart."

–G.F. Handel, *Giulio Cesare in Egitto*, Act I

Orfeo's scales rose and fell, clear and fresh as the warbling of Weber's beloved blackbird that filled their inner courtyard with song. His artistry was far greater than the bird's country cousins'. Here on the farm, the females did not require any refinement from their future husbands. A dozen trills, satisfactorily executed, and they would lower their guard. It was during these serenades that Singer the cat was best able to decapitate the plump, insouciant suitors. All it took was a leap, which was followed by a peep. There were so many males around their house in Bernau that the females, with their dull plumage, had only to choose those who could keep clear of the cat. But sooner or later, Singer would catch the warbler he had his eye on. In the meantime, he would go about his business, never forgetting which little heads he would lay as an offering at the feet of the one he loved.

On the way back to Bernau, Weber had wracked his mind: how could he possibly relate what had happened at the castle? With Orfeo sitting beside him, he realized that never, between him and Kirsten, had he felt emotions that could compare with what he had just experienced, even though the singer had not responded to a single one of his allusions at the Mainz. What might have gone on between them had he been free, he wondered. Would the *musico* have behaved in the same way, with his constant evasions? His two relationships shared two qualities: they were uncertain; he did not know whether he was loved. Quickly he corrected himself: how could he possibly consider his ties with Orfeo as a relationship? On his part, there was that same raging will to possess. When he was not in Orfeo's company, when he could not imagine what he was thinking, he felt shivers of anxiety. The desire to hear him declare his love. Kirsten had ways of signifying her affection, but she never told him "I love you." Nor did Orfeo; in fact, the idea did not even appear to have occurred to him. So often he seemed remote, far off in another world, his eyes lost in the distance. He barely heard what Weber was saying, then turned to him with his stage smile. He answered Weber's questions with monosyllables, with a calm, carefully rehearsed voice, so different from the voice he had used during his crisis, the voice that had so drawn Weber to him.

With Orfeo, he wondered if he were not confounding love and passion. For even if the singer remained locked up in his own world, he could no longer live without him. For all that, there would be times when he paid attention to what Weber was saying, as he had at Würzburg. If the singer were only a fleeting passion, it would soon flicker out. Kirsten would always be there; she was someone he could count on.

Doubts still gripped him: Orfeo had established contact with the world beyond the thick hedges of the villa. Weber could not forget the way the young violinist had looked at Orfeo during the concert. There would be many more such glances. Men as well as women would succumb to the *musico*'s charms: to his voice first of all, then to his person. Weber could never be sure of Orfeo. If he left Kirsten to live with Orfeo, he would have to live in uncertainty, in the constant fear of losing him; he would face the guilt of having destroyed the tranquility he'd so painstakingly constructed out of habits, of afternoons on the veranda listening to the warbling of the blackbird.

The previous evening Orfeo had said, before switching off the light, "I shall always be grateful to you for rescuing me from the grave of my childhood. I am so happy la Signora chose you. You like music, my music. Here at Weissenfels, I made up my mind that it was time for a first test. If I'd asked you, you wouldn't have let me do it. I know it. It was easy to convince them to perform a little addition to the concert. I sang them 'An die Einsamkeit.' They were speechless. I knew then that it would work. I had a terrible attack of nerves, but I convinced myself this little concert wouldn't commit me to anything. If I'd failed, there wouldn't have been any damage."

Those words he had spoken in his detached tone, as though he were solving a mathematical problem. So that was Weber's great rival: music itself. The muses Euterpe and Polymnia, melody and lyric. Where did he fit in? Was there a place for him? Weber lifted a hand from the steering wheel and sought that of Orfeo, who took it gently, in a gesture of friendship that hurt far more than if he had pushed it aside. Weber concluded sadly that he was suffering the pain of first love. He felt as though he were riding a rollercoaster, plummeting from euphoria into despair. The singer kept slipping through his fingers. Perhaps he would come to love him one day. Until that time, it was necessary to give him all the room he needed, not to fence him in. Orfeo's outburst of impatience on the evening before the concert was not something Weber would easily forget. For all his youth, the singer knew exactly what he required. La Signora had been right: Orfeo was not only a musician of extraordinary talent, but he also learned quickly, observed, and drew his own conclusions. Perhaps his intelligence was cold, perhaps the singer's heart had become hardened by the trauma he had suffered many years ago, perhaps he was simply using Weber as a pawn in a game he would not reveal. Weber was thinking that the most terrifying thing about love might be the realization that the intensity of one's own feelings was not reciprocated.

When they entered the boutique, Kirsten's eyes flicked from one to the other. She handed them a note. "Ah, there you are! What were you up to anyway? The count called; everyone's looking high and low for Orfeo. He sent me an article from the *Bamberger Kurier*, totally off the wall. No one knows who's hiding behind that voice. They asked the musicians, but they only knew his stage name. So, what now?"

She listened attentively as Weber related the concert to her, while Orfeo browsed through the boutique. Orfeo needed rest, he added; he was taking him to Bernau. She went on, "It sounds like there's some kind of revolution going on down there. They were fighting for tickets for tonight's concert. From early this morning a crowd was gathering on the lawn in front of the main building. The count told me some people camped out all night in the seashell cave in the formal gardens. This morning, they wanted to use his showers, would he serve them coffee and croissants! When he told them the singer had disappeared, there was an uproar. Everybody was talking at once. Who was that singer? Where did he come from? The count asked me to tell you that he feels he's been deceived, that he's always kept away from singers; they always cause a hullabaloo."

Seeing her husband's somber expression, she added, "You should phone him. Tell him you had nothing to do with it. Our singer is indisposed. He's got a sore throat, whatever."

Orfeo joined them and placed a statuette of a black cat on the counter, a fine reproduction of an ancient Egyptian sculpture.

"I've always liked cats," he muttered, hesitatingly. "I don't know any other creature that's so discreet."

His right hand caressed the sleek body, followed its arched back, touched its paws.

"As long as mine," he said. "How much is it?"

"What do you mean, how much? It's a gift."

He perused the small objects on display in the show window, pointed to an old Bakelite penholder in eye-catching colors, a relic of the 'thirties "This is for you, if you would accept a little gift from me. It works, I hope."

Kirsten lowered her head, blushed. When she pulled out an inkwell from beneath the counter and dipped the pen point in it, she looked for all the world like a little girl unwrapping her Christmas gifts. In capital letters she wrote "ORFEO," then her own name, followed by Weber's. After which Orfeo had no choice but to describe the concert down to the tiniest detail. She sat on a stool. From time to time she said, "How I would have loved to be there!"

He promised he would sing "*Che puro ciel*" for her, next time they were in Bernau.

And all the while, she fondled the penholder, as Orfeo looked on with amusement.

After Orfeo and Weber left for Bernau, Kirsten stayed in the boutique for a bit longer, then closed earlier than usual and returned to the apartment. Weber would not be back before ten o'clock that evening. She prepared a light supper, brought out her writing pad, and sat down on the sofa. It was as if her pen was writing by itself.

The telephone rang several times. She let it ring. The caller left no message. Later, she gathered up the sheets of paper, placed them in the drawer, and lay the pen down beside the tape-recorder atop the writing pad. She would soon need to buy another. Her energetic handwriting had already filled a respectable stack of paper.

She awakened around midnight. Weber had just come in. When he got into bed she caught the odor of musk. For Orfeo, it was a kind of talisman. When he was feeling sad, he poured a few drops into his bath water; the scent spread throughout the house and clung to his clothing. Kirsten lay still, breathing regularly. She wanted to wear the same scent. Then Orfeo would be with her, close to her, anytime she desired. She could imagine him, lying there close to her. A dead woman's perfume handed on to her student, absorbed by another man, and finally by her. She would always have a tiny flask of it with her, and from it the Genie would spring, as in the stories of Aladdin. And this Genie would do exactly as she commanded.

Weber rolled over onto his side, his back to her, throwing off the covers, a pillow between his knees. Later, he would draw the covers back, mumbling in his sleep. Ever since the first night they had spent together one summer evening in her student apartment, he would follow the same ritual. He would always complain about being unable to sleep, but as soon as he dropped off, he would become an inert mass. In Husum, her parents slept in separate rooms. In Kirsten's eyes they were right to do so; it was so much more civilized. It wasn't at all pleasant to hear someone else's stomach growling; to repair a night's damage the morning after. Until Orfeo had come into her life, she had been relatively indifferent to Weber's body close to hers. But now because of Orfeo everything changed. Orfeo's voice, his odor, his eyes, his movements drove her wild, now that she could see him regularly at Bernau.

How often she thought of the open neck of his shirt, of the spot where his faintly tanned skin shaded into white, of his shoulders and his chest. She longed to press her lips to his flesh, to bite into it. At those instants her stomach knotted, she clenched her fists, a pleasurable hurting sensation shot through her. She would get up and leave the room, and take a seat on the bench beside the door, as his song rang out across the threshold.

* * *

131

There were always noises at the farm, the birds, the chickens, the clinking of cowbells in the pasture. But nature seemed to hold its peace when he began to sing; even the dogs dared not bark. Each time, Kirsten felt as though her body was disintegrating, liquefying, with a sensation of icy heat in her entrails. To look at him at such a time would have betrayed her. In his presence she had learned to adopt an impassive expression, allowing nothing to show.

She was never alone in his company. Weber and Frau Schäuble were always there. Weber suspected nothing, she was sure of it. He adored the singer, and could think of nothing but Orfeo's career. The night before, she had devised a new expression, "the Orfeo effect." Had she been at Weissenfels she would have been able to let herself go, for the first time. No one would have paid attention to her madness. Kirsten did not know how much longer she could hold back. For eight years now, Weber had provided her with security, a semblance of stability; up until now, he had been her refuge. Where she came from, in the north country, men looked at her, unsmiling. But he, he truly loved her. In bed he had been a disappointment at first. There, the ritual was always the same, unvarying. Even before they began their life together, she had been obliged to explain, to show him what she preferred in love. He had been abashed, like a humiliated schoolboy. But ever since, he had performed regularly, doing exactly what she asked of him.

In Schleswig-Holstein, her first lover had taken her like a bull, panting atop her. It had only lasted a brief instant; she had been startled, then shocked when the man had pulled away. He was good-looking, handsome as a god. She did not stay with him for long. No one could accuse Weber of being good-looking; he was getting thick around the middle, but she had grown accustomed to him.

At Bernau, it was hard for her to look at Orfeo when he stood beside the piano, legs apart, his right arm on the instrument, his left arm at rest, without a superfluous movement, head thrown back in defiance. Despite that terrible injury of his, he had attained full mastery of his body. He was an athlete. His lungs must have completely filled that barrel chest. His movements were deliberate, measured. When she was seated on the bench beside the door, she could tell exactly the movement he would be executing as he sang one portion of an aria or another. She would think of his hands, and of what she would feel if they were to slide along her body. She imagined unbuttoning Orfeo's shirt, caressing his chest, smooth as a woman's. Once she had caught a glimpse of Orfeo's chest, of his tiny white breasts. His skin must be as soft as her own.

Slowly, Kirsten subsided. One hand under his pillow, legs bent, Weber was asleep. The air coming through the balcony door was coolish. He stretched out his hand to pull the coverlet over him.

She clenched her teeth to keep from screaming. She could only wait.

Two days after their return, Weber and Orfeo began preparing for the international baroque music competition organized by the Friedmann Foundation and held every three years at Starnberg, not far from Munich. The stakes were considerable; the level, demanding. The winners of the first three prizes would not only win substantial awards, but would be offered contracts by the agents of Europe's greatest and lesser opera houses. Conservatory graduates from around the world would be present of course, as would outsiders, the fondest hopes of still unsung professors who could expect to attract other students if one of their own were to win a prize.

According to Weber, it was the only specialized competition of its kind. Instead of obliging participants to perform works from every musical period, from the Renaissance to the modern era, the Friedmann had adopted a formula much closer to the reality of the marketplace. Singers themselves had long developed a preference for one genre or another, for one historical period or another. In response, the Foundation established three distinct competitions, one devoted to the 17th and 18th centuries, the second to the 19th with emphasis on Italian opera, with the third open to lovers of contemporary music, from Schönberg on. So successful were the results of this policy that there had been a steady increase in the quality of the candidates.

The elimination round consisted of a program of thirty minutes maximum. If the judges could not reduce the number of finalists to six, a semi-final round would take place.

At Orfeo's request, Weber registered him under his stage name. In the space for "teacher" he wrote down la Signora's name. Under "voice," he indicated "counter-tenor," specifying "alto."

"I'm certainly no counter-tenor, but since my classification doesn't exist any more… In any event, if I call myself an alto, I won't be lying."

They turned in the application forms just prior to the deadline. Only six weeks remained before the competition, to be held at the end of the first week of September.

"This is the only competition that can help you. Anywhere else, you'd have to sing German *Lieder*, French *chansons*, English or American melodies. Better still, the Friedmann allows you to choose what you want to sing. Most places, there's an obligatory program for the elimination round. But don't forget, everybody has the same advantage. I know for a fact that this year there are plenty of foreigners. I've had a look at the list. The two Germans aren't dangerous; I know their teachers. The French don't scare me; people here don't care for their light voices. But you never know. It can happen, someone can cause a sensation. I know the French judge, he's a real sonofabitch. He could try to give one of his protégés a boost. For you, the threat isn't only Italy, but from the British schools too. Their students are top-notch. For the last few years, they've been winning all the top prizes. The Italians are still turning out magnificent voices, with superb technique. Beautiful sound, but without emotion. Remember la Signora's insisting you had to have *il sen-ti-mento*? Once they can produce a perfect sound they forget their gut feelings. You, you've had the best of the Italian and the German schools."

Weber added, "Be careful. Don't think you've got first prize in your pocket."

They spent several days drawing up the most advantageous possible program. For the four elimination-round arias, Orfeo selected "*Cara speme*" from Handel's *Giulio Cesare in Egitto*, followed by "*Gelido in ogni vena*" from Vivaldi's *Farnace*, then Ulysses' aria "*Del terreno, nel centro profondo*" from *Achille in Sciro* by Johann Friedrich Agricola. For the fourth choice, he was torn between an English aria, "*O give thanks to the Lord*" by Pelham Humphrey and "*Sia pur d'amore*" from Attilio Ariosti's *Artaserse*. Finally, he settled on the Italian aria.

Should he reach the finals—Orfeo made a face when Weber mentioned the possibility of failure in the elimination round—he would present, "as an appetizer", a vocalise by Porpora, written by the great Neapolitan master for his finest student, Farinelli, followed by one of Handel's most celebrated battle arias, "*Vivi tiranno*" from Rodelinda, where his vocal agility could shine.

"Sure it's spectacular, and they'll never have heard anyone sing it quite like I can. That aria is usually sung by a mezzo. I'll add on a few little ornaments that no one else can do without weighing it down."

Then, it would be "*Deh, per questo istante solo*" by Mozart. "I know it so well I can't fail; besides, it's a splendid contrast to the Handel."

They were torn between "*Che puro ciel*," with which Orfeo had triumphed at Weissenfels, and the aria "*Ah di sí nobil alma*" from Mozart's *Ascanio in Alba*. Finally, Weber prevailed. "You were magnificent in the Gluck. I already told you so; I was completely bowled over." He wanted to add, "That was the aria where I realized I love you." But he said nothing.

As his fifth piece, Orfeo picked Glauco's aria from *Polifemo* by Giovanni Battista Bononcini, "*Voi del ciel numi clementi*." He seemed to be enjoying himself.

"And to finish them off, I'll do '*Non temer: d'un basso affetto non fu mai quel cor capace.*' Plenty of grit, and a lot more rousing than Malcolm in *La Donna del Lago*, don't you think?"

Weber begged to differ. "To start with, its 19th-century; what's more, Rossini is completely different from the great arias you've already chosen. If you ask me, it won't look serious."

"Not serious?! He's one of the greatest musical geniuses of all time! Mozart's heir!"

They argued back and forth until Weber conceded.

For an eventual encore—Weber doubted it, Orfeo was certain there would be—he would sing one of the choicest, and one of the longest, most demanding pieces in the repertoire, "*Taccia il vento e la tempesta*," an aria by Riccardo Broschi, Farinelli's brother.

"That should shut them up. If '*Taccia*' doesn't convince them, nothing will."

They had a serious disagreement over another matter: what to wear? Orfeo, who was a bit superstitious, wanted to appear in 18th-century dress, in a pink frock coat this time, which he considered more flattering than the light blue he'd worn at the castle, but of identical cut. It had been a gift from la Signora, and it brought him good luck.

Weber wouldn't hear of it. "I've attended enough of these competitions; I know how the judges would react. It's a serious matter, this one! It's not some kind of show. If you appear in costume, they'll be irritated with you right off; you won't have a chance. They'll eliminate you for nothing, don't you understand? If they interpret your costume as a challenge to their authority, your goose is cooked."

"I don't agree. The girls wear lovely dresses and plenty of make-up, and the men all have to dress in the same black uniform. Plus, it just isn't my style. I'd feel constricted. The collars are always too tight, so are the coats, always too snugly fitted. I'd pop the buttons when I breathe. When I'm wearing my own costume, I can adjust the tie so that I have a good five centimeters of play, and it doesn't even show. Plus, I can move about as I like."

Weber held his ground. But in a tuxedo rental shop in Freiburg, the salesman was stymied by Orfeo's physique. Nothing fit him. His shoulders called for one size, his sleeve length another, his waist measure yet another. If he wanted enough room to breathe, they would have to unstitch the back of the coat, if by good fortune they could find one. As for the trousers, they were simply hopeless, either too short or too baggy.

"Now you can see why la Signora had everything made to measure!"

Orfeo was enjoying himself. Finally, he dragged Weber along to the old Lebanese tailor's close to the cathedral, where they took his measurements and noted the necessary adjustments. The suit would be ready on time.

For the first time, he pulled out his cheque book, and rounded off the total handsomely. The tailor saw them to the door, bowing as he went.

So began a period of intense effort. Weber had applied for a holiday in order to devote himself to rehearsals, but that would have upset everybody's plans at the newspaper; his editor turned him down. The first week, he got up at six-thirty, while Kirsten was still asleep. He worked with Orfeo from eight o'clock until twelve-thirty, when Frau Schäuble decided he'd had enough: "You're going to tire him out, the poor boy!" By then, it was lunchtime. She set up a wide parasol beside the house, sheltering a table and chairs. When she realized that Weber would be eating at Bernau every day, she delved deep into her cookbooks, and whipped up meals "for husky lads who need all their strength." During their ten o'clock snack break, Singer would reluctantly leave his place at the threshold for a bit of hunting, but would come back as soon as they returned to work. By now the cat let Weber touch him.

Every day, Weber left for Bernau a bit later. One Friday, as he was rushing back to the office, he almost caused an accident. He asked Kirsten if she didn't think it would be better for him to drive out to the country at night and sleep over at Bernau. That way, he and Orfeo could eat breakfast earlier and he could work with less fatigue. He wouldn't have to break the speed limit on his way to the newsroom either.

"Of course I understand. For him, it's a crucial competition. You should do everything you can to make it a success."

When he called home two nights later—he'd forgotten to bring along the recordings that he wanted Orfeo to hear—neither she or the answering machine answered. When he called her at the boutique the following day, she told him she'd been out. Weber asked no questions.

He had given up his attempts to remind the *musico* of the incident in the room at the Mainz in Würzburg. His own recollections had begun to fade.

As soon as Weber moved to Bernau, they set up a work schedule. Orfeo would do his exercises first thing in the morning, then warm up his vocal chords. Only after that would the rehearsal begin.

At times Orfeo would move from his usual place beside the upright piano to look at the score. He would bend over, and place his left hand on Weber's shoulder. At these moments, Weber felt a surge of intense pleasure, closer to pain perhaps; he hoped that the singer would never lift his hand. But Orfeo would straighten up, and resume his normal position. One day, Frau Schäuble came in without knocking. Orfeo was explaining a passage from *Achille*, by Agricola. Their heads were almost touching. At her loud "Good morning" Orfeo stood up, ill at ease; he was almost blushing.

Later in the day, after lunch, Weber encountered Frau Schäuble on his way to the car. She said, "If you only knew how good he feels when you're here! He's so sad when you leave; he hardly sings at all in the afternoon. Says he'd rather read."

Weber listened to her, startled. She paused, then went on, "This is a boy who needs love, tons of love. Look, a woman knows these things. I can tell, he's never really had any to speak of. I try to give him what I can, but I don't know how to go about it. And just when I get the feeling he's ready to open up, if you know what I mean, he snaps shut. Gets tense all of a sudden, like he'd swallowed a stick. It's like he doesn't want love. But he needs it, you listen to me. You want to know what I think? He feels all alone out here. When he's expecting you for the weekend, you and the missus, he waits there beside the farmhouse to get a glimpse of the car. Then he hurries back inside, and pretends to be surprised when you arrive."

Kirsten kept them company almost every weekend. For a long time Singer tolerated her, nothing more, until the last Sunday in August when, to everyone's surprise, he walked right up to her, stretched out his neck with a curious look on his face and his ears laid back. Then he rubbed his back against Kirsten's legs, just as he did with Orfeo and, since their return from Weissenfels, with Weber. Frau Schäuble couldn't believe her eyes. "Well, look at that! Now you're in his good books too! Can you tell me what's up with that cat? I raised him, but until lately I could never get close enough to pat him. Now he doesn't even hiss any more; he even lets my son-in-law touch him."

Kirsten was happy. She'd slipped a vial into her handbag to add to the collection hidden in her dresser drawer in Freiburg. All she had to do was open it when the mood struck her, and the Genie would pop out, ready to do her bidding.

If Bad Krozingen was, as Kirsten put it, "a second-class spa for the old and the decrepit" where even the city park had a dreary, mournful look, the little town of Starnberg, only twenty minutes by car from Munich, was exactly the opposite. The sails of pleasure craft were like joyful notes against the bright blue of the lake. The rolling countryside had a serene, prosperous look, scattered about with villages where the houses were decorated with motifs drawn from local legend.

Starnberg had a country air about it, even though the nearest farmhouses were still some distance away. This was the heart of traditional Bavaria, with all the modern comfort and opulence of the

Munich upper-middle class that would spend its weekends in the luxurious country houses lining the lake.

From the back seat, Kirsten had assumed the role of tour guide. She had described Stuttgart, Ulm, Augsburg. They made a brief stop at Schleissheim, but Orfeo had reacted coolly to the chateau, with its broad white façade and ponderous bulk. Even in Munich, at the Königsplatz, which Kirsten described as one of the loveliest public squares in any German city, he retreated into an uneasy silence. The museums with their colonnaded entrances, the neoclassical buildings overrun by tourists with their ceaseless chatter, the heavy, abundant meal they'd eaten in a chic restaurant next door to the Cuvilliés Theatre: nothing pleased him. He picked at his plate, with a bored, discontented look. When the waitress, a girl in Bavarian costume with breasts almost bared and generous hips, asked him if he'd enjoyed the meal, he replied, with the boorishness he was capable of at times, "Well, you can see for yourself I didn't!" It was something la Signora could have said. Then, they strolled down the Ludwigstrasse, but even the show windows of the luxury boutiques couldn't catch his eye. For reasons neither of them could understand, he continued to withdraw into himself. Several times, Weber attempted to ask him a question, but he remained silent, throwing him not so much as a glance.

When they reached Starnberg, they stopped at the offices of the Foundation, beside the market square. There, an employee located two rooms for them in the Zum Reiter, a small hotel in the village of Percha, only ten minutes away on the other shore of the lake.

"Everything's been booked solid for months!"

In a reproachful tone, she'd added that late registration always caused problems.

She handed them a copy of the program, a handsome brochure printed on glossy paper, all prim and proper. It was clear that the Foundation had spared no expense. Inside were photographs of each contestant, a brief biography, and the program they would present during the elimination round. Orfeo leafed through the pages excitedly, muttering at how ugly his photograph was as he dissected the photos of each of the other competitors in his category, which consisted of three female altos and one counter-tenor. He knew none of them.

Before taking up their rooms in Percha, they stopped off briefly at the concert hall, which was close by. It was a small church of the kind found everywhere throughout the region, decorated in white, gold and blue, with a capacity of perhaps two hundred and fifty people. The orchestra would be located three steps up from the floor. Chairs had been set up at the end of each pew, and even around the organ, a handsome period instrument. As they were alone, Orfeo sang a trial scale; he felt better already. The sound filled the church. All that remained to be seen was what would happen when it was full of people.

They spotted the Reiter from its signboard, a rearing bay horse within a horseshoe. From the terrace of their rooms, they could make out, far off to the left, a large cross in the lake, not far from shore. The owner of the pension told them that it marked the spot where King Ludwig drowned. Later that afternoon they took the path that followed the lakeshore. Guard-dogs bristled against the fences. Here and there, on spreading lawns, a few people were visible, seated in the shade, not turning to observe the passersby. Orfeo said he would like to visit one of Ludwig II's most spectacular castles, at Herrenchiemsee, later.

Kirsten spoke. "We should have gone there earlier in the season. Weber took me to see it once, it was truly extraordinary."

Orfeo encouraged her to continue, "So, what happened that night?"

"Well, Weber had an invitation to a dinner concert. For a visiting head of state, or something like that. We showed up at the pier at seven-thirty, along with at least two hundred other people. They put us in launches, ten at a time, and ferried us out to the island. From the lake, you can't see a sign of the chateau. Then, all of a sudden, the trees open up before you and you think you're seeing a *fata morgana*, the Château de Versailles, plumped down in the middle of an island in a Bavarian lake. We climbed up a huge staircase. Then they showed us into a hall of mirrors that's even longer than the French original. Ludwig II was a fervent admirer of the Sun King, you know. There was this immense room, full of set tables, waiters in period costume, and an orchestra that was playing ... Weber, what was it they were playing?"

Her husband, who was strolling a few steps ahead of them, said, "Haydn, Mozart, Gluck, Rameau, Handel. Nothing but orchestral music; no singers."

She resumed, "That's right. So we started to eat, as night was falling. At Seebrück, before we boarded the boats, the heat was overwhelming. But at the chateau, with its tall glass doors thrown open, a breeze was blowing in off the lake, and when you added up the music and the meal, it was just wonderful. Ah, what a magnificent evening! Afterward we explored the chateau, which was lit up with thousands of candles. I don't like the paintings of that period, but I understood then that the frescos and the paintings were made to be seen by night, that the king lived only by night, do you see what I mean?"

She paused. It was the first time she'd spoken at such length. Orfeo said, "How I would have loved to be there, with you!"

She looked at him, transfixed. After a moment, she whispered, in such a low voice that only Orfeo could hear, "How I love being here, with you ..."

He said nothing, but smiled at her with a sidelong glance.

A low wall blocked the path. To their left spread the grounds of the decidedly less regal chateau of Berg, where Ludwig II had been interned. Just opposite them loomed the cross, protruding from the water.

CHAPTER EIGHT

*Such haughty beauties rather move aversion than
engage our love.*

–G.F. Handel, *Saul*, Act II

The first three competitors had been assigned to the sacristy; the others waited their turn in the reception room of the presbytery, which was linked to the church by a covered passageway. All together, they were twenty-four, whose order of appearance had been drawn by lot. Orfeo drew number seventeen and would perform on Saturday, late in the afternoon. Before leaving him, Weber suggested that he converse as little as possible with the other competitors, and concentrate on what he would hear, and on what he would then do. Kirsten was barely able to control her nerves. Without a word she kissed him on the cheek.

The judges were already in their places, seated in front of the organ. They included Kristina Gunström, music critic at the *Aftenbladet* and professor at the Stockholm Conservatory; Guy Ritchie, professor of singing at Bloomington; Guillaume Collebon, professor at the Conservatoire de Lyon; Giuseppina Parini, director of the Siena Musical Academy, and Georg Bender, artistic director of the Frankfurt Opera. The Swedish critic was also an excellent harpsichordist; the Frenchman, a musicologist of international stature. The other three had enjoyed prestigious careers as singers, and frequently sat as members of international juries.

Weber knew Bender, Collebon and Parini from other competitions where he'd been a jury member himself. Bender was the gruff type, but fair. After productions at his opera house which Weber had reported on for his newspaper, they had often taken dinner together and had almost become friends. The Italian, beneath her white, red and black cadaverous makeup, eyes so caked with mascara that she could not allow herself even the suggestion of a tear, had the appearance of a mad woman, but she also had an impressive ability to seize instinctively on a candidate's weaknesses. She was capable, too, of monumental outbursts of temper. But Weber was most concerned about the Frenchman, a dry, slim fellow who had written several works about 17th-century opera. Collebon had the faculty of knocking even the most promising musician from his pedestal with solid, devious, logical arguments; he was also a man who never withdrew a judgment. Weber hadn't met the others. Gunström, a tall, elegant brunette, had a reserved look about her. Ritchie, a solidly-built man with a bull neck, had a reddish complexion of the kind that betrayed a lifelong dedication to the pleasures of the table and the flesh.

The elimination round, which would take place on Friday and Saturday, drew a sparse audience; the church was only three-quarters full at most. Under no circumstances were the competitors allowed to mingle with the public, but they could listen to the others sing from the waiting room and the sacristy.

On Friday evening, Orfeo had confided in them, over a generous meal on the terrace, "I'm worried about the Polish girl, Nina Klescewska. Lovely transitions, and a register almost as wide as mine. Her aria 'Cortese il cielo non più' from Graun's Cleopatra e Cesare is impeccable; she sang us an extract. I don't know why. To intimidate us, maybe. It really sounded lovely; I doubt I could have done better. What's more, she's really nice, laughing and smiling all the time. She studied with Kinsky in Warsaw and then worked with Ingrid Fischer in Berlin. But be prepared: if she makes it to the finals, and I'm sure she will, she'll sing 'Una voce poco fa' from the Barber to cap it off. According to her, the judges were rankled because it's early 19th-century. It could have hurt me too, since I'll be singing 'Non temer' from Maometto, from only four years earlier. I don't know how she managed to keep it in her program. But it saved mine; they didn't say a word. She ends with a sensational high B that seems to go on forever!"

Weber did not tell him that most judges don't like to eliminate the student of a colleague on a technicality—you never know when you'll be needing somebody's help. But he did remind him that he had his doubts about the Rossini. All the other contestants had previous experience in international competition, and several of them were gold medal winners. They knew the rules of the game, ostensibly straightforward but full of fine print, restrictions and insider practices that Orfeo could not have been aware of, especially since Weber had decided not to give him a crash course. Nor did he say a word about judges who would stop at nothing to undermine a candidate who might outshine their favorite.

The voices from Eastern Europe—Hungary, Russia and Poland—were solid instruments, proof that their teachers were masters of their trade, even though they practiced it in difficult conditions. Then there were the English. Before the competition began, the organizers requested the audience not to applaud between arias. But when a young Hungarian soprano sang *'Eia mater, fons amoris'* from Pergolesi's *Stabat Mater*, the entire hall, as if electrified, broke into enthusiastic applause. The young woman had delivered a profoundly personal version, leaving aside any of the pretensions of "historical truth" that so often condemn contemporary interpretations to a pseudo-baroque straight-jacket. She used an almost subliminal vibrato, coloring the Latin text with a sensuality suffused with deep sorrow that transformed the Madonna into an emotionally compelling mother. And she was only twenty! A Czech bass had sung *"Voici les tristes lieux que le monstre ravage"* from Rameau's *Dardanus*. In seconds, the singer had not only recreated the essence of the scene, but had transposed it to modern times. How would the judges possibly choose between so many budding talents, Weber wondered.

He was relieved when the Austrian counter-tenor missed the mark with his version of *'Cara speme'* from *Giulio Cesare in Egitto*. His voice was colorless and cold, and his transitions from one register to another reminded one of an adolescent in the throes of a voice-change crisis. At the end of his presentation, the audience broke into a humiliating chorus of throat clearing. A tenor, followed by an English soprano, brilliantly executed pieces by Purcell, Haydn and Mozart, but never touching the audience.

Orfeo's turn came on Saturday afternoon, shortly before three-thirty. Weber thought he could detect a certain boredom in the hall;

by now the public would be satiated, overflowing with notes. People were looking at their watches, yawning, fanning themselves with their programs to stir the air. Those who had not brought cushions shifted position on the hard wooden pews. A tired audience can be dangerous: the connection between the hall and the singer can break; even the best voice can hit a wall of indifference, freeze, lose its flexibility, weaken and fade out. These were things the judges were not supposed to take into account, but they could not help but observe how the audience was responding.

When Orfeo launched into his version of *"Cara speme,"* there was an audible shift in the hall. Of surprise, first of all; it was what Kirsten called "the Orfeo effect." The audience had undoubtedly been expecting another counter-tenor, perhaps even less experienced than the Austrian, who had been successful in other venues after all. Not only that: to present the same aria, from the same Handel opera, that had proved a competitor's downfall could have been seen as a gesture of defiance, even though everyone knew that the programs had been decided well before the competition.

From his first notes, slumped backs straightened; other spectators leaned forward. His voice—now sweet and warm, now grieving yet without affectation—suffused the church. Weber traced the trajectory of his vocalises as they intermingled and intertwined with perfect clarity, each note identifiable, like a mathematical proof transposed into sound, limpid, edging on coldness, tracing a sharp contrast with the languor of the text, and with its harmonic structure.

When it was over Weber glanced at Kirsten. Neck stretched forward, head held high, she sat motionless with almost painful attention. Crumpling the program in her hands, she was staring at Orfeo so intently that Weber began to fear the same stupor that had struck her when she'd heard him sing for the first time, at the villa.

He sang the next three arias in the same style. It was as if he was seeking to create a distance between himself and the music, to prove that he, too, existed. Unlike his performance at Weissenfels, he projected now a sense of self-control. There was not a sign of nervousness, not the slightest hesitation in his attacks; his vocalises were precise as clockwork. The energy he projected into the hall was restrained, yet it conveyed the promise of much more to come, of a vocal richness inexhaustible, as though he were barely cracking open an immense treasure chest.

After his rendition of Ariosto's "*Sia pur amore*," as the final note expired, the audience sighed. During the aria, the director and the musicians of the chamber orchestra had glanced at Orfeo with an expression of disbelief. Then, the tiny church shook with furious applause. Weber risked a quick look at the judges. Gunström, eyes closed, seemed lost in contemplation, still immersed in the aria. Ritchie was even ruddier than usual. Parini—it was a serious breach of discipline—was applauding like a woman possessed. Bender had bowed his head, while Collebon sat there motionless, his face as blank as an invoice. Kirsten sought out Weber's hand; there were tears in her eyes.

"Makes no difference whether he wins or loses. He's the best of them all."

As he stepped off the stage, Orfeo stood aside to allow the Polish girl to pass. She was solidly-built, the perfect likeness of the great singer, of tomorrow's diva, dressed in a heavy, green velvet gown that caused her to sweat copiously. Still fresh and smiling, he bowed elegantly to Klescewska's hand, and then exited through the sacristy door to continued applause. She, in a gesture of generosity, followed him out and brought him back, then kissed him on both cheeks. This time, there were cries of "Bravo!" mixed with the first calls for an encore. Orfeo turned on his heel, squeezed the soprano's hand, and disappeared.

Nina Klescewska was stunning. Hers was a voice of extraordinary prodigality, located somewhere between alto and mezzo, where one could barely detect the possibility of a contralto, and with a power that contrasted sharply with Orfeo's restraint. Now that voice came rolling through the church like a thunderclap. It was a voice of bronze, a gilded voice, full and throaty. If Orfeo conjured up images of heraldic beasts of far bygone days, Klescewska was the embodiment of a power that Weber struggled to define in words, before settling on "telluric." This young woman was straightforward in her emotions, generous almost to excess. But what linked her to Orfeo was this: at every instant, the love of music shone through. Everything had been thought out, internalized and mastered by the one, everything rushed out, violent, impetuous and demanding in the other. Her "*Venga pur, minaccia e trema*" from Mozart's *Mitridate* was a demonstration of courage coupled with vocal pyrotechnics of the highest order. Weber had to close his eyes. He preferred to imagine a *musico* singing that aria, not necessarily Orfeo, but certainly not a substantial woman in a long velvet gown, her face thick with makeup. But he had to concede that her voice had moved and energized him. It was impossible to extract himself from her spell; he let himself go, just as everyone else had done. When he opened his eyes, he was startled to see her still standing there in front of him, just as before, in that ugly gown of hers, bowing right and left to acknowledge the applause. Then she presented an extract from one of Handel's Italian cantatas, sang Monteverdi's "*Solitudine amata*" and ended with what she knew would be a crowd-pleaser, Gluck's "*Che farò senza Euridice*" in the Viennese version. Weber was irritated: he was convinced that only Orfeo could sing that aria, and that it should become his trademark. But she interpreted it beautifully. The hall offered her a lengthy standing ovation. The ideal human voice would be the marriage of the two temperaments, Weber thought; it would be capable of expressing a broad range of emotions, and combine the register of a fine female alto with that of a tenor whose high notes would not conceal the warmth of his chest voice.

After Orfeo and Klescewska, the public seemed anesthetized. The final four competitors paraded past uneventfully, in a kind of pleasurable indifference. Then, it was time for the verdict.

The judges deliberated at length. The orchestra had been dispersed for a half-hour when Bender emerged to say that there would be no semi-final round; the five finalists had been selected. First the women: the young Hungarian, the Pole—at her name, several "Bravos" rang out—and three men, the Czech bass, the French tenor whom Weber had found pleasing to the ear but rather too piping, ending with Orfeo. Again, the applause rang out. They left the church.

As they walked out, Bender told Weber, with a note of fatigue in his voice, "I must talk to you, this evening. What hotel are you staying at?"

"The Reiter, in Percha."

"Fine. I'll call you at around seven o'clock, if that's all right with you? Please understand that I shouldn't be seen in your company right now."

Orfeo was just coming out, still dressed in his stylish black suit. He was chatting with Klescewska; they seemed to be having a fine time. The young lady had traded her gown for a pair of jeans and a white blouse. Her breasts swayed as she walked, and her jeans left nothing to the imagination.

Kirsten perked up, "Someone should tell her not to wear that thing again. It's frightful and ridiculous!"

But Weber wasn't listening. He had fallen silent, a worried look on his face. He asked Kirsten if she could take Orfeo to dinner. He was expecting an important call.

Back at the room, he stayed close to the telephone. Bender was right on time.

"I must tell you that we've got a problem with this young man of yours. Listen carefully: even before we began our deliberations, Collebon objected to Orfeo being there at all. I'll spare you his remarks about the Austrian. He *loathes* counter-tenors, it's as simple as that. True enough, the other young man is nothing to write home about, in a manner of speaking. But when we began to evaluate Orfeo, Collebon went into a rage. He is convinced that Orfeo's voice is fine enough, but totally artificial, and above all, too forced; give him two or three years, four at the most, and he'll be finished; best to forget him now. In France, he's always been dead-set against that kind of voice. Now, he's taking his crusade on the road. He's determined to stop Orfeo tomorrow, at any cost. He describes his voice as 'absurd.' He wouldn't stop shouting 'Absurd, absurd! His voice is a monstrosity, an absurdity!' He even ended up claiming his timbre and his register reminded him of a castrato. See what I mean? Except this imbecile isn't the only one who's never heard a castrato! Anyway, no matter, he behaved like a fool. What I think is that he has an old score to settle with Ferrone-Oragagni. Something must have happened between them years ago. Something about a student from Lyon that she flunked, or maybe they had a fight about God only knows what. He detests Parini; in fact, we were afraid they'd come to blows—just picture the situation! In fact, she gives as good as she gets. By the time we were through, she was cursing him like a madwoman. She's convinced he's an Italian-hater."

Weber's heart was pounding. La Signora's work could be destroyed by a single jury-member, for a long time to come. The telephone slipped from his hand, he was shaking. It was all over. He'd always known that the Frenchman would bring Orfeo down.

Bender continued, "He's threatening to leave the jury if Orfeo sings tomorrow. Giuseppina Parini called him an old fool and a boor. For her, a beautiful voice is a beautiful voice, and if it breaks down three years later, well, that's too bad. If he sings tomorrow like he did today, there'll be an uproar in the hall. Kristina Gunström didn't even dare to look at Parini, she was so embarrassed. For her it was like a marital spat. She shrank down in her chair and kept on saying, 'Come now, come now!'"

Bender seemed almost to be enjoying himself. Weber was already thinking of what he would tell Orfeo if the competition turned sour. Quarrels were inevitable among some jury members, especially if they had old scores to settle. Administrators selected judges with divergent views in order to get the best possible results. In the final analysis, a jury verdict is always a compromise. If one single juror walks out in protest, it can even launch a musician's career. It had happened more than once.

After catching his breath, Bender continued, "Parini called him a chauvinist who knows nothing of music. She couldn't care less about his quirks. She threatened to tell all to the press tomorrow if he walks out. She would make him look ridiculous, his career in Lyon would be finished. She defended Orfeo like a lioness. I've seen her with the gloves off before, but nothing to match this afternoon. The rest of us, we just sat there with our mouths closed. It was two furies going at it hammer and tongs. You had to be there! Gunström, Parini and me, we voted for Orfeo to advance to the finals, but Ritchie took Collebon's side. He's always had a weak spine. He admires Collebon, who's a regular guest of his in Bloomington. In return, he gets invited to Lyon. I hear Ritchie has a little apartment there, and never brings his wife along."

Another long pause. Weber could hear him chuckling. Before Bender wandered off into gossip about the American's private life, he wanted to get an idea of Orfeo's chances, realistically. "But that's mind-boggling! I never heard of a judge eliminating a singer because of his register! Can't you convince Collebon how foolish his attitude is—and I'm choosing my words carefully. He's not making any sense! What does he have against counter-tenors? Pinch me, I'm dreaming! I know the guy; he's influential and he's dangerous. Do you think the same argument will start up again tomorrow? Just how serious is this threat of his? Will he really pull out of the competition if Orfeo sings in the final? It would be a scandal, which maybe the Foundation wouldn't mind terribly."

Now Bender was thinking out loud, "Hard to say. No, we haven't said a word to the Friedmann administration. If we fight to the death, we'll never get invited back, which would be a pity; they really pay well. But Collebon, he's such a Jacobin that he'd cut off his own head before he'd back down. Funny, for a guy from Lyon! Maybe he'll try to convince Gunström, but she really appreciated Orfeo's performance. But I just don't know her well enough. No danger with Parini; she can't back down now. But if he can convince the Swede, Orfeo's goose is cooked. Three to two. I'll try to see her this very evening."

Bender paused again. Then came the attack that Weber had been expecting since the phone rang. Bender's voice suddenly turned soft, pliant—more than enough reason for suspicion. "Tell me, though, just who is this lad? Where on earth did the old owl turn him up? As far as I always knew, she didn't train singers, only pianists like you. So, what is it with this voice of his?"

Weber could not keep silent much longer. He knew Bender well enough, but he was far from sure that he should tell him the truth that the Frenchman had intuited. Discretion was hardly the rule in the closed little world of music. In fact, it was a world that thrived on rumors and backbiting, where every rumor was greeted with cries of delight. The nastier and spicier, the louder the laughter. But if he said nothing, he would awaken Bender's suspicions. So, in a slightly irritated tone, he said, "You're wrong. Ferrone-Oragagni was a vocal coach before she started her career as a pianist. And Orfeo was the last passion of her life. She happened on him by accident, just as she was casting off her last piano student. She trained him using the methods of the period. But whatever the case, Collebon just doesn't know what he's talking about. Orfeo is a natural alto, one of those rare voices, just like Klescewska. They sing almost the same repertoire. In fact, the girl has a clear advantage over Orfeo: she can sing masculine as well as feminine roles. Of course, he could do the same, but on the stage today, well, maybe he wouldn't be all that credible. There are only two things that set them apart—Orfeo's broader register, and their temperaments. Not to mention their vocal techniques. They're both born musicians. Magnificent voices, stage naturals. Did you see the little to-do when she followed him? She must have been scared silly after Orfeo's performance. But she didn't let it get to her. I don't believe there's any such thing as a perfectly spontaneous singer. There's always an element of playing up to the audience, a bit of staging. Anyhow, the crowd ate it up. They're both young and enthusiastic. And both of them have a superb instrument."

Prudently, Weber stopped there. By suggesting that Orfeo would be less credible on stage in a feminine role, he'd attempted to tip the scales toward the Polish girl. He had to admit that Orfeo's presence in the competition had skewed the rules: his condition gave him all the advantages; he stood head and shoulders above all the other contestants, except for Klescewska, whom nature had given an incomparable voice. If Bender were to learn the truth, he would have no choice but to side with Collebon. He would immediately size up the enormity of the deception, and would turn against it. The scandal that would be sure to follow could only rebound against him, Weber. Hadn't he assisted la Signora in her work?

In a surge of anger, he said to himself that such an exceptional singer should not be punished for his "nature," in the Renaissance sense of the term. Why should a human being's sex influence our judgment of him? What did it matter if a fossil like Collebon was still mired in his timeworn prejudices? So he trumpeted for all to hear how much he hated counter-tenors. Well and good. But why, exactly? Everyone else had welcomed Orfeo's voice enthusiastically; the public adored him. At Weissenfels the audience had been delirious. True, he had not presented Orfeo as a *primo uomo* because he, Weber, had feared the consequences. If any ill were to befall Orfeo—the false tolerance that kills, that put-on pity that assassinates—he would be responsible.

Suddenly, Weber felt weary. Had he made a mistake in so carefully concealing the singer's identity? If he were to tell the truth now, la Signora's dream would be smashed to smithereens; her last and greatest success would be obliterated. No one would support him, except perhaps for Parini. Who could tell whether she'd intuited something; she was just unhinged enough to do it. Orfeo could have a nice little career in Italy, as a curiosity. A handful of opera houses would mount productions featuring him, but not La Scala, not La Fenice, not the Maggio Musicale, not Rome. Genoa, Naples? Perhaps. Naples had always had a weakness for aberrations. After all, the very first *musici* were products of that city's conservatories. Collebon called his voice a "monstrosity," an "absurdity." The public would come to hear a monster, just like it would rush to see a bearded lady or the world's greatest strongman. But for how long? No, what had to be done was to make a place for Orfeo in the world, as a natural voice, a phenomenon unlike any other.

If he were to tell Bender the truth, tomorrow Collebon would be shouting from the rooftops that this "monstrosity" must be nipped in the bud. That voices like his, that had been "shamefully pieced together," had no place in today's world. Collebon knew perfectly well that the greatest voices are the result of long, exhausting efforts, where the teacher works on the student's natural attributes, his physiological configuration. The truth was that every great voice was "pieced together"; even the finest natural instruments cannot avoid the long years of training under a teacher's guidance. There are times when we believe we are hearing a revelation; someone with a magnificent voice, who has just emerged from the hinterland. People line up to hear him. One or two years later, because he has asked too much of his instrument, the singer cracks. He slips back into oblivion. And if his voice doesn't fail, he will end up in the hands of a competent teacher.

Collebon would eliminate the *musico* with extreme prejudice the moment he could muster the slightest proof of his difference. All because of this bloodhound, Orfeo would be liquidated and Weber would lose everything he'd built up over the years in this hard, spiteful, fiercely competitive world. The affair would shadow him to the end of his days. People would whisper, "He's the one who tried to launch that bizarre creature, you know, the one who ..." No, he had to stand his ground, admit nothing. One of Kirsten's favorite little maxims popped into his mind: "Concealing is not lying."

He bit his lips and took a deep breath when Bender said, "What made him pick that stage name? That's another thing Collebon doesn't like. Really, there's nothing about your singer he likes. I've never seen such a deep aversion to somebody. But, on that score, he's not completely off-base. A name like that is unusual, especially for such a young person. If you ask me, it's even a bit pretentious."

Weber seized the occasion. It was the last lifeline, the last chance to save Orfeo.

"Oh, you know, he's wild about mythology. When he read how Orpheus could charm everything, even the stones, and how he almost defeats death, he adopted the name. I think he sees it as more like a title. Not to mention that his real name is really impossible."

Weber suddenly hated himself, for he had just betrayed the person he loved. But it was better to throw that portion of Orfeo to the lions, rather than sacrifice him completely.

"His real name is Lennart Teufel. He's from a small town in Baden. That's where Ferrone-Oragagni heard him for the first time."

"Teufel, you say? Really? Well, you're right. No way he could have any kind of career with a name like that. Now I understand why he picked the name he did."

Bender enjoyed demonstrating his mastery of the classics, "Not bad, not bad. The Orpheus of antiquity falls for a dryad who dies after snakebite. He can't quite manage to bring her back from the netherworld. An incomplete, isn't that what Freud would call it? No wonder he's inconsolable, swearing up and down he'll never care for another woman. Well, in my book, you should think twice about any widower who says things like that. He takes a seat on a rock, but he can't stop whining. Makes everything around him weep. But, tell me, at what stage exactly is this Orpheus of yours? This afternoon, it struck me he found his Eurydice. A bit on the robust side, isn't she? I wonder what she'd look like in nymph's clothing?"

He broke into a raucous laugh. Weber held back a sigh of relief; now Bender was following another trail.

"Then, the Maenads tear him to pieces. They aren't about to forgive him for not loving women! His head and his lyre wash ashore on the island of Lesbos, and you know what that means? They say the nightingales sing more sweetly on that island than anywhere else in the world. Go check it out! It's not only for the nightingales that the women of Lesbos ..."

He stopped, laughed again. Weber was at the end of his tether. He wondered how he could put up with Bender for a second longer.

"In any event, I really love your young man's voice. A phenomenal register, like you say. I've never heard such a perfect counter-tenor. He's almost a sopranist. Nobody will make much of that silly name of his. All that matters is the voice, right? That little devil of yours is a prodigy. Must leave you now. Got to get my hands on Gunström before Collebon does. See you tomorrow."

And he added, "Mum's the word, right? If you talk, it will cost us both plenty."

Bender hung up. Weber stared at the handset, stunned. The danger had passed. For the time being, at least.

He stepped into the bathroom and splashed water over his face. When he saw Kirsten's toiletries, he suddenly felt safe, secure. How good it was to feel her so close to him. Suddenly, towel in hand, he stopped still.

Faintly perceptible, he picked up the scent of musk in the air.

He went downstairs, and found Kirsten and Orfeo at their table.

"You don't look well," she said. "Bad news?"

"No, everything's under control. It was a colleague of mine; we had some business matters to settle. I'm a little feverish; it's nothing. I'll be better tomorrow."

Orfeo was in fine fettle. He ate and drank with the satisfaction of someone who has done a good day's work. A cool breeze was blowing off the lake. When they began to shiver, they got up and left the terrace.

CHAPTER NINE

L'angue offeso mai riposa
"The offended serpent will not rest"

–G. F. Handel, *Guilio Cesare in Egitto*, Act II

Sunday was hotter than the day before. Orfeo really ought to warn Klescewska about her gown, Kirsten cautioned Weber; if she insisted on wearing something as heavy as yesterday's, she was likely to melt. But Weber couldn't care less about her gown. He was in a state of extreme nervous tension: Orfeo's fate hung in the balance.

Even the aisles of the church were filled with chairs; on instructions from the Institute, the sacristan had set them up. After the previous day's elimination round, word had gotten out. The finalists were not to be missed. The sacristan had to raise his voice to disperse the listeners who had gathered on the stairs leading to the organ loft and drive them out onto the front steps. The high, small windows just beneath the ceiling were open and the doors thrown ajar. Many latecomers had taken seats outside on folding chairs, in the sunlight, under bright-colored parasols.

It was ten o'clock. The finals would be divided into two parts, men and women alternating. In the morning, the Czech bass, then the Hungarian, followed by the French tenor. At two o'clock, Klescewska, and at two forty-five, Orfeo.

From the start it was apparent that people had come to listen to the last two singers perform. They gave the bass a decent reception, but no more. The Hungarian was less successful than she had been on Saturday; her voice sounded tired, even though her rendition of Haydn's "*Ave Regina*" was honorably sung. The French tenor drew polite applause for his musical inventiveness. The arias sung by the first two contestants were from *Griselda* by Bononcini, followed by lesser-known excerpts from *Artaserse* and from Graun's *Arsace*. The Frenchman had selected a magnificent aria by Telemann, "*Lieto suono di trombe guerriere*" in a curious transcription for tenor. But the audience's heart wasn't in it. People shifted on the uncomfortable seats, cleared their throats, coughed, crossed and uncrossed their legs, keeping impatient track of the program, as it seemed to creep forward. As usual, there was a constant fluttering of programs as people fanned themselves. It was as if they were in a hurry to get it over with, to move on to serious matters. At twelve-thirty, some members of the audience pulled sandwiches and bottles of water from their pockets. Some stepped outside the church for a quick stroll in the cemetery, pausing to rest on the gravestones.

The crowd's impatience had created a festive atmosphere. A sausage wagon was parked a few paces away from the church steps. It was not long before the garbage cans began to overflow with plastic plates and cups. The concert-goers quenched their thirst with beer or lemonade. The acrid odor of burned grease hung heavy in the hot afternoon air. How far removed it was from the refined atmosphere of Weissenfels, Weber told Kirsten. Here, the audience seemed to be made up of all kinds of people. Young people wearing African jewelry, gleaming rings in their ears, lips and noses, hair bleached, strolled around in groups, standing out against the older regulars who traded knowledgeable comments about the music they'd heard. Weber thought of the punks he would run into, early afternoons on the banks of the Dreisam. Everybody gave them a wide berth. Here, like there, an invisible wall loomed between the generations. Weber overheard a gentleman of a certain age telling a woman, "Well, it's comforting to know that these young people are interested in classical music!" But they moved in a broad circle to avoid them. Weber thought of Vera as well. A glimpse of those young people and she popped into his mind, maybe because she was part of their world. He never asked Kirsten how her friend was doing. And Kirsten hadn't said a word about her.

Orfeo got up that morning with a faint hoarseness in his voice.

"There must have been ground nuts in the dessert; I should have been more careful. And the air was damp in my room. But it's nothing. Nothing, really! Don't look so sad! You know perfectly well that singing isn't only a matter of vocal chords. Don't worry, everything is going to be fine."

Delighted to see that he was ready, Kirsten gave him a hug. Then he disappeared into the sacristy, his slender frame clad in black, one hand in his pocket, walking with a hint of awkwardness, with that hesitant pace of his, that distinctive slide, head held high. In the other hand he carried a bag with a change of clothing "for after the show," as he put it. She returned to the interior of the church where she encountered Weber. He had a worried look on his face, and whispered to her in a hoarse voice, "Let's keep our fingers crossed. He'll need it."

From her very first notes—"*Dopo un'orrida procella*" from *Griselda*, then "*Dite, oimè*" from Vivaldi's recently discovered *La fida ninfa*—Klescewska was sublime. She was in extraordinary form; her vocal brilliance and the agility of her voice drained the blood from Weber's face. To the disapproving looks of the older members of the audience, the young people in their fanciful outfits applauded wildly after each piece. After her fourth aria, a superb interpretation of "*Dopo l'orrore*" from Handel's *Otone*, the first cries of "Encore!" rang out. When she sang Rosina's cavatina, "*Una voce poco fa*," she mimed the text, mincing about on the stage and throwing knowing glances at the conductor as if they were lovers. In the coloratura sections her technique flirted with the outer limits of the humanly possible. She had an effervescence that Orfeo did not possess, and the momentum of a well-trained charger; her shoulders were streaked with sweat. Her gown was identical to the one she'd worn the previous day, but in royal blue tulle, without jewelry, and with a deep cleavage. Immediately after her last note had died away, the young people started shouting and whistling, as though it were an American rock show, which caused Weber no end of irritation.

When she left the stage, it was as though the hall was still panting.

"This is terrible for Orfeo. All her arias were written for *primi uomini* except for the Rossini. This girl is really mind-boggling," Weber whispered to his wife.

Nervously, Kirsten was smoothing her skirt, the same one she'd worn for her first encounter with Orfeo. The singer had noticed. "You're right. I put it on to commemorate that day. I'm a little superstitious, you know. This dress is a good luck charm for me."

Kirsten had methodically torn the program to shreds, and rolled the pieces into little balls that she deposited in the hollow of her skirt, between her thighs.

"She's too good; he can't win," she muttered under her breath.

Orfeo kept the crowd waiting. When he stepped through the stage door, Weber and Kirsten understood why he'd used the word "show." He was dressed in his 18th-century costume, the one in pink silk, with the long-tailed, gem-encrusted frock coat. On his head, he wore a powdered white wig; his face was made up in white and red, a beauty spot on his cheek just below his right eye; on his ring finger, la Signora's immense gold ring; white stockings, light tan patent leather pumps with shiny buckles. Weber could not suppress a low moan. By dressing this way, he was violating all the unwritten rules of the competition. If such a thing were possible, he would irritate Collebon even more. But Kirsten, who had never seen him in period costume, whispered, "He's adorable; magnificent! He's more beautiful than all of them."

In costume, Orfeo seemed to incarnate the fantasies of the century he loved so much. In fact, he had immediately made his position clear: *he truly belonged to that age*. Taken aback at first, the hall fell silent, then broke into clapping and whistling. Even before he began to sing, mouths had begun to water in anticipation.

Orfeo nodded to the harpsichordist who would accompany his first piece. The vocalise by Porpora floated skyward, pure and serene, in a soothing *adagio*. Not a trace of hoarseness in his voice. One note followed another, elegant, delicate, barely separated by his quick intake of breath. In his high notes there was a transparency, a clarity that Klescewska did not possess. The low notes enveloped the audience as though the singer had cast out over them nets of silk, holding them motionless. After the Polish girl's power, Orfeo's voice suffused the hall with a restrained, measured delight, like a breath of sweet, fresh air. Two philosophies, two schools were meeting in combat: if Klescewska was the embodiment of physical performance, in the manner of a well-muscled acrobat, the heritage of the 19th century, Orfeo showed the way along another path. He had left vocal virtuosity far behind him, relegating it to the category of that which could be taken for granted, something any self-respecting singer knew how to do without exceeding his limits. With him, the audience rediscovered the underlying emotion of melody, that which struck directly to the heart, rousing it, or soothing it.

So striking was the contrast between the two styles that Weber felt reassured. A quick glance at Kirsten, then, leaning forward, at the other faces around him, gave him even more reassurance. His wife was radiant with happiness. The audience were holding their breath, motionless, breathing through their mouths. Weber had anticipated a reaction from the young people he'd seen earlier that morning; there was not the slightest reaction. His heart missed a beat. So, they'd come to support the Polish girl. Orfeo, impassive, launched into *"Vivi tiranno,"* where the notes of his vocalises followed one another, as distinct as pearls on a string yet bursting with masculine energy and pride, in a perfect legato. Weber drank in the precision of his notes, of his hand and body movements; the complex whole of the voice, of perfect breathing, of gesture drawn from baroque art, drew him deeper and deeper into that singular discipline to which Orfeo had submitted for twelve years.

Nothing moved, not so much as a hand.

Toward the end of Sextus's rondo, *"Deh, per questo istante solo,"* Weber heard a muffled disturbance from the back of the church. Turning his head, he saw that a gentleman had taken sick. Several members of the audience helped him outside, pushing their way through the people who could not find a seat inside and who stood there blocking the doorway. It was as if they cared little about what might happen to the man with the livid complexion. They moved to one side reluctantly, their gaze focused on Orfeo who was completing his aria. When he sang *"Che puro ciel,"* which they had worked on together, the *musico*'s hands described exactly the same slow, hypnotic arabesques that they had in rehearsal. His eyes were focused on a point just above the organ stall, his head held high, shoulders thrown back, as he followed Gluck's exquisite melodic line, overpowering in its simplicity.

When it was over, Weber glanced at his wife. She had heard the same aria before, but now she sat motionless in a posture of abandon, hands open on her knees. As he bent over to retrieve the program he'd let slip to the floor, he saw the same expression on other faces; the same relinquishing of the self, the same mixture of happiness and sorrow. The men had adopted an impassive look, but their lips were trembling as much as the women's. Then, suddenly, in the absolute silence of the hall, from the rear of the church, a voice rang out: "Magnificent! Magnificent!"

Silence fell once more. Orfeo had not moved; he stood there in total concentration, his eyes half-closed. He motioned to the director whose head was turned toward him in an attitude of expectation and submission, and launched, almost without transition, into Brocchi's "*Taccio il vento*," a change from the printed program. Weber congratulated him inwardly for the change. The Rossini would have been too sharp a break after the coherent succession of arias. Taking such liberties would earn him another reprimand from the judges, but Weber could not care less. All that mattered was the hall. Over-whelmed by the music, it held its collective breath. The cry from the rear of the church had been an outburst straight from the heart, which prefigured what was to come. Orfeo concluded the aria, one of the finest that Brocchi ever composed for his brother, in which Farinelli could combine his fabulous technique and his innate sense of the dramatic. Now, in turn, Orfeo left his own instrument far behind; now the long *messa di voce*, the prodigious vocal leaps demanded by the score became the new framework from which pure music sprang forth. It was Apollo leading Euterpe, the melding of beauty and artistry.

He bent forward, and held the position for several seconds. The audience understood that it was over. As the singer slowly exited the stage, the first full-throated cries of "Encore!" echoed through the hall. With them came a chorus of whistling, high-pitched and intense, from the young people scattered through the church. Others were slowly getting to their feet, resurfacing, joining the ovation. People were shouting now, laughing, stamping their feet, shaking their hands. This crowd was even less restrained than at Weissenfels; raucously, aggressively, it demanded Orfeo's return. Already some members of the audience had climbed over the balustrade that separated the sanctuary from the nave. The first wave intermingled with the musicians, who recoiled in fright. The conductor hurried toward the sacristy, opened the door and appeared with Orfeo. From his pew Weber noticed how pale the singer was, even beneath the thick layer of makeup, how extreme his exhaustion. He bowed once more, and raised his arm as if to call for quiet. Silence settled over the church, but with reluctance; it was as though the audience, by tacit agreement, did simply not wish to be still. After a hurried consultation with the harpsichordist, Orfeo sang the second vocalise from Porpora, a marvel of simplicity in which a single word would have been one too many. When the thunder of applause rose up again, the cries of "Encore" roaring out with an almost threatening cadence, he brought his hands to his throat, shook his head, bowed one last time, and vanished.

He had sung for more than fifty minutes, full out, with virtually no rest. The conductor followed him; the members of the orchestra slipped through the narrow passageway behind the altar.

The judges had been forgotten. No one noticed that they had disappeared. Someone in the crowd was shouting "Orfeo! Orfeo! Orfeo!" Soon everyone took up the cry, shouting it imperiously, over and over again.

One half-hour later Bender appeared on stage, the sweat running down his face. "Ladies and gentlemen, if you please!" he called out, several times.

In the short moment of silence that followed, he blurted out, "I wish to inform you of the jury's decision. Third place, François Bertaux, France. Second place, Veronica Gabor, Hungary."

No one moved. It was as if the church had suddenly emptied. In a lower voice he added, "First place, Nina Klescewska, Poland."

He pulled a kerchief from his pocket and mopped his face. It may have been this gesture that forestalled an immediate reaction from the crowd.

"We have awarded a special prize to Orfeo, Germany. We thank all the competitors for taking part, and you, true lovers of music."

Then he fled.

For a few seconds, the crowd appeared to be thunderstruck. Then, one of the young people shouted out: "Unacceptable! This is unacceptable!" People rushed toward the sacristy door, but it had been locked from the inside. Then they dashed outside, ran around to the back of the church and flooded into the parish house; it was empty. The contestants and judges were gone; they found the parish priest, who asked them to leave. Weber, who had remained inside the church, watched as the young people came back, in a fury. Now they were grabbing the folding chairs and smashing them against the backs of the pews.

So, Collebon had won. That special prize had fooled nobody: not only had the Frenchman bumped his protégé up to an honorable third place, given the prestige of the competition, but he had also downgraded Orfeo. Confronted by the enraptured public, the judges had not dared to dismiss him openly. Perhaps a small recording company would sign him to a contract, print a thousand, perhaps fifteen hundred copies, and then nothing more would be heard of him. It was a premeditated assassination, an act of legalized, public murder, a death sentence carried out in front of witnesses. If he had even the slightest concern for his own career, Weber would have no choice but to accept their reasoning. In the world of music, every-thing—almost everything—boiled down to a question of credibility. It mattered little whether the crowd adored its god. The true gods, those who remained invisible, wanted nothing to do with a passing craze; their sole concern was that the rules they had established be followed. This singer, who had come out of nowhere, had thrown everything off. With his heavenly voice, he was a threat to the established order.

Shaking with chagrin, Weber stalked out of the church where, in a fury, people were turning everything upside down: pews, chairs, flower arrangements. He was looking for Bender.

Orfeo understood perfectly. He threw himself, still wearing his stage costume, upon the bed in his room. Seen close up, the spangles shone less brilliantly, the makeup on his face was grotesque, the beauty spot had disappeared. Kirsten was sitting beside him. When be broke into sobs, she got up, and caressed his hand, which he held close to his chest.

There was nothing to say. Kirsten had not grasped the full impli-cations of the jury's verdict. For her, it was simple: the decision was unjust, he should have won first prize. She wanted only to console the singer; his pain and heartache terrified her. She went into her room, found a bottle of facial cleanser, and got to work. Slowly, Orfeo's face emerged from beneath the mask of makeup. She took off his wig, combed his damp hair, unbuttoned his collar and undid the complicated knot of his lace-trimmed tie. But he still seemed to be gasping for breath. She brought him a glass of water, made him drink. It was hot in the room; she fanned him with a piece of folded newspaper. That seemed to comfort him for a few moments, then he began sobbing once more, and even the touch of her hand on his forehead, his cheeks, his neck and his chest could not console him.

When she noticed that Weber was not budging from the pew where they'd been seated, Kirsten had quickly made her way out of the church through the raging crowd. She rushed to the parish house and entered the sacristy before Bender could lock the door. Collebon had leaped into a car along with three other judges. They all looked aghast. The French tenor and the Hungarian soprano had also decamped. Only Klescewska, still in her concert gown, was looking after Orfeo, who had collapsed on a prie-Dieu, legs stretched straight in front of him. The Polish girl knelt beside him, talking to him gently. Bender stood off to one side, mute. When he saw Kirsten he blushed a deep red, greeted her perfunctorily and walked out. Kirsten snapped at Klescewska, "Help me get him out of here. After that, I'll take care of him."

They coaxed Orfeo to his feet, then shoved him into the first taxi in the lineup outside the church. They spoke not a word. When they stopped in front of the hotel, Klescewska told her, "I'll hand him my prize tomorrow, in front of everybody. It's his. We'll find out just what happened. When I arrived, I was sure I'd win. I didn't know anything about him, never heard a word ..."

Taking him in her arms, she kissed Orfeo one last time. Kirsten only wanted one thing: for that fat girl, with that disgusting gown of hers, her sport bag, her smell of sweat, her makeup, her thick black hair, her energy, her cannibal's smile, to get out of the taxi and to get out fast.

* * *

163

Once he was alone with Kirsten in the room he'd begun to weep, harder and harder. She made no attempt to console him. She drew a tub-full of water, added bath salts, went down to the desk to buy a bottle of brandy, helped him sit up and drink a gulp, which made him cough. Then he said, with a weak smile, "Ah, if la Signora knew I was drinking that stuff! She'd really let me have it!"

Then he added in his high voice, eyes filled with sadness, "Anyway, from now on, I can eat and drink whatever I like. And go to bed as late as I like."

"No, no, what are you saying? Just try to relax now, and we'll see what tomorrow brings."

Kirsten poured him another tumbler of brandy, then pushed him into the bathroom. From behind the door she heard him slip into the tepid water, the sound of water lapping against the sides of the bathtub, then silence. After a few minutes, she opened the door and stepped in. Before her, on the floor, lay his garments, wrinkled, as he had dropped them. Orfeo lay there in the half-opaque water, which gave off a mingled scent of algae and lavender. He was asleep, his head lying on the edge of the tub. She could make out the shadowy traces of his nipples and of his penis, toward which thick reddish and bluish rope-like scars converged. She turned her eyes aside, then bent down to pick up his costume: his shirt, tie, stockings, underwear, shoes. Out of the corner of her eye, she spied a golden glimmer on the surface of the water. It was la Signora's ring, which he still wore on his finger. Everything about Orfeo looked elongated to her, his arms, his hands, his legs. He'd bent his knees, and they protruded from the water like two smooth, white bumps.

Kirsten left the bathroom. She laid his garments on the chaise longue in her own room that stood in front of the small writing desk, carefully folding each piece. The tailor had done a fine job. The frock coat was a masterpiece of *trompe-l'oeil*; when he wore it, the singer's shoulders no longer sloped, and its slim-fitted cut concealed his hips. The silk itself was faded rose in color, and soft to the touch. You would have sworn it came from a bolt of fabric at least two hundred years old. It had a slightly rough texture and smelt of musk and dust. His breeches had been cut from modern material, with an elastic waistband that would allow abdominal breathing. The tie was a marvel, a rare piece of Flemish lace, perfectly intact. Kirsten had sold a few such pieces herself.

She returned to Orfeo's room and waited. All was still at the Reiter; from one end of the building to the other, not a sound could be heard. Outside the window stretched the lake, like a broad mirror across which boats with blue and white sails glided in silence.

Suddenly she took fright, leaped up and opened the bathroom door to make certain that he had not slipped beneath the water. But Orfeo's head still lay atop the edge of the tub, the rays of the afternoon sun shone through the window, reflecting off the white tile walls. He was asleep, his lips parted. His chest rose and fell with a regular rhythm, appearing and disappearing in the water.

Silently, Kirsten undressed, then lowered herself gently into the water, her eyes fixed on Orfeo's face. The bath water had cooled. With a shiver, she opened the hot water tap, drew back to avoid scalding herself, and with gentle sweeps of her hand circulated the warm water, barely touching the sleeper's leg; she felt his finely textured skin, like that of a child. Then she slipped further down into the water, maneuvered herself between the open thighs of the *musico,* and placed her feet on either side of Orfeo's chest. Without opening his eyes, he stretched, and grasped her ankles. She turned off the tap; the water was now comfortably warm. At that same moment she felt Orfeo's hands slithering up her legs, like snakes curling along the inside of her thighs, then his hands reached out and touched her sex. Their bodies slipped deeper into the water, then Orfeo's torso emerged. He wrapped his legs around Kirsten, drew her to him without opening his eyes.

Slow and hesitant at first, their little game became more impatient, more imperative. Over and over again they kissed, clinging fast to one another. From time to time they would run more hot water, to warm the bath, then abandon themselves once more. Orfeo's caresses were totally unlike Weber's, and nothing like Vera's finely polished technique that had seemed to her the height of sensuality. As a woman, Vera knew what would give Kirsten pleasure. Vera had nothing of Weber's invasiveness; he was capable of giving her only what she asked for, nothing more. And yet, her nights spent with Vera had quickly settled into an agreeable routine. Upon awakening, she would find herself asking for more. With her, for the first time in her life, Kirsten had made love with no other care than the pleasure that she could give to her partner.

Now, she seized the initiative. Orfeo followed her lead, and introduced her to sensations she had not even imagined could exist. Her hands slid across his torso, caressed his soft, warm chest; it was as though she were touching herself. When Orfeo came into her she smiled: she was with the man she loved. The snake had bitten her; it made no difference, for at that precise moment she was fully alive, because she was in love.

They dried each other off. Dressed, seated at his bedside, she massaged Orfeo's thighs, her hands following the path of his scars. A door closed in the corridor. Perhaps Weber had come back. She stood up.

"I've got to find out what happened. Don't worry about anything else. He'll understand. Just like I understood when I saw you come into the boutique after your trip to the castle. Weber loves you. I know he does. It only bothered me for a little while. I love you just as much as he does, only differently. No less."

CHAPTER TEN

Ma dove andrò? E chi mi porge aita?
"But where shall I go? Who will bring me help?"

–G. F. Handel, *Guilio Cesare in Egitto*, Act III

Weber corrected Kirsten: Klescewska would do nothing of the kind. It would be folly for her to give up her first place to an outsider no one had heard of. She'd suffered more than her share of disappointments. There had been her first singing competitions at the provincial level, then in Warsaw, losing to singers no better trained than she was, but who could bandy about the names of their teachers like hunting trophies. She had concealed her disappointments, and bared her teeth in a finely constructed smile when what she really yearned to do was to fly at the throats of her tormentors. When it came to her professional future, she had long realized that there would be no pity for losers. In a dog-eat-dog world, they would be quickly forgotten. In the sacristy, she had cared for Orfeo under the tender, admiring eyes of the onlookers.

She knew, too, that her physique would not work to her advantage. Her power of seduction lay entirely in her voice. When she heard Orfeo, she realized her only hope would be to silence him by whatever means possible, right there, on the spot. For his voice was like an echo of hers, but purified by an artistic mastery that he possessed to a degree that she would never attain. There was no way she could rival a singer like that. Never in her life had she been so terrified before a final round. Then had come the totally unforeseen decision that had neutralized him—for the moment, at least. To conceal her joy from this born artist was a masterpiece of dissimulation.

Now, with a contract from Bender in her pocket, her ascent was assured, providing her voice held. In her nervous excitement, she had revealed to Orfeo that lately she had been pushing her voice to the limit. Some arias, which had been originally written for a *primo uomo*, called for the kind of exertion that left its mark: a sore larynx, a sensation of blocked resonators, the fear of nodules on her vocal chords: the bug-bear of any singer. Two years ago, she had heard a counter-tenor's voice break during a recital: a pure nightmare. For every one hundred fine voices, perhaps one or two would make their way to the marketplace. For every thousand, one would become famous. Perhaps she would be the one, "la Klescewska." Frankfurt would be her launching pad; while she remained there, she would cast her nets. Then would come Hamburg and Berlin, in that order. Then the other great houses: London, Vienna, Milan, New York. Weber intuited that as far as she was concerned, the eccentric upstart with the superb, unbreakable voice, with the technique she could never hope to equal, could go to hell. Let him go through what she'd been through, let him learn to cope with the reversals and the injustices of the trade. Orfeo had admitted to her that this was his first competition. She'd told him that she was jealous of him for having a protector who had been able to present him at the Friedmann because it meant he had not had to claw his way up the ladder like everybody else. But in the end, all the protection had been for naught. She had won the first prize. And the contract.

From the sacristy Nina had heard the acclamation of the public, and had caught the note of madness after the final vocalise from *Porpora*. It threw her into despair. She would never be able to attain such purity of sound, with her thick vibrato that she'd inherited from that harridan Frau Fischer in Berlin, who had pushed her voice so hard.

The next day, the press had words only for her. Orfeo's name was mentioned only in the *Süddeutsche* and the *Frankfurter Allgemeine*, described as a curiosity, as a promising singer, with all the usual adjectives. All praise was for the winner. She was a "natural star," as if such a thing existed in the music business. The two other prizewinners were given polite mention. In a few days, music lovers would remember only "la Klescewska."

* * *

Starnberg, Munich, Augsburg, Stuttgart, Karlsruhe, Freiburg. Their return was a painful one, punctuated by long pauses along the autobahn. Weber left the driving to Kirsten and moved to the back seat beside Orfeo. The singer kept an obstinate silence. When Weber attempted to take his hand to comfort him, he pulled it back and turned his head away, toward the window, his gaze empty, his face drawn, such deep sorrow in his eyes that Weber did not dare to approach him again. Before, when he had one of his "nervous fits," as Gertrud had called them, he would let himself go easily. Now, he had withdrawn into himself, creating a vacuum that Weber could no longer hope to penetrate. As Kirsten described the cities they passed not so much as a smile crossed his lips, not even a reaction. Finally, she gave up and fell silent, glancing continuously toward the rear seat. Orfeo's face would suddenly turn the color of dry earth; they would pull off the road for him to get a breath of fresh air. When they reached Freiburg they took the ring road; Kirsten suggested that he spend the night at their apartment; Bernau was at least another hour's drive away. For the first time since they'd left Percha, he spoke, "I never want to go back to Bernau. Never, never again."

He went upstairs with them and immediately withdrew to the guest room. They could hear him taking a shower in the tiny adjoining bathroom, then silence. Kirsten and Weber tiptoed about. They were certain he was sleeping. When Kirsten knocked on the door to invite him to share their supper, she heard him sobbing.

"He's crying," she whispered. "What are we going to do? I never thought the outcome of the competition would hit him like this. For me, his special prize still counts for something."

"Don't you get it?" said Weber, in exasperation. "He was rejected by a jury whose competence no one dares to question. That honorable mention is like a mark of shame, a signboard hanging around his neck, which proclaims: 'Beware of this man. Keep your distance.' It will be terribly difficult for him to recover. Can't you see he's been completely thrown off balance? He was sure he'd win; he *knows* he's the best, better than anybody else. That Polish girl—goddamn her!—betrayed him. But that's normal in this cutthroat milieu, and I don't blame her for it. She's got her career to think about, and nothing else. Orfeo would have done the same thing in her place, and he knows it.

That bastard Bender only cares about his next star. Nope, everything's shot to hell, for the time being anyway. And I don't have a clue about how to get him out of this mess. It's serious, all that's happened. We'll have to wait at least a year before launching him again. For the moment, he's a burnt-out case. People have long memories in the music world. And nasty tongues."

Kirsten's back was turned. She rummaged through the little cupboard beside the baby grand, pulled out a bottle of port and filled two glasses. Weber did not see her hand shake. In an attempt to conceal her dismay, she spoke to him in a harsh tone. "But don't you think he should do something else between then and now? Something to keep him busy? Don't you see that he's living in the past? Since he's been a kid, all he knows is Monteverdi and Handel, and God knows what else. Poor guy, he doesn't have a clue about the world you've plunked him down in, much too soon. You and your competitions! There must be other ways for him to get a start. Can't he just show up at some opera director's and sing? It was criminal to keep him there, in the villa. That crazy old witch, locking him up in a world of baroque opera! As if there was nothing else. Wake up! He's never had the slightest contact with the world except through his television screen! For him, everything is illusion. Put yourself in his shoes! He needs life, real life; he needs to meet people his age. To go out, to do the shopping, to be on his own for a change. We've got to let him go, get it? He has to figure things out for himself."

Furious now, she lit a cigarette and stepped out onto the terrace. It was a beautiful evening. The rooftop ventilators had drawn the hot air from the apartment. Weber felt the same discomfort he always did when Kirsten spoke to him in that tone of voice. But she was right. He couldn't help but admire her practical, combative spirit. There was no way she could understand how terrible Orfeo felt, of course. She knew nothing of the musical world and had never suffered a defeat in her life. Everything had been easy for her from her earliest years. With her qualities of observation and her good memory for detail, the antique business had been a natural match for her. And in case of need she could always turn to her family or to her friends, maybe even Vera. On the other hand, she was right about Orfeo's contact with the world. Weber realized he had treated him as though he were just another conservatory graduate. But even in that, he'd been mistaken: at the conservatory, you have to move ahead, one step at a time, take part in competitions, win the first prize in the final round. Orfeo had never been exposed to reality.

But Weber knew, far better than anyone else, whence the *musico* had come. He had never forgotten la Signora's terrible judgment when she had let him go years before: "*Your hands won't do what you hear inside your head. They never will. It's time to think of something else.*" Her words would remain with him until his death. In a few short sentences everything had collapsed around him: the past, the present, the future. In seconds she'd plunged him into total disarray. When he'd left her, Weber did not believe that a safety net existed for him. He had been fortunate; music would remain his field. His first dreams had been shattered into a thousand fragments. But he had survived.

What else could his *primo uomo* do? Even now, the most vicious possible accounts of the competition would be circulating, in whispers, by word of mouth, scabrous details increasing as they went. He knew how the rumor mill worked. Had he not taken part in the assassination of musicians? Dropped insinuations in the right place and at the right time, a wink, a chortle, a cruel, incisive, vaporous word.

How could Orfeo possibly make his way in this world? Should he move away, live alone in another town? What could he hope to do? Weber could feel the ache returning, the same ache that he felt when he tried to imagine life without the *musico*. "Absurd, a monstrosity." Collebon's words flashed through his mind, and Bender's betrayal. He felt his courage slipping away. On the way back to Freiburg, he'd considered participating in other competitions, even engaging a celebrated teacher for Orfeo. But what would that accomplish? What else could he possibly learn? Another vocal coach would try to impose his own methods, would put him through the wringer, maybe even destroy his perfect voice. He had already made the repertoire his own. What now?

In a fit of powerless rage, Weber clenched his teeth until his jaw muscles began to ache. How he wished he could have spoken to Kirsten about his feelings of anguish, but she would not understand him. She would rattle off a series of commonplaces. "When one door closes another one opens" or "One day at a time." For her, there was no such thing as a catastrophe, no problem without a solution. Not to mention that awful "Time heals all wounds."

By now, he was almost certain that she was aware of his feelings for Orfeo. That afternoon, their eyes had met in the rear-view mirror. It was unlikely that she had not noticed how he had reached out to console Orfeo, and how the singer had abruptly withdrawn his hand. He thought he'd detected a distant smile; it was not the one he feared most, the smile with a hint of mockery, with the condescendence of a princess of the North. It was the smile she always wore when they made love and he seemed to satisfy her. He'd noticed that ever since their long walk along the shores of the lake at Starnberg she spoke much more freely in Orfeo's presence. She had cared for the *musico* after the competition. That evening, when he'd returned to the guest house empty-handed after spending hours looking for Bender who, he was convinced now, had gone into hiding to sign a contract with Klescewska, Weber came upon Kirsten in their room, writing. She often pulled the Bakelite pen—she always kept it with her—from her purse, for the pleasure of touching it. It was so pleasant to hold, she claimed; she should have gotten one years ago. Whenever he came in she screwed the cap back onto the pen, gathered up the sheets of paper and slid them into her purse. He wondered what she was writing.

Now everything was ruined, destroyed. He had acted without fore-thought, hastily, in everything he had undertaken. La Signora had warned him: "Don't turn him into a circus act!" But every competition was a succession of circus acts under the big top, the trainers on one side, the trained animals on the other. He hadn't wanted to wait, to draw up a more solid, cautious strategy for introducing Orfeo to the world. The old lady had died before her time and he, he had not lived up to her expectations.

His hope that Orfeo would succeed, that his rise would be meteoric, never forgetting what the singer's glory might have brought him in turn, had been almost violent. His failure was that he had done everything backwards. Instead of acclimatizing this strange being from another age, he had exposed him unthinkingly to the world of today. He had allowed himself to be seduced, first by the voice, then by the body, then by the shadowy depths of that troubled soul. When Orfeo favored him with a smile, he was grateful. There had been times at Bernau when his happiness became almost too much to bear; several times after a particularly touching aria, when the singer stood close to him, he had to leave the house to conceal his emotions. Physical desire gave way to a feeling that was both diffuse and specific: reality vanished; he felt as though he were at home in the music. So pervasive was the sensation that he belonged to a bygone era that at the merest intrusion of reality—the ring of the telephone, Frau Schäuble's voice, the noise of farm machinery—he nearly flew into a rage. When Orfeo would lean forward over a score, tracing a line of music with his slender index finger, when Weber would catch a whiff of his acrid scent, he would think not only of the villa and the moments of happiness that he had experienced with la Signora, but of his fall, and his dismissal. He realized that when he was working with and for Orfeo at Bernau, he thought he might redeem himself in her eyes. For she lived with them still, her presence hovering constantly in the air.

When he returned to the house to resume work, Orfeo would throw him a sidelong glance, then lay his hand on his shoulder in a friendly gesture that hurt him. It was almost the same gesture Weber had used to comfort the little hunchback at boarding school. The first time he had done so, Weber had broken into sobs and laid his head against Orfeo's stiffened chest. Later, he learned how to control himself, so that he would not feel the singer's withdrawal. But for the most part Orfeo would wait for him calmly, leafing through the score. Then they would resume their work, with nothing said.

One day the musico had presented him with an aria from Vivaldi's *Giustino II*, "*Ho nel petto un cor si forte.*"

"It's exactly the way I feel when I'm with you," Orfeo said.

The text read: *So strong is the heart in my breast that I find supreme pleasure when faithless fate places me in danger's path. Risk I adore, nothing do I fear. Not for me to be swayed by vague hope of martyrdom nor happiness. Ask me only to fight, and to feel no terror.*

But the musical score contradicted *Giustino*, "the small just one": the composer had peppered his melodic line with tiny, worrisome notes. The hero's bravura is little more than a façade behind which lurks fear of the ordeal that awaits.

Still, for an entire day the aria had lofted Weber into the clouds. He had believed that Orfeo had chosen that particular piece to tell him in music what he could not express in words. Weber had taken pains not to mention the dissonance between text and melody. He had rejoiced in Orfeo's apparent optimism. At noon, Frau Schäuble had brought them bunches of grapes. Orfeo had plucked the individual grapes, which he tossed to Weber. They laughed when Singer started to chase the ones that fell to the floor, like a playful kitten.

But all that had happened at Bernau, outside the world.

Orfeo wept all night.

At Bernau, Weber and Kirsten had learned the details of Orfeo's life at the villa, in bits and pieces that he let drop, almost against his will. They had come to realize that he could not live outside of la Signora's shadow.

When pain tore through his thighs, the old lady would draw her chair up beside his bed. There she sat, giving him what she called her "energizing waves," hushing him at the worst times when the pain became too much to bear and he would cry out. Even after the crisis had passed and he fell asleep, la Signora would not move. When he awakened, with the first sunlight that streamed through the yellow curtains into the room, the first thing he would see was the shapeless figure hunched over in her chair, wrapped in her housecoat, so tiny that her feet barely touched the floor. How he detested her for witnessing his weakness; how he loved her, for she alone could give him reassurance, and courage.

"It's a passing thing, you'll see. In a few years it will be over; you won't hurt any more. It's your age that makes it that way, not the accident. You're growing so fast, my little bean plant! Think about all the children who are *really* sick, in their wheelchairs, with cancer, the ones who are bald after all those horrible treatments. They're much worse off than you. Courage, *piccino*, I'm here beside you."

By the time he turned seventeen, he had begun to develop nervous tics. He was convinced he was ugly; he looked upon his body with horror, like something he could not manage. The needlepoint of scar tissue that converged on his genitals threw him into crisis after crisis.

These la Signora wrested him from by the sheer force of her will.

"You have a wonderful life ahead of you, don't forget it for an instant. You survived the accident, you're alive. That's all that matters. There's no one like you; you have a divine gift, the gift of fortune. Nothing can match your voice, your gift for music. In three or four years, you will be the best in the world, I promise you."

In her company he had learned to keep silent, to speak as little as possible of his hurt. But when the pain began again, his difference came crashing down upon him with a violence that not even la Signora could assuage. In those moments, he would cry out, "And what if I lose my voice? Who can assure me I won't lose it, maybe even tomorrow? What else am I good for but music? I couldn't even find work as an accompanist; I just don't have the knack. And if I don't lose it, who's to say people will even want to hear me sing? I've got a woman's voice but I'm not a woman. And I'm not a man either. I'm nothing. Everybody will make fun of my voice; I won't know what to tell them."

At times, she had been unable to find words to console him. But she did teach him how to lower his register to avoid raising suspicions. She had also taught him how to strike an inner balance in a single breath, to shift from song to speech in a matter of seconds, to move swiftly from controlled emotion to reality. Weber and Kirsten discovered one of Orfeo's secrets: his ability to concentrate with extreme rapidity. He used his natural voice only for singing. In conversation he would adopt his artificial voice, a pleasant alto of the kind that one often hears among radio announcers. Had it not been for that voice, someone would have detected his true condition. But during his crises his high-pitched voice would take over, and he would become once again a wounded child.

La Signora was not the only one who knew how lonely he felt. She had never forbidden him from inviting his old schoolmates over. He had cut off contact with them himself. Before, they had always been together, like a gang. Now he lived alone in a villa, with neither father nor mother; his aunt never came to visit, he had a private instructor. He sang; they did not. They had new toys, they ran, jumped; he did not. He was no longer like them.

Cut off from the world. *Cut off*: the words that defined him best.

During his lessons la Signora had sometimes been so harsh that she seemed not to love him. "Look at you! Look at those hands! Why do you lift up your arms like that? You're not begging, you know! Above your shoulders, you hear me? Again! Look straight ahead. Not at me! I'm not worth looking at. Your jaw! Let your jaw relax! And lift up your palate, for God's sake!"

Throughout the years of his musical training, her compliments had been few. Most of the time she did little more than point out his mistakes. "No need for it to go to your head," she said. "If lies make you feel good, you'll have plenty, later. But not from me!"

And so it had gone, for twelve years.

Often he had wished she would fall over dead. She suggested they attend concerts, go to the opera in Freiburg, but he refused. He was convinced his infirmity showed on his face. Everyone had someone. He only had her, a wrinkled fake grandmother with a strong smell and a Babel of three languages.

For her eightieth birthday, shortly before her death, he had sung for her an aria he'd learned on his own, "*Ombra adorata aspetta*" from Zingarelli's *Romeo e Giulietta*. This was the aria that Crescentini, one of the greatest *primi uomini* of the age, had performed for Napoleon and Josephine. The Emperor, who was no crybaby, wept when he heard it, and asked to hear it several times over. La Signora forgot the torment of her own pain: "*Piccino*, it's perfect. You are ready. Now you can fly, alone."

He had never been so happy in his life. The compliment, from that hard woman, carried him along for several days. Never again had he sung the aria, in respect for her memory.

Weber and Kirsten hardly knew what to make of these scattered pieces of an immense puzzle. There was one crucial element missing in what they knew of him:

Orfeo had no need of love.

What he needed was admiration.

The exploration of Kirsten's body at the Reiter had satisfied Orfeo's longstanding curiosity. With la Signora he had never spoken of women. Whatever he had learned came first from books, and then from television. In the villa's modest library he came upon 17th- and 18th-century novels, mostly in French, written in a convoluted style where "it" was never identified. He finally realized what "it" was when he came upon an illustrated volume hidden behind the other books. He read it from cover to cover in a single night and returned it to its place. He was startled, but felt not the slightest excitement. Early on, after the accident, he had learned what the consequences of his condition would be.

Kirsten's body and her sex made no great impression on him; he was fascinated by her changing expression, by the hardening of her nipples, by the way her slender, muscular body shuddered. Her body was much like his own, he reflected, only better proportioned. When he penetrated her, her spasms frightened him at first; he thought she was in pain. Then she relaxed. When they emerged from the bathtub Kirsten had kissed him again, but the sensation of her tongue searching his mouth was disagreeable. The thought of Weber's body had crossed his mind at that moment, but he felt no desire whatsoever to caress him. If his skin were as rough as his hands, it wouldn't be pleasant at all. He didn't like his receding hairline, his shiny, oily bald pate. Weber's outbursts of delight and his tears after a particularly successful work session always seemed excessive to him. He couldn't understand why Weber needed to touch him, to take his hand, to squeeze it.

Orfeo felt no desire. Loved no one. He felt affection for Weber, Kirsten and Frau Schäuble, the same affection he felt for Singer the cat. Admiration and compliments were all he sought. They had been his only reward during his years with la Signora. The ultimate realization of his seductive power had come at Weissenfels, where he experienced an adoring crowd for the first time. It had been like a meal for the gods; he had drunk deeply of the applause, the cries, the people crowding toward him, arms outstretched. No, he loved no one; he loved only the crowd when it shouted his name. He had luxuriated in the tumult, in the multitude of eyes that devoured him, in the human tide rising around him, in a state of excitement. When they drew close, his sex hardened. And when the first hands reached out to touch him, he felt an upsurge of sensual pleasure, a delicious feeling of domination that he experienced anew at Starnberg. At first, the silence between arias disturbed him; why were people not applauding? He could not understand. And yet he was in far finer form than at Weissenfels. Following la Signora's advice—"Never look them in the eyes!"—he

177

focused on a mid-point above the main entrance, between the organ, the judges and the audience.

Then came the cry: "Magnificent!" From that moment on, that incomparable sensation had swept over him. The public now lay at his feet, and he knew it.

He, too, had forgotten the judges. Their verdict filled him with impotent rage. Why did they not succumb, just like everyone else? Klescewska was very good, even excellent; but he knew she was not his equal. He detected signs of weakness in her voice that would have troubled la Signora. A faulty technique that amplified her volume; maybe it was something learned from an incompetent instructor. Or perhaps a flagrant misinterpretation of the music itself.

He understood that Weber could not have been clearer: he had been burned, badly burned, and the burn would take time to heal. But who would help him cross the desert of an entire year? He could not do it alone. He knew no one. Suddenly, in his head, he heard Caesar's aria *"Dall'ondoso periglio"*: *And where shall I go? And who will bring me help? Where are my troops? Where are the legions that paved the way to so many victories?* Handel had written it for the incomparable Senesino, one of the most beautiful voices of the age, a *musico* with a register almost identical to his own.

A tiny cohort of hate-filled, ignorant judges had defeated him. He had lost his troops, his legions. He would have to raise others, somewhere else. They would not be from that closed little world.

La Signora was right: he would have to accept his pain, not fight it. Pain would always win out, always. Better to avoid it by ruse, or as Kirsten would say, "by opening another window."

Orfeo finally felt at peace.

It was too soon to say what he would do. But this time he would do it alone.

CHAPTER ELEVEN

Uccidetemi, dunque, da le speranze mie povero derelitto!
"Kill me then, poor creature, by all hope abandoned!"

–F. Cavalli, *La Calisto*, Act II

In the weeks leading up to the competition, Vera had done everything to gain Kirsten's confidence. Weber had been away most of the time, his energies concentrated on rehearsing with Orfeo. He had dropped by the office in late afternoon to look after pressing matters, often too rapidly. He had neglected some of his responsibilities to a dangerous extent: he hadn't read a book for weeks, had hardly listened to a recording. Luckily, he had been able to dredge up all-but-forgotten essays from his files, and whip them into shape for publication.

Vera hated the scent of musk, which now it seemed Kirsten was unable to part with. She'd recognized it of course, but chose to say nothing. Except that after a night with her friend, the odor seemed to stick to her skin. It was impossible to disguise; the only way to get rid of it was a vigorous scrub in a hot bath.

Their trip to Starnberg had annoyed her. And since their return Kirsten's attitude toward her had changed. She would hardly let herself be touched, she had become withdrawn. Furious, Vera realized that as long as Orfeo stayed at their house, as long as Weber was at her side, there was no place for her.

One Monday morning Vera dropped by the boutique. Kirsten mentioned that Orfeo would now be living with them indefinitely. It was time for him to "find out about life" and to make his own life over. Of the failure at Starnberg, and the bath at Percha, she said not a word. Nor did she reveal that Orfeo would not be returning to Bernau, that he was no longer working, either alone or with Weber.

Kirsten had told Orfeo, "But Frau Schäuble will miss you. Singer too."

The answer was as quick as it was curt. "They'll survive."

Orfeo wanted none of the clothes that were left at the country house. He bought himself a new wardrobe. Kirsten brought his tuxedo, which hung in a corner of the closet, back from the cleaner's. When she handed it to the singer, he shrugged his shoulders.

"Would you like Weber to bring your cherub?"

"No."

Two weeks after their return to Freiburg, Vera told Kirsten, "I thought I saw your singer at the Unicorn. I'm not absolutely sure, but I thought it was him. What's he up to, anyway?"

She searched Kirsten's face for a change of expression. Kirsten turned away, mumbling, "Orfeo's his name. And he's not *my* singer, as you put it. He sings for everybody. But you always refused to come to Bernau with us to hear him. I'd be very surprised if he went to the Unicorn. His music has no relation with what you play at your club."

"But you've never come to dance at my place! You always claim the dance hall gives you the creeps. Okay, you were there once, when it was empty. But just wait till I open the new addition; you've *got* to come. Hey, I'll invite all three of you. It'll be great, I'm planning a fantastic evening. I'm calling the new place the Twilight. How does that strike you? Not bad, eh? Okay, it's a bit fusty, a bit decadent, but not too-too. I've already hired a small orchestra, students from the conservatory. I already mentioned the idea I think. Classical music. I want to see if it'll work. Next door, in the big dance hall, I'm organizing a rave; it'll be a wild night. The biggest yet. There'll be a group from Berlin, real hard rock, plus some new acts we don't even know about yet. Ah, before I forget it, that guy Litow, your husband's colleague, he's amazing. Boring and ugly as a toad, but really amazing. He knows everyone."

She took Kirsten by the shoulders. "What's bothering you? You can tell me. You look unhappy. In any case, if it's him I saw, Orfeo I mean, he's hanging out with guys I don't like at all. Straightedge, if you get my drift. They don't drink, don't smoke, don't fuck around. So they claim, at any rate. Except the leader. Can you beat that? I think your singer is hanging out with a bunch of fringe cases."

She was right; Kirsten was unhappy. Orfeo was using the guest room, but she rarely caught a glimpse of him. He was normally an early riser, but he would still be sound asleep when she left for work.

She and Weber talked it over; he was as concerned as she was. He'd spotted him a few times, late in the morning, his face puffy with sleep, his eyes red-rimmed and distant, in a foul mood. He tossed down a glass of water, then went back to bed until Weber left the apartment for work or to meet Kirsten at lunch time.

"Don't you think it's time to get back to work? You haven't sung for weeks."

"I've got better things to do."

"But what about Frau Schäuble, what about Singer, the mountains; what about us?"

Obstinately, Orfeo kept his right hand in the pocket of his bathrobe. And when Weber attempted to touch his shoulder, Orfeo shoved him away with a look of exasperation. It was at that moment that Weber noticed a large 'X' on the singer's hand.

"What's that?"

But Orfeo had already turned away.

At the office, Weber asked Litow, "A big 'X' on the hand means what?"

Litow, who couldn't pass up an opportunity to shine, "How could you possibly know, you're into classical! It's a mark of straightedge identity; these young people are sick of the world. In their eyes, it's completely rotten. Just between us, they're not entirely wrong. It's not so much a philosophy as an attitude. They're into hardcore, which can be tough on the ears. Your friend came to see me about hiring a straightedge group for next month. If you could see what they're singing! Real hard stuff. But where did you see that 'X'?"

Without answering the question, Weber asked, "What do they do? How old are they?"

"They're mostly teenagers, but a few are over twenty. Except for the musicians, who end up with the cutest girls. They're easy to spot. Baggy low-rise pants, cheap sneakers, T-shirts with slogans all the way from 'pro-life' to 'straightedge never dies,' if you see what I mean. Some of them have piercings all over. But they're not punks; they're tougher, and their ideas aren't so dark. They're for animal protection, and lots of them are vegetarians. Until they've had enough. Then in one night they throw everything over, get drunk out of their minds and fuck like madmen. But as long as they're pure, they look down on everybody else."

He walked off. Weber was stunned by what he'd heard.

Weber and Kirsten resumed their meetings on the banks of the Dreisam.

They pretended that their life was unfolding just as it had before. But when Weber spoke of the future, a note of disquiet crept into the conversation. Kirsten tried to reassure him: Orfeo was "going through a phase." He had never had a normal adolescence like other young people of his age; it was time for him to "let go." Her detachment gave her husband some relief. But in reality, she was just as worried as he was. Orfeo's moods had become hard to bear, a dark cloud seemed to follow him wherever he went. He never spoke to them, and disappeared into his room the moment they returned home. As the weeks went by, they noticed that his behavior had a pattern: he came home in the wee hours, slept, got up and washed, had a bite to eat, then vanished. He never told them where he was going, whom he was seeing.

They ended up organizing their lives so as to cross his path as little as possible.

It was mid-October. The grapevines on the Schlossberg had begun to change color; the fall would be mild. Orfeo gave no sign of changing his routine. Weber had attempted to bring him back to music by playing new recordings. Once he played la Signora's transcriptions on the baby grand. Orfeo didn't react to the recordings, and when he saw the transcriptions he turned pale, then hurried into his room, slamming the door behind him. After that incident, the keyboard cover remained shut.

One day, when they stayed later than usual on their park bench, they spotted Orfeo among a group of young people; he stood out like a dark spot against their elaborate paraphernalia. Many of the boys sported shaved heads or hair dyed in violent hues. Most of the girls had long hair and and wore cheap plastic jewelry. When Orfeo saw Kirsten and Weber he waved, then got up, unsmiling, and followed the others beneath a bridge.

The following day Weber asked him who they were.

"They're my friends. Some of them are good musicians. Not the kind you know. They accept me. They can understand."

Weber was not about to give up. "What do you intend to do? Do you want to go with them? Would you like me to help you rent an apartment downtown? Wouldn't you be more comfortable alone with them?"

There it was once more, that sharp pain that shot through him, burning. But the singer said nothing.

Ever since Starnberg, he no longer smelled of musk.

One day they went back to Bernau. They contrived to bring him along on the pretext that they had to close the country house before winter. It would be an opportunity to say goodbye to Frau Schäuble. The farmer's wife was delighted to see him; no sooner had they arrived than she took him in her arms. Orfeo pulled away from her and lifted Singer onto his lap. For an instant the cat stiffened, sniffed his pants, then began to work his paws up and down on his thighs, like a baker kneading his dough, purring and peeping. As he stroked the cat's coarse coat. Orfeo said, in a low voice, "At least he loves me, and he doesn't ask questions."

Kirsten attempted to bring the past to life again; in vain. She learned that love moves in circles, that it was an obtuse desire to live over and over again the first happy moments shared with the loved one. Orfeo's attitude was one of cold politeness; he arranged never to be alone with her. One Sunday, when Weber was at the newspaper, she knocked on his door, but there was no answer. When she opened the door she saw Orfeo stretched out on the bed, eyes closed, headphones over his ears. She could hear a rhythmic whistling. She touched him on the shoulder. "What are you listening to? It doesn't sound to me like your repertoire."

Calmly he switched off the music. She repeated the question.

"It's another kind of music. You wouldn't understand."

In exasperation she pulled him from the bed and led him over to the chest of drawers in their bedroom, opened the drawer and showed him the stack of papers, the cassette with the recording of their first conversation, the vial of perfume. He recoiled, brows furrowed, "I'm sorry for you. So sorry."

Then he hurried back into his room, slamming the door violently behind him.

When Weber returned she pretended to be asleep.

There was no one she could talk to. Especially not Vera. Vera had sent them magnificent invitations to the opening of the Twilight. When Kirsten showed him the painting on the card, a red-headed woman with a classic *fin de siècle* appearance, Weber grimaced. "Looks more like a self-portrait to me. And what a name, Twilight! What is it with this craze of using English? The whole thing's a fake, from top to bottom. Depressing, too. If I were older, I certainly wouldn't go for a drink in a place that advertises something that's about to end."

"You don't get it," said Kirsten. "Vera told me she's testing a new concept. A bar for people who like to talk, with a relaxed atmosphere, like in a tea-room. A bar for intellectuals, with newspapers and magazines. Afterwards, some clients might want to dance, so they can cross over to the Unicorn through a corridor. She's done the market research. It'll be a success. You'll see."

Orfeo didn't even mention his invitation. Of late, he'd been coming in at "impossible hours," according to Kirsten. But he would crack the odd smile. He stayed with them long enough to eat breakfast, then left for one of his mysterious "engagements." When Weber became too insistent, he told him, with a twinkle in his eyes, "Just wait; we're working on something really good. You'll see when the time comes."

"Who do you mean, 'we'?"

Orfeo had looked up toward the ceiling and sighed.

At the opening, Weber realized he hated everything about the Twilight, the bouncer at the door, the people who crowded around Vera, the pretentious style of the place: tables and bar in mahogany that was too red, too thickly varnished; a counter made of hammered copper that shone atrociously; chairs in black wrought iron that were a pain to sit on; windows made of bottle-bottoms that vainly attempted to soften the gaudy atmosphere. Squeezed in against a medium-sized grand piano, a small group of musicians was playing innocuous music that nobody was paying attention to. Trays of petits-fours and appetizers were circulating. Guests could drink sparkling red or white wine, beer, fruit juices, mineral water. Good-looking girls were distributing pins with the bar's logo, the profile of a redhead in baked enamel. When Weber removed it from his lapel he pricked his finger. The pin punctured his skin; it began to bleed. He cleaned the wound in the washroom. In irritation, he told himself that everything that came from that woman was dangerous.

Vera was wearing a smart creation in white silk that set off her tanned skin and highlighted her henna-streaked hair. The guests, mostly mature men with their wives or their mistresses in tow, ate and drank with gusto. They pretended to appreciate the paintings from Kirsten's boutique, admired the curiosity cabinet with its stylishly lighted pieces of mercury glass. Weber didn't like the jewel-laden women, the elegantly dressed men, all chewing, swallowing, smoking, and chattering. The cream of the town. A few nodded in his direction, others greeted him. He attempted to be sociable, but his concern about Orfeo wouldn't let him rest: the singer had refused to join them; he had "better things to do," he said. Kirsten stood in a corner, eye-catching in her little black dress, surrounded by a handful of single men.

By ten o'clock only a small group remained. Weber had hidden his wounded hand in his coat pocket, embarrassed by people's glances when they saw him applying his handkerchief to the bleeding finger. All of a sudden, he spotted Litow, who said to him, "Are you coming? Vera has a surprise for you, on the other side."

Weber's first reaction was not to budge. The first and only time he'd set foot in a disco, he'd emerged half-deaf.

"Good Lord, it won't damage your ears for good! Don't tell me you can't stand a bit of rock music," said Kirsten, impatiently. "Don't be a snob, come along with us. Vera will get us a seat by the DJ, above the dance floor. Whoever wants to, can dance. If you don't like it, you can go home after a half-hour, okay? It's no big deal really. Can't you be polite just this once? Me, I'm staying. Tonight I'm going to have fun."

They made their way down a short flight of stairs and followed the subterranean corridor that connected the Twilight to the Unicorn. Weber felt as if he was far beneath the surface of the earth. First they went even deeper, then turned upward again. Their progress was tortuous, as if they were constantly avoiding obstacles, even other buildings. At every corner, the fake torch-light lamps Vera had installed cast blood-red shadows on the walls. A strange smell pervaded the place, a mixture of mold and freshly applied stucco. The walls oozed moisture; the guests had to jump over puddles of dark water. Someone whispered, "We're under the Dreisam. Can't you hear the sound of flowing water? This is no place for claustrophobics."

Soon a vague vibration filled the air, growing stronger as they moved along. Suddenly they came to a steel door that blocked the entire corridor. Vera opened it.

Weber, who was just behind Kirsten, took the blast of sound head-on. He wanted to stop, but the others pulled him forward into the unknown. Fear gripped his throat.

They could not see the outer limits of the space they'd stepped into, illuminated by bolts of green and blue lightning. Above their heads, shafts of white light slashed like knives through the dark vault, then swooped low, playing across the heads of the dancers. What terrified Weber most was the music, the beat from the loudspeakers. His thorax throbbed like an echo-chamber, the bass notes set his ribs vibrating. His breath came in short gasps; the hellish din had knocked the wind out of him. He looked around for Kirsten, could not find her, then caught up with the others who were pushing their way through the crowd. With the riff of an electric guitar he understood the source of the lightning that was crackling over the dance floor: the dancers were holding flexible light-sticks, illuminated in a way he could not determine, and were waving them to the rhythm of the drums.

Weber was learning what a rave was.

The dancers' bodies were steaming as if they'd stepped straight from a pressure cooker. It was cold; from high above a polar draft enveloped them. Almost all the young men had taken off their shirts. Tattoos covered their torsos; sparkling rings pierced their flesh. To his surprise, they held their glow-sticks in one hand, a water bottle in the other, drinking frequently. No one gave him a second glance; they seemed utterly absorbed in executing sets of incongruous movements. It didn't seem like a dance at all, more like an extraordinarily violent form of gymnastics—arms thrown high, shoulders rolling, heads thrown back, eyes half-closed, mouths agape, chest muscles straining, hips and thighs carrying out movements that totally contradicted what their upper bodies were doing at the same instant. They wore strange fluorescent baubles around their necks, stuck into their ear-lobes, their lips, their nostrils, their eye-brows. The girls were wearing bracelets and necklaces of outsized multicolored plastic pearls, like children's gifts. Some of them were sucking fat lollipops. Judging by their glassy, empty eyes fixed on no point in particular, and by their jerky movements, all of them were there to abandon themselves to the music, sung by a hoarse-voiced vocalist.

It was hard to estimate how many dancers might have been in the hall; perhaps three thousand, crowded in almost on top of one another. Litow put his hands to Weber's ear and shouted, "What a sensational rave! Word must've gotten around. These kids are from everywhere. The last big rave party was in Frankfurt, there were more than five thousand. But this one is really a monster!"

To the left, atop a broad podium, a handful of musicians were playing, their movements identical to the dancers'. A nearly naked man was shrieking into a mike, while two others were whipping their guitars, whose roar was absorbed by the crash of the immense electronic percussion section. Weber attempted to pick up a few words. He thought he heard "tomorrow will take us," "I'm losing control."

Finally the group from the Twilight climbed the stairs to a glass-enclosed cage several meters above the dance floor. Beside them, in another cubicle, the lighting engineer was hard at work. The women in their lightweight dresses were shivering in the cold. The DJ, a skinny individual with a shaved head, was wearing a heavy sweater. The green light of the console cast a sickening glow over his angular face. For an instant, when he bared his gums in a grimace, Weber thought he was seeing a pin-studded skull. The DJ nodded at Vera and pressed some buttons. The sound became slightly less deafening. Weber spotted Kirsten; she was staring at something at the far end of the hall. Amid the swirling ballet of beams of light sweeping across and above the dance floor, there remained a single immobile point, surrounded by an aura of white light: the head of the unicorn, the gleaming horn protruding from its forehead. It hung directly across from the podium where the musicians were just winding up their number.

Then the music halted abruptly, the spotlights stopped their sweeps, the dancers steadied their glow sticks. A melody welled up, Weber could not tell from where, like the beginning of a fugue.

"Ah, this is going to be great! You'll love it. For insiders only. The composer's a guy called Turilli, an Italian who takes his inspiration from the classics. Nothing like the techno the kids are so wild about. Wonder how they'll react? It's got nothing to do with a rave. All they want is metal, in all shapes and sizes. With their ecstasy capsules they can dance all night long. This is going to be something."

Weber turned away in irritation. He didn't have the faintest idea what Litow was talking about. He had no idea what the expressions "techno" and "metal" meant, and he didn't have a clue who "the kids" might be. He didn't like that voice in his ear. Litow's breath, reeking of food and alcohol, made his stomach turn.

All at once, the spotlights flared, and zeroed in on the podium where another group of musicians had taken their places.

It was then that he saw Orfeo.

The *musico* had put on his most sumptuous costume, the one he'd worn for the competition in Starnberg. In the blinding white light the precious stones on his frock-coat sparkled fire; the silk glistened like metal. The other musicians, two guitarists, a saxophone, a drummer and a keyboard player were dressed in black. For the rest of the fugue Orfeo stood motionless, then nodded to them. He brought the microphone to his lips, and began on a single high C-sharp, long and pure, that slithered through the hall like a snake. After the violence of the music that had preceded it, that single note, imperceptible at first, grew louder, finishing in an almost inaudible whisper without faltering. It was the longest, most beautiful *messa di voce* that Orfeo had ever executed. On the dance floor, no one moved. Everyone was waiting. The drums and the guitars launched into a rapid intermezzo picking up the theme of the fugue. The glow sticks remained immobile. But a deep rumble began to rise up from the crowd, like a collective murmuring. Orfeo began a text in Latin, sung up-tempo, then switched into English. It was a solo; Weber thought he understood the words

"We are the kings of the northern twilight," in the shape of an aria with frantic vocal pyrotechnics. Then something happened that he'd never seen before: while the singer's voice performed breath-taking leaps across octaves in a display of extraordinary agility, the crowd began to sing along with him, a simplified version of the melody. It was like the Italian lyric theater in the age of the greatest singers: a celebrated air, well known by all, would be repeated, bringing stage and audience together.

Kirsten took Weber by the hand, "Come with us!"

He shook his head, unable to move. The sense of foreboding that swept over him when he stepped into the cavernous dance club had been a premonition: the same scene they had witnessed at the castle would be repeated here. Except that here, the audience was made up not of people of a certain age listening politely to a surprise as a climax to a concert, but of young people who had come for "the night of their lives," as Litow put it. Their motionlessness seemed to him even more terrifying than their frenzied movements before Orfeo appeared.

Litow said to him, "Magnificent! Amazing adaptation! Where did that lead singer come from? Never heard anything like it. Fabulous. Got to hand it to Vera! What a find!"

Litow stepped aside so Kirsten could make her way down the stairs with the others to reach the dance floor; then he took Weber by the sleeve. "Stay. We can see everything from here."

High above the floor only Weber, the DJ, Litow, Vera and the lighting engineer remained.

Almost without transition the instrumentalists began another number, with a much more aggressive rhythm. The glow sticks began to move, shouts began to echo through the darkness.

"It's 'Black Dragon.' At least I think it is. But they've made a lot of changes. It's better than the original." Litow was shouting now.

Smiling, eyes glowing, Vera leaned impassively over the DJ's console.

Orfeo's voice soared high, sharp as a knife, on the edge of hysteria: *Black dragon fly high, regain your past, lost in the fire, the fire of hate.*

Then came the refrain: *His day will soon come ... your reign will fall ... burn to pay what you've done to us all!*

The piece was almost over. The gyrating spotlights converged now on the podium, the crowd had gathered beneath it, hypnotized by his voice. Orfeo's movements were slow and deliberate, the same movements he had mastered during the long years in the calm of the studio at the villa, in sharp contrast with the other musicians, who jerked back and forth like men possessed. The DJ spoke rapidly with Vera, who shook her head. Orfeo had let the microphone drop, the musicians had stopped. When the first dancers clambered up onto the podium, the DJ threw a disc onto the turntable and set it in motion.

Litow cried out, "It's *KoRn*, the best guitarists in the world!"

The confusion was total: as the loudspeakers blasted out waves of sound to a furious rhythm, Weber looked on as the crowd overran the podium. They captured the musicians and threw them into the extended arms waiting beneath them, then threw them back into the air like so many toys. There was nothing innocent about their game. The wilder the music became, the more violently the musicians were thrown into the air, like rag dolls. Horrified, Weber watched Orfeo's progress. Although he could not make out his face in the constant sweep of the spotlights, he thought he could see the *musico* laughing, or shouting, or singing, with pleasure, pain or fear, his mouth open wide. They'd torn away the first pieces of his frock coat, then ripped it to shreds. By the time he had reached the middle of the hall only his shirt remained.

"Watch out, things are getting nasty." Litow's forehead had broken into a sweat. But he was still smiling, eyes focused on the musicians as they were passed along atop the heads of the crowd. Vera was holding the DJ's arms, stopping him from removing the recording. The music was so loud that, in spite of the insulation of the glass wall, Weber had begun to sway from side to side. The din of the guitars was ripping at his eardrums. His only thought was to throw himself into the crowd to protect Orfeo, but Litow held him back. "There's nothing you can do. Can't you see they're totally out of control? Let 'em go. Nothing bad usually happens, they're only kids paying tribute to the group. Don't worry; your wife will be all right."

The center of the whirlpool had reached the far end of the hall, beneath the unicorn's head. The six bodies were bobbing up and down above the sea of heads; then one of them suddenly dropped beneath the surface, followed by the others. All of a sudden the music stopped.

The DJ had shoved Vera away from the console and stopped the disc. For an instant Weber heard nothing. He thought he'd been struck deaf. Then he heard shouts of "Hey!" accompanying the movements of the arms that where throwing the remaining two musicians into the air: Orfeo and the drummer. They were all but naked. Now Weber could hear the *musico*'s cries distinctly. What he heard were cries of absolute terror, of pain beyond endurance. In wave after violent wave the dancers threw him into the air, over and over. In the spotlight beams Weber could see now that Orfeo was bleeding: his arms, his torso, his neck, his legs were covered with wounds, as though he had been lacerated by one thousand fingernails, torn by one thousand teeth.

The drummer had vanished.

At the precise instant that Weber placed his foot on the first step, eyes turned toward the unicorn, a throaty "Hey!" rang out, and they tossed Orfeo higher still. Weber could not tell if the dancers, mostly girls, had thrown him toward the long, pointed horn on purpose, or if Orfeo had simply attempted to escape the madness beneath him. He collided with the horn, which slid the length of his arm and pierced his torso beneath his shoulder blade.

Orfeo hung there suspended above the milling heads, a butterfly on a pin.

Epilogue

They had to unscrew the unicorn's head from the wall. A curious procession formed: Orfeo on a stretcher, a long, sharp horn in his chest, and the white head of a gazelle held by sweat-drenched young men and women.

He was hospitalized for a month.

One day, Vera visited him with a lavish bouquet of flowers. For several minutes they had traded meaningless words, never admitting how deeply they loathed each other. After she left, Orfeo asked the nurse to remove the flowers; they were making his head ache. For all that, no sooner had he begun to improve than he had resumed using la Signora's perfume. Weber would come to visit him in the morning, Kirsten afternoons.

In early December he returned to Bernau. He never wanted to see Freiburg again, nor live in any other city. He had everything he could wish for: music, a piano, recordings, nature. Now he began to study the composers of the 19th century, and even discovered those of the 20th.

After Weber told her what had happened at the Unicorn, Frau Schäuble cared for Orfeo day and night. After a certain time, he let her cradle him in her arms before leaving him for the night. He even joined her on long walks, and seemed to be quite cured. But no sooner did he find himself in a group, no matter how small, than he began to tremble and turn pale.

One afternoon as he was walking alone down the country road, Orfeo met some school children. They plied him with questions: what was his name, what was he doing here in Bernau. He answered them in a serious voice, without a trace of panic: they understood that he was sorrowing. From that day on he would wait for them, at the same place.

Singer the cat enjoyed playing with the long tapes from a handful of audio cassettes that were all that remained from Orfeo's adventure in the world of a music that was not of his day and age. The cat would tangle the strands of shiny brown plastic into jumbled balls, throwing them into the air and batting them under chairs. From then on, Frau Schäuble would immediately discard the cat's most recent handiwork. The *musico* felt ill when he saw the head of a bird, the drops of blood.

There were times when he would join the Webers, late in the evening, at the Bad Krozingen mineral baths, when everyone else had left. The warm water of the great pools do him good, he says. Orfeo floats on his back, his head barely out of the water, in that echoing hall where the dim lights blink from the ceiling like so many stars.

Author's Note

This book pays tribute to voices whose sound could not be preserved. The sole exception is a sad, almost caricatural recording by Moreschi, the last *musico*, his voice ravaged by age, dating from the early 20th century. Still, the listener can detect the vestiges of an art form, and of an era when music lovers were quite differently disposed toward artifice than we are today, when audiences were almost unimaginably thrilled by the vocal acrobatics of singers whose range and dramatic capacities were being constantly expanded by the composers of the 17th and 18th centuries.

They could be found everywhere: in 1780 more than two hundred *musici armonici* were singing in the churches of Rome alone. Some of them crossed over to opera, with uneven results. The great singers were trained in conservatories, primarily in Naples and Bologna. We know of the enormous efforts and the extraordinary discipline that lay behind these incomparable voices, but our knowledge has come to us only through the often vague accounts of their contemporaries.

In 1870, a Papal decree forbade the mutilation of boys.

The reader will have noted that I have not used the word *castrato*, with all that it implied, particularly during the Ancien Régime in France. I have preferred to use the terms *musico* and *primo uomo*: far more accurate designations, which are also accepted outside of Italy. The voices of those stars, whose fame exceeded by far that of the best-known singers of our era, wielded a near-hypnotic power over their audiences, who celebrated them as the incarnation of the vocal art.

To avoid unduly burdening the text, I have not mentioned, except on rare occasions, the names of the librettists or poets, most of whom are forgotten today. They can be found in the program notes of the recordings listed in the discography.

The voices of several modern-day counter-tenors that particularly inspired me as I was writing this book: David Daniels, Jochen Kowalski, Andreas Scholl, Gérard Lesne, Daniel Taylor and others, not to forget the admirable performances of a few select *prime donne*: Montserrat Caballé, Marilyn Horne, Ewa Podles, and Cecilia Bartoli, to name but a few. I hope that the reader will be tempted to listen to one or more of the arias that are mentioned in the text.

Acknowledgements

I would like to thank the students of the Quebec Conservatory of Music and their teacher, Jacqueline Martel-Cistellini, for their generosity, as well as Bernard Labadie, Robert Weisz and Irène Brisson who gave me judicious advice on the selection of the works of music I have quoted. Peter Woodford lent me long-distance support as I was writing. Two friends, MDs Josée Villeneuve and André Collet, put their scientific expertise at my disposal by illuminating the physiological aspect of Orfeo's character.

My thanks go as well to translator Fred A. Reed whose task has been especially difficult since the book tries to transpose the magic of music into words, thus creating emotions the reader can feel in his own heart and mind.

The English version of this book would never have seen the light of day without my publisher, Simon Dardick, and my editor, Andrew Steinmetz. From the first reading, they both believed strongly in this novel. I am deeply grateful for their thorough and complex work on a manuscript that needed time before it was ready for publication. Combined with Bruce Henry's extensive knowledge of the 17th and 18th centuries, their insight and advice have been an enriching and very pleasurable experience for me.

Discography

Bartoli, Cecilia, *The Vivaldi Album*. Il Giardino armonico, Giovanni Antonini, Decca, 1999.

Daniels, David, *Haendel: Operatic Arias*, Orchestra of the Age of Enlightenment, Sir Roger Norrington, Veritas, 1998.

——————, *Sento amor*, Orchestra of the Age of Enlightenment, Harry Bicket, Veritas, 1998

Genaux, Vivica, *Arias for Farinelli*, Akademie für alte Musik, Berlin, René Jacobs, Harmonia Mundi, 2002.

Kowalski, Jochen, *George Frederic Handel, Italienische Solokantaten*, Akademie für alte Musik, Berlin, Capriccio, 1991.

——————, *The Masters of the Opera, 1642-1771* (Mozart, Handel, Hasse, Gluck, Monteverdi, Rameau), Laserlight, 1993.

——————, *Berliner Opernkomponisten* (Friedrich II, Graun, Agricola, Bononcini, Hasse), Kammerorchester Berlin, Max Pommer, Capriccio, 1987.

Mozart, W. A., *La clemenza di Tito*, Choeur et orchestre de l'opéra de Zurich, Nikolaus Harnoncourt, Teldec, 1994.

Scholl, Andreas, *Heroes*, Orchestra of the Age of Enlightenment, Sir Roger Norrington, Decca, 1999.

Taylor, Daniel, *Lamento*, Theatre of Early Music, Atma, 2002.

——————, *Handel: Sacred Arias*. Arion, Monica Hugget, Atma, 2000.

Turilli, Luca, *King of the Nordic Twilight*, Limb Music Product (L.M.P.), 1999.

35th Anniversary Year

1973-2008

Véhicule Press
www.vehiculepress.com